'Seen th[...] and
d[...] he o[...]
and the burdens of inherit[...]
messiness of a single human life in all its joy and heartbreak'
Claire Lombardo

'Crisp, haunting and intelligent. Beneath the surface of this
booze-soaked, small town, dive bar novel lies a devastating story
of loss, guilt and grief. Bruno's narrator proves a dark, funny,
unflinching companion as you descend with her, step by step,
towards the revelation of what has led her to the bar tonight'
Stephen Markley

'It's rare to read a novel that takes such an unflinching look at grief, self-
recrimination and the way people try to put themselves back together after loss'
Lydia Kiesling

'Each character in *Ordinary Hazards* bears the weight of their history, and
Bruno shows how even the most devastating secrets deserve redemption'
Fatima Mirza

'Quiet but emotionally engaging, this atmospheric novel has a raft
of enduring characters ... Bruno has a gift for observation which she
uses to produce a haunting examination of love, loss and grief'
Fanny Blake, *Daily Mail*

'Impressive ... a beguiling portrayal of grief'
Prima magazine

'Devastating'
Woman's Way

'A kaleidoscopic novel of the best variety, spinning into
and out of itself as it explores grief, love and loss in ways
that will haunt readers long past the last page'
Shelf Awareness

'Bruno shows a masterful talent for sketching both the outlines and depths
of depression, guilt and self-loathing ... A spellbinding portrait of grief'
Kirkus Reviews

Anna Bruno is a writer and teacher at the University of Iowa's Tippie College of Business. Previously, Anna managed public relations and marketing for technology and financial services companies in Silicon Valley. She holds an MFA in fiction from the Iowa Writers' Workshop, an MBA from Cornell University, and a BA from Stanford University. She lives in Iowa City with her husband, two sons and blue heeler. *Ordinary Hazards* is her first novel.

ANNA BRUNO

ORDINARY HAZARDS

SCRIBNER

LONDON NEW YORK SYDNEY TORONTO NEW DELHI

First published in the United States by Atria Books,
an imprint of Simon & Schuster Inc., 2020

First published in Great Britain by Scribner,
an imprint of Simon & Schuster UK Ltd, 2020

This paperback edition published 2021

1 3 5 7 9 10 8 6 4 2

Simon & Schuster UK Ltd
1st Floor
222 Gray's Inn Road
London WC1X 8HB

www.simonandschuster.co.uk
www.simonandschuster.com.au
www.simonandschuster.co.in

Simon & Schuster Australia, Sydney
Simon & Schuster India, New Delhi

A CIP catalogue record for this book is available from the British Library

Paperback ISBN: 978-1-4711-8488-8
eBook ISBN: 978-1-4711-8487-1
Audio ISBN: 978-1-4711-9140-4

Interior design by Erika Genova
Printed and bound by CPI Group (UK) Ltd, Croydon, CR0 4YY

For Parker

We were victims of the tyranny of small decisions.

—*Alfred E. Kahn,* economist

5PM

THE FINAL FINAL IS the kind of bar that doesn't exist in cities, a peculiarity of a small town that has seen better days. It is so called because it's the last bar on the edge of town. The final stop after the final stop: The Final Final. By last call, there's no place to go but home. The college kids head up the hill to the dorms and the working folks find their way to the outskirts, where they can afford to own property or rent for cheap.

The antique tin ceiling is the nicest thing in the bar, a sharp contrast to the vinyl floor, manufactured to look like wood, cracked and knotted. Vinyl isn't fooling anybody, not even a bunch of drunks at the end of the night. But we all like the ceiling. The tin tiles belong in an East Village watering hole or a Tenderloin speakeasy. Polish and decay. I'm not sure how, but the black tin makes me want to stay so much longer and drink so much more—indeed, black magic.

I stare into my drink, and my peripheral vision catches movement around me, bodies adjusting on stools, sips of whiskey and long swigs of beer, wallets opening. Time is ours now—time for a first drink and a second, time to take the edge off. We've paid our daily dues, taxes have been levied, and we naively believe these hours belong to us and us alone—they are borrowed from no one—and they will remain in our possession until last call, and beyond last call, until we give them up to sleep, and to the morning, and then, once again, to the man, but only until five o'clock tomorrow, when we reclaim what is ours.

On the edge of my stool, arms resting on the thick, old wood bar top, gouged and scuffed by the drunks who came before, I feel this split in my being, like a schism. There are two of me: the woman I am and the woman I used to be. I wonder if these versions of myself can both exist, as if in two dimensions overlaid, or if they erase each other entirely: two extremes that average out to nothing more than middling. I close my eyes and the smell takes over—booze and dish soap—and I am *her*, the old me, and I can almost picture *him* walking through the door.

A gold band adorns my left ring finger. I haven't taken it off. I'm playing with it, turning it around and around with my right thumb and index finger. I am more alone now than I was before because back then, *before*, I felt love, my body's experience of this state: alive, my cheeks flush from the warmth of another, my lips red from a hard kiss, my muscles relaxed from endorphins; and *after*, I remember love, my mind's recollection of this state: dead, a thing of past experience, beautiful but fleeting, a hummingbird that floats in place and then, in an instant, vanishes, never to return. The problem is not that I live in the past, the *before*; the problem is that I live in the present, the *after*.

LUCAS AND I MET five years ago, here at The Final Final. I'd been living upstate for less than a year at the time, adrift. I walked into this neighborhood dive to meet Samantha, my oldest friend, only to find she had sent a man in her place. He had messy, longish brown hair and a trimmed beard, and I remember he was wearing shorts because I thought it was an odd choice for a date, until I realized my presence was as much a surprise to him as his was to me. It was a blind-*blind* date, meaning we were blind to the notion of it—we hadn't agreed to it. I received a text. It read, *Emma meet Lucas. I'm sorry I can't join you but I know you'll have a smashing time!* We caught each other looking at our phones. Lucas knew I was Emma, and I knew he was Lucas. He looked up and smiled, and we were both immediately grateful.

My first impression? I could have sworn he was Canadian. He was profoundly kind and unapologetically socialist—and by that I mean he didn't believe money was the barometer of success—qualities that were alien to me and, at the same time, deeply attractive. In him, I'd found a Canadian-at-heart, who would never say *eh* or make me watch hockey. He was *The One*.

When Amelia delivered his third whiskey, Lucas raised his glass toward no one and said, "Lord, give me chastity but not just yet." Surprise must have registered, ever so slightly, on my face. He looked down into his glass.

"St. Augustine," I said, smiling, pleased with myself for catching the reference. He looked relieved. Lucas and I would eventually be able to read each other's minds, but not yet. This was our first date, and there was a bit of first-date awkwardness—the good kind of awkwardness, the I-like-this-person-and-I-don't-want-to-fuck-up kind of awkwardness.

Amelia filled my glass again too. We were on pace.

"Ahhh, I get it, Emma," he said. He stared deep into my face, not my eyes but my whole face. "For a second I thought you were worried I drink too much, but you drink too much too."

"Get what?"

"That look you just gave me," he said.

"What look?"

"Promise me you'll never start playing poker," he said. "Because I think I could fall for you. And it would be a real tragedy if you lost all our money playing poker."

I punched him on the arm. His bicep was firm. He wasn't a big guy. His body was lean and taut, a runner's body. He had masculine, hairy legs—strong calves and a great ass. I was attracted to him.

"Ouch."

"You didn't answer my question," I said. "What look did I give you?"

"Surprise," he said. "You weren't expecting me to know St. Augustine."

I'd been in The Final Final a couple of times before this blind-blind date, but I'd never noticed the flock wallpaper behind the bar, deep red with a gold-leaf trellis pattern, vintage and probably expensive when it was chosen. This backdrop suited Lucas, who seemed to me, even at this early meeting, to be from another world. The way he sipped his whiskey and talked about philosophers and pushed that flop of hair back on his head. It wasn't that he belonged in another generation; quite the contrary, it was that he belonged in my generation but in a different dimension, where people weren't brainwashed by social media. In Lucas's dimension, minds were meant to wander, exploring various curiosities, and friends enjoyed long, uninterrupted conversations.

"Is that what I was thinking? You can read all that in one micro expression? Maybe you should quit the drywall business and become a fortune teller," I said.

"More like a mentalist. Sure, I think I could if I wanted." He pointed subtly, through his body, to a couple sitting at a high-top table. "First date. He's trying too hard; she's being polite. There will not be a second."

"Well, it doesn't take a genius—"

"So you're telling me you weren't surprised?"

"Not even a little bit," I said. Then I thought about our friend Samantha and specifically why she chose to bring us together in exactly this way, the blind-*blind* date. If she'd done it differently, I would have asked her what he did for a living, and she'd have said something coy like, *He works with his hands*, and I would have pressed her and she would have told me but she would have qualified it with color commentary, *He's brilliant*, and she would have been right but we would have already diminished him by the very need to qualify, and Lucas was a man who did not demand qualification.

As he walked me home, our arms brushed against each other a few times, and I felt a rush of teenage giddiness. I told him it was my thirtieth birthday.

"A blind date on your birthday," he said.

"I thought I was meeting a friend," I protested.

"Mission accomplished," he said. He asked for my number but was so flustered he could not figure out how to get it into his phone. I took a pen out of my purse and wrote it on his hand. By the time I changed into my pajamas and washed my face, I knew he'd managed to get the number into the phone, where it belonged.

A FEW MORE LOCALS show up. Five o'clock is quitting time in our town. The clientele is mostly men—the regulars. Occasionally groups of girls come by for shots. They are from the university on the hill. This is their first stop as they make their way downtown.

Amelia has dark-brown hair and you can tell she's pretty under all the makeup. She's been working here since she was eighteen, twelve years and counting. According to New York State law, bartenders at places like these—places that don't serve food except bar nuts and bags of potato chips—must be twenty-one, but back then everyone just looked the other way, even the cop who dipped in from time to time. Small-town liberty.

I've never seen Amelia dressed in anything but black hot pants—skin tight and short—and low-cut tops, even in the dead of winter. She dresses this way at the grocery store and the dog park too. I run into her sometimes.

She is the best bartender in town. She knows what you drink and when you're ready for a refill. She pours whiskey generously. She makes a good martini. I think about all the secrets Amelia must be in on. She must know things about Lucas I can't even imagine.

All the regulars drink their same thing all night. Cal drinks Bud Light from a bottle. As he drinks his piss beer, he talks about his "bunker," which is his basement, filled with guns and ammo, rice, water, and canned goods. He never takes off his maroon sport coat, even when the bar gets hot, because it conceals a handgun in a holster, which rests about midway up his left side, between his belt and his armpit, so he can reach in quickly with his right hand. There are two Peters. Fancy Pete drinks white wine served in individual portioned bottles, like you see on airplanes, which Amelia unscrews for him, and he pours into a wineglass. Short Pete drinks gin and tonics. Fancy Pete makes his own pants and furniture and Frank Lloyd Wright–type lamps. Short Pete is tiny, smaller than a petite woman. No one calls him Tiny Pete, though, only Short

Pete. I drink bourbon, almost always Maker's Mark, because it's as close to perfect as I've found.

Cal is talking about Jimmy, Lucas's best friend. Lucas and Jimmy grew up together, played on the same soccer teams, drank twenty-four packs of Busch Light in the cemetery after dark. Jimmy is a line cook at the greasy spoon up the street. He's thirty-five but he looks older.

"He fancies himself a chef," Cal says.

I wonder if Lucas talks to Jimmy as much now as he always did. There was a period when he called him about three times a day. Jimmy: the human encyclopedia. Whenever Lucas had a question about history or current events, he called him. It was pretty obvious he used these requests for information as excuses to call his buddy. Perhaps it was a male thing, I thought—needing an excuse. Later, when I knew Lucas inside and out, I came to understand that he called Jimmy for Jimmy's sake—that it was Jimmy who needed to be needed, and that Jimmy loved rattling off information as much as Lucas enjoyed absorbing it. The truth is probably somewhere in between—the two men needed each other, albeit in different ways.

"Yesterday he was in here talking about salmon with pickled radishes and foamy tapioca balls," Fancy Pete says.

"Foamy tapioca? No self-respecting man would eat that," Cal says.

"Lucas would." Fancy Pete chuckles.

Foam is a big deal in New York City right now. I don't say that, though, because I don't want to remind these guys I'm from Wilton, even though it drips from me here.

"I got breakfast at Jimmy's place this morning, and I tell you what— there wasn't one tapioca ball in the place. Every last one of us ate eggs and bacon with a side of black coffee," Cal says.

All the locals call the diner *Jimmy's place*. That's not its real name and Jimmy doesn't own it, but he's always there so it's his place. There are days, when his eyes are especially puffy or when he tips up his hat to scratch his scalp, hair greasy and unkempt, that I'm sure he's slept there. When Jimmy leaves the bar, he goes back to the diner and cleans up the kitchen for an hour or so, rectifying details the closer—some college kid, drunk or stoned—missed. Then he preps for tomorrow, which comes so fast. Jimmy's place opens at six a.m. So, for Jimmy, a night's rest is often a nap on the two-seater couch in the back office. I picture his enormous frame splayed on top of it, legs bent over the armrest, going numb. My feelings about the way he lives are ambivalent—pity for the discomfort of his situation but also a strange, misplaced envy because he has found a way to avoid those hideous dreams that leave a person worse off for having slept.

"Man," Cal says, "this town is full of tapioca balls these days. Jimmy can serve foamy balls to tapioca balls. Might get stuck in their beards, though."

I can't help myself. "The foam and the tapioca are two different things."

He moves his head from side to side and snaps his fingers. Cal's hands are thick and sturdy, and one of his fingernails is black: a workman's hands. Under his maroon sport coat, he's wearing an old golf shirt with the embroidered logo of his general contractor business. He must have a few of these in rotation because he wears them just about every day until the temperature drops and then he switches to old flannels. His wrist is adorned with an expensive watch. Large and gaudy, the watch draws attention both because of what it is and the man who wears it. It suits him, and at the same time, it doesn't.

"I'm just saying: tapioca is one thing—your mom probably makes pudding with it—and foam is another thing," I say.

"Now you're talkin' about his mom?" Fancy Pete says. "Hey, Cal, tell your mom I'll eat her tapioca any day." He rocks his body back and forth like he's riding a horse and pretends to slap it on the ass.

"Shut the fuck up," Cal says.

Cal is in his late thirties. He was a few years ahead of Lucas and Jimmy in school and didn't play soccer, so he ran in different circles growing up. He met a girl in high school, Evie. They got married at twenty-two and eventually had a daughter. They named her Summer because she was born in July. I don't know all the details, but when Summer was just a toddler, Evie hit the road, late to follow some unapologetic jam band that had peaked in the late nineties, Widespread Panic or Phish.

I never once heard Cal complain, not even when they divorced. He loves Summer too much, sees her as a gift from the ex-wife or God or both, and everything he does, in and outside of the law, is because of her and for her.

Cal is a tradesman at heart but also a hustler. Straight out of high school, he got a job tying rebar for various projects, most notably for an undulating concrete wall that cuts through the park in the middle of town. He is proud of this job and talks about it to this day. He refers to it as "my wall."

He tied rebar for minimum wage for a year or two, until one of the old-timers from the bar took him under his wing. This all went down long before I set foot in The Final Final, but as the story goes, Cal needed work so he asked the old-timer if he had anything. The old-timer saw something in Cal, and without children, he had no one else to whom he might pass his business. So he sold Cal everything—his clients and all the equipment— for ten grand, which Cal borrowed from his dad. Then the old man worked for Cal, watched him grow the business.

Most people think of inheritance as money handed down, but not Cal. For him, inheritance is earned like everything else.

WHEN LUCAS AND I had just started seeing each other, Cal told me he didn't understand him. "You know how much money I contracted out to Murphy's Drywall last year?"

Apparently, Cal was pushing several jobs a year to Murphy's Drywall, big jobs, making up maybe a quarter of their business. According to Cal, Lucas was never the one who submitted the estimate—each time the bid came from Lucas's dad. Cal saw Murphy's Drywall as a cash cow. He saw it as Lucas's birthright. And for the life of him he couldn't figure out why Lucas wasn't taking on more responsibility there, why he acted like paid labor.

"Lucas is a turnip," Cal said. I remember this specifically. It struck me as an odd thing to come out of Cal's mouth, not because he was talking about Lucas, but because it reminded me of something my father would say. He loved to call women, whom he found ineffectual, *pumpkins*. And though he had never called Lucas a turnip, I had no doubt he would, given an appropriately impudent mood and a couple of whiskeys.

There was something quaint about comparing people to fruits and vegetables. Lucas would have found it funny.

I didn't agree with Cal but I let it pass.

For Cal, more so than any of the other regulars, I feel a certain loyalty— not friendship, but not far off. He gave Lucas sound advice early in our relationship, advice born out of clear-eyed devotion to his daughter, and maybe also to his ex, even though she'd left him. Without his advice, I'm not sure Lucas and I would have worked through an early hurdle.

When we first met, Lucas was in a relationship with someone else: Angela.

Lucas and Angela lived next door to each other growing up. Angela's mother helped the Murphys with their taxes, and later, after she graduated with an accounting degree from the U., Angela took over the role. Lucas was sure she'd never traveled outside of Upstate New York, where most of her family lived, never even to the city.

As kids, they did kid stuff together. Back in the early nineties, Lucas apparently called for a pizza and then went outside where she was playing and typed in the order as a note in his TI-81 calculator, telling her Pizza Hut had this amazing new system. When the delivery guy showed up, it blew her mind. Later, he let her in on the joke.

They had that kind of history. By her late twenties, Angela's feelings for Lucas were abundantly clear. For his part, he liked the attention, the text messages with heart emojis, the constant prattling on about celebrity chefs and recipes, the certainty that he had someone who would always be in love with him. He insisted there was nothing romantic between them. He told me, again and again and again, what they were: Just. Good. Friends.

Eventually, I found out he'd slept with her a few times right after college.

Cal knew this. There were people at the bar who knew things about Lucas I would never know because they'd been around for all the years when I had not. They'd seen Lucas bring women here, and they'd seen them replaced. All of us, myself included, had these kinds of histories, but I'd grown up in Connecticut, graduated from Harvard, moved to San Francisco for five years, then back to Harvard for my MBA, then Manhattan, which is the place that instantly felt like home.

Lucas never liked being told what to do, so Cal didn't tell him what to do. He asked him what he wanted. And Lucas told Cal he wanted me. And Cal told him that if he wanted me, he'd have to let his friend Angela go. There was no way around it.

Cal didn't do this for me. He did it for Lucas. I think he understood that keeping one foot in a relationship created a kind of stasis. Still, when I found out he gave Lucas this advice, I felt like he had my back, and feelings are more powerful than facts.

EVERYONE SEEMS CONTENT TO be at the bar now, and nowhere else. There is a shared easiness, almost an audible sigh. The day is done. Bring on the night.

Cal and Fancy Pete are still talking about Jimmy's culinary experiment.

"So Jimmy wants to put tapioca and foam on salmon and charge me thirty dollars for it?" Cal says.

"It's a texture thing," I say. "I'd try it."

"Of course you'd try it. You and Lucas would line up at the door for that crap." Cal sees me frown. "I mean, separately—you'd line up separately." A necessary clarification.

"Talk to your ex-wife about it, Cal," I say. "Tell her you know all about molecular gastronomy. It might turn her on."

"Shoot, I'm open to suggestions. I haven't gotten laid in two months"—Cal looks at Fancy Pete—"and the blow jobs stop after you have a kid together." A warning.

"I hear the street vendors in New York are putting mustard soy lecithin foam on hot dogs," I say.

Fancy Pete takes the bait. "Foodies are like Forrest Gump with a box of chocolates. They think food should have a plot."

"They tweet about it until a pipeline diverts their attention," Cal says. "All pipelines are objectionable." He calls out to Summer, "We'll take French's over foam any day, right, Beautybelle?"

She puts a little thumb up. The gesture seems so grown-up, an acknowledgment and a sarcastic dismissal of the stupidity of the conversation all at once.

I pretend to gag. "Yellow mustard peaked in the nineties."

"Your face peaked in the nineties, honey," Cal says. I walked right into it.

I ignore him and look at Fancy Pete. "Who'd Jimmy make salmon for, anyway?"

"Himself, I guess," Fancy Pete says. "He's always trying stuff out in the kitchen."

I can picture that—a midnight meal at the diner. He should invite a woman to join him next time.

"I tell you what," Cal says. "Making a plate of salmon at midnight and owning a restaurant are two entirely different things." He looks at me because I am the only one at the bar who makes more money than he does, and for that reason, he respects me.

"So what?" I say. "Sounds to me like he's living his dream whenever he finds the time."

I place a coaster on top of my drink and excuse myself.

———

THE BATHROOM SMELLS LIKE fake pine needles. Normally these types of smells—factory scents—make me nauseous, but somehow I don't mind it here. The ladies' room is always clean enough. There are no drips of piss on the toilet seat or scraps of paper on the floor. The lighting is dim. I look great in the mirror: milky, clear skin, absent the weariness—ashen pallor accented by reddish, under-eye puffiness—revealed elsewhere by fluorescent bulbs. There is wood paneling next to the toilet, which has become a canvas for old carvings. I trace my finger over one that I made some time ago: *HERE WE FIND HAVEN AND HAUNT*. Under it: *EMMA+LUCAS* and a tiny heart, gouged deep in the wood, permanent.

I yank up my jeans, wash my hands, and look hard at the woman in the mirror. If I concentrate on the fake pine needle smell, really let it in, I can see her for a moment, the woman I used to be.

Thirteen unanswered text messages cascade across my phone. The content of the messages is pleading, urgent. My business partner, Grace Hu, isn't worried about work; she's worried about me. But I don't want to do anything tonight. I swipe left to dismiss the most recent one: *CALL ME*.

———————

MANY OF MY DECISIONS, big and small, that led me here trace back to my friendship with Grace. Grace: head of private wealth solutions at a bulge bracket bank by the age of thirty-three. Grace: one of *Fortune*'s 40 Under 40. Grace: devoted wife and mother. Grace has always been special, and, in her orbit, I wanted to be special too.

I noticed Grace for the first time in my statistics class, freshman year at Harvard. From my vantage in the back of the lecture hall, I observed her sitting in the front row. She wore sweaters with the shoulders cut out and, one day, appeared sporting a buzz cut, which only she could pull off. Her hair has grown out since then, thick and jet-black, usually pulled into a loose braid. She has the mind of a fox, the elongated neck of a swan, and the focus of a bird of prey.

Born into a working-class family in Ohio, Grace was both valedictorian and captain of her high school track team, and this was what drew me to her: her otherness. I called her *Ohio*, a term of endearment. She stayed in Boston after graduation, only trekking home to the Midwest for Christmas holidays. Eventually, the nickname fizzled out.

In college, we ran together often, typically at night, ending on the empty, lit track, where we did crunches and leg lifts and discussed our dreams. *Married by twenty-eight. Kids by thirty-two.* True for Grace but not for me. *Corporate jobs in New York or Boston.* I studied economics and Grace studied applied mathematics. We didn't know it at the time but we were learning how to use money to make money, which was both hardwired into my DNA and a consequence of Grace's roots.

Senior year, I took Grace home over spring break. The timing of our visit to Connecticut was less than ideal. Unbeknownst to me, my mother had discovered my father's infidelity just days prior. While he hid out in his condo in Manhattan, my mom lorded over the vast, empty house, eating only saltines and pickled herring, the food my dad hated most, and washing it all down with Connecticut's finest gin.

When Grace stopped gawking at the marble staircase and messing around with the intercom system, she insisted the place had an echo, which wasn't true, but it was so big and empty it probably seemed that way. She kept saying, "Echo, echo, echo . . ." softer each time. We had a good laugh. I promptly raided the liquor cabinet, which was fully stocked because Mom was on her way to becoming a raging alcoholic. At my insistence, we holed ourselves up in my bedroom all day, passing around a bottle of vodka and popping pills I'd bought from some douchebag at a frat party before we'd left campus.

We left my room only when we heard Mom yelling at the pizza guy for banging on the front door. "I don't eat pizza, you ape!" Mom shrieked through the intercom.

The pizza guy didn't know to push and hold down the button when he spoke, so his muffled voice called back through the door. "Extra-large pepperoni mushroom for Emma."

"Emma!" Mom yelled. Her voice rang loud across the intercom. Even drunk out of her gourd, she knew which button to push.

"Calm down, Mom. We got it," I said. Grace and I slid across the marble floor of the atrium in our socks. I shoved precounted cash into the hands of the pizza guy, grabbed the pie, and said sorry before slamming the door in his face.

My plan was to whip back upstairs, as fast as we'd descended, but my mom said, "Emma, why don't you and your friend eat in the kitchen?"

Mom wore one of her designer outfits—a knee-length skirt and sweater cut like a jacket—St. John by the looks of it. She'd left off her rock and stacked thick gold rings on both hands. The clothes and jewelry were a charade—she wasn't going anywhere. The tip-off? Her stocking feet. Either she'd kicked off her heels hours prior when she poured her first drink, or she'd never put them on in the first place.

It took all of five minutes for Mom to start in on Dad. Her skin was grayish and dull, and when she raged, her wrinkles deepened. Somehow she still possessed weatherworn beauty, the kind of beauty that photographs well, the sad kind. I wanted to spare Grace the worst of it, but I'd brought her under this roof. We were stuck. The look on her face screamed, *Is this what it's like to be rich?*

"You know, she's twenty-one," Mom said. "Younger than you girls. And look at you! Children! She didn't even bother with college. Two years of fashion school and straight to letting her boss fuck her in the ass. Did you know he always wanted to do that?" This was a new kind of vulgarity from my mom's lips. She'd never have uttered these words sober. She considered herself a dignified woman.

I tried to steer the conversation. "Mom, Grace is my roommate. We met in stats class freshman year—"

"I've heard so much about you—" Interrupting herself midthought, Mom asked, "Are your parents still together?"

Grace said, "Yes, but my mom's been in Taiwan for the last six months." When Mom didn't respond, she added, "Taking care of her mother."

In her present state, my mom didn't care about Grace, her mother, or her mother's mother. She perseverated like a crazy person. "Can you believe him? The louse. It's disgusting, picturing him with a twenty-one-year-old. Taking Cialis to keep it up. That bastard is going to embarrass the family. You watch. The girl will end up suing him for sexual harassment."

This seemed like a reasonable prediction at the time, though over the years my mom would be proven wrong. That twenty-one-year-old secretary stuck by the man she'd stolen—she's with him even today, thirteen years later.

I wanted to tell Grace this wasn't my mom. She was a proper woman who didn't cuss or talk about anal sex. It was just the gin talking. But Grace was a smart girl and would have known that was only a partial truth. Whatever meanness ran deep in Mom's arteries ran also in mine. I judged my father harshly too, and words escaped my lips that were every bit as unkind.

The three of us gorged ourselves, and when we were done, Mom insisted we try a proper gin and tonic with a curled strip of lemon zest and three juniper berries. I never invited Grace to Wilton again after that.

Back then, neither of us predicted we'd go into business together but in hindsight it feels inevitable, in the way romantic relationships seem fated unless you catalog every intention and step along the way, reminding yourself it was all your doing: *you chose this life.*

I SETTLE BACK ONTO my stool and remove the coaster from the top of my glass. Then I text Grace back a lie: *Driving home from the city. Let's talk before the markets open in the a.m.*

She could call me out on the fact that I routinely take calls on the road but she won't.

Grace and I run a hedge fund. We have two hundred million dollars under management, and Grace is pushing hard to raise more capital. If the universe had whispered some version of this future in my ear in my early twenties, I would have believed it but there's no way I'd have predicted my circuitous route, the sweat and tears and pain, the good luck and bad—all the ways I love Grace and how much I resent her.

Three dots appear on my screen. Whatever she's typing is taking too long, which means the message will annoy me.

After college and before grad school, I spent five years working in California. I commuted from a shared apartment in the Mission District of San Francisco down the peninsula to my Silicon Valley office. One afternoon I dipped out early to have beers with friends on Baker Beach. As I drove back into the city on the 101, I noticed several dead birds alongside the highway, big black birds. There weren't thousands of them or anything but there were enough to notice. I remember thinking to myself, *We're gonna have an earthquake tonight.* It wasn't that I thought dead birds were some fantastical, ominous sign. It was simply that these birds were dead because they'd been disoriented. They'd flown into traffic. And they were disoriented because they were more in tune with the natural world than we were.

There was a minor earthquake that night. We felt it when we were sitting on the beach. I hadn't told anyone about the birds, but when the earth shook, I understood.

For some reason, the dots on my phone make me think of those dead birds.

Grace writes, *Will you be available by 9 p.m.?*

No further explanation. If she set up a conference call at nine, it must be with Singapore. We have an investor there, a dot-com billionaire. Grace can handle the call herself. I turn vibrate off and place my phone facedown on the bar.

The Yankees are playing, and though I can tell no one really cares too much about it, we all look toward the TVs when there is a lull in the conversation, which is most of the time.

————————

THE LAW OF NEPOTISM dictated I had a job on Wall Street waiting for me when I finished business school. I moved to New York with an MBA from Harvard and a chip on my shoulder. Back then, I was dating an artist who lived at Ninety-Ninth and Lex, right around the time when people stopped saying, "You don't want to go above Ninety-Sixth." Rich white people still said it.

Labeling him an artist was generous, I'll admit, analogous to calling a guy a garbage man because he empties the can in the kitchen once a week at his wife's behest. Trash duty isn't a job he gets paid for, and it isn't a hobby, because hobbies are activities people enjoy. But nevertheless, he takes out the garbage so he's a garbage man. My artist boyfriend's relationship to art was similar. He dabbled in installation art, creating lopsided structures and telling everyone who would listen, "My medium is gravity!" He claimed to be working on his magnum opus but he wouldn't show it to anyone and complained when people didn't take him seriously. He also slept on a queen-size air mattress because he was a hypochondriac, deathly afraid of bedbugs.

Naturally, I figured it was a good idea to crash with him for a few weeks as I got my bearings.

On my first day, I made my way to the Ninety-Sixth Street subway station in heels and a pencil skirt, turned a blind eye to the rats, willfully tolerated the smell of piss and garbage, and emerged at ten minutes 'til eight to find a tower in the financial district that was to become my home for eighty-plus hours a week.

My father had set up a meeting with the woman who was supposed to be my mentor. He told me I should get to know someone who'd "done well for herself in a man's world." I was shown to a conference room on the thirty-seventh floor.

The view was, as one might expect, a glimpse through other towers. I pushed my chair up to the window and looked down at the street below: black suits, heels, shoulder bags. There was rhythm in the monotony.

The woman—her name was Pamela—entered the room and we made small talk. She'd found her way to banking because she saw a job posting that included the word *research*. After three years in research, she'd become an analyst, and after that a VP.

She drank coffee like it was a job requirement. At one end of the room, there was a service table with coffee and pastries. There were two pots of coffee, one regular, one decaf, which the staff periodically refilled, and five rows of cups, four deep. The room did not seat twenty people. At the time, I saw this merely as an incongruity. Only after I met Lucas did I assign the smallest extravagances to a category of corporate buffoonery.

Pamela picked up the pot of regular and brought it over to the conference table, placing it directly in front of her. She filled her cup and emptied three packets of artificial sweetener into it. Instead of taking one or two sips and setting the cup down on the table, she sipped rapidly, in intervals of four or five. She put the cup to her lips and held it there: sip, sip, sip, sip, sip. Then she put it down for a beat, half the cup depleted. Before the cup was completely empty, she refilled it to the brim, dropped in three more packets of sweetener, and repeated.

In a profile, which I came across much later, I read she was abstinent from alcohol. This made sense because if she drank booze anything like she drank coffee, she'd end up parking her car on her lawn or drinking gin out of her coffee mug at ten o'clock in the morning.

Something struck me. She looked like me, though her bone structure was dissimilar. She had a round face and a small nose—men would have found her cute when she was younger. My cheekbones were more prominent and my chin had a slight cleft. My hair was long and dark and hers was dyed blond and cropped short. And yet, we were sisters. We were two women in an office that was 74 percent men, 89 percent not counting reception. We wore black skirts and black nylons and black heels. The feeling I had, the je ne sais quoi, wasn't our features or what we were wearing, though. It was where we came from.

"My father worked with your father for many years," she said. "Your dad wrote my recommendation for Harvard Business School."

Her name was Pamela Randolph Walsh. Maiden name: Randolph. Pamela had grown up in the same neighborhood as me in Wilton, Connecticut. She was maybe five or six years older so I didn't know her in school, but I'd heard the name Randolph. It had been in the news. When I was about twelve—Pamela would have been a junior or senior in high school—the police raided the Randolphs' cul-de-sac mansion. I rode my bike over to see the spectacle. There were about ten police cars on the circle and in the long driveway, and one or two on the lawn. By the time I rolled up, they'd already entered the house. A neighborhood kid told me they'd had the place surrounded, guns drawn.

We read about it in the papers the next day. Walter Randolph was allegedly the kingpin in Connecticut's largest sports bookmaking operation of all time. Randolph and his associates were purportedly netting nearly five million dollars a month.

Pamela looked out the window while I wrapped my mind around

these details. I couldn't tell if she knew how much I knew until she smiled.

"Lucky for your old man, my dad used code names in all his ledgers," she said. "Lucky for me, your dad was grateful."

"And lucky for me, you are grateful?" I said. In my mind, I was mocking her but it rang earnest.

"No one here knows," she said. "It wouldn't look good for the firm: daughter of a bookmaker. Compliance would take issue."

"Why keep Randolph as your middle name?" I asked.

She shrugged. "Number one: it's a common enough name. Number two: no one in this business cares about your family unless they care about your family." She said this matter-of-factly. She had my dad's recommendation and the Harvard pedigree, which was quite enough for anyone around here. After fifteen minutes with her, I could tell she was one of those people who work their butts off—eighty-, ninety-, sometimes hundred-hour weeks. The bleach in her hair covered up the premature grays, but despite its roundness, her face looked older than it should have, more weathered. I had to remind myself she was only in her early thirties, midlife crisis still distant on the horizon.

The idea that she'd kept the name because it was common was her lie, though—I could tell. She was either proud of where she came from or she loved her father (or some combination of the two), and though she'd taken Walsh because she did what was expected of her, she was unwilling or unable to part with what she was: a Randolph, daughter of a bookmaker.

She looked at the clock on the wall. "The market opens in thirty. I need to cut this short," and then added glibly, "Best of luck to you, Emma."

"Thanks," I said, thinking, *What a gal!*

"Look, I'm not here to help you. That's not my job. Your dad did something for me because my dad did something for him. Even Steven. I can promise you that I won't get in your way." Investment bankers do mentorship like deadbeat dads do parenting.

I tried to picture myself in her shoes, and I was, almost literally, wearing them already. Her experience, not within these walls, but outside them: waking up in the morning, checking her phone on the nightstand for something, anything, that happened in the five hours that had ticked by since the last time she checked, before she allowed herself some semblance of sleep, and then—in the absence of a firestorm, which she would have known about already because some young analyst would have called and woken her—letting the rush of warm water from her fancy showerhead run over her face. This would be her last calm moment of the day. This was what I cared about. I did not care about the male colleague who said she was hot enough to want to be around but not too hot to distract him, just the right amount of hot. I wasn't concerned with some wide-eyed notion of doing good in the world, something beyond moving money around, making the rich richer. I actually looked forward to the boozy, coked-out nights, clubs and strippers, house music and bottle service. But none of this mattered to me as much as the experience of waking up as Pamela Randolph Walsh. The waking up with myself in this life was the unbearable part.

She had a high tolerance for pain. I did not. She went back for more. I did not. That was the difference between her and me.

Pamela swiveled her chair away from the table, stood up, and walked out without looking back. She didn't smile or shake my hand. From behind, she was perfect. I had the feeling I was watching an actress playing her as she walked away. Through her silk blouse I could see the curvature of her back, which was slightly concave at her waist, accentuating her round ass. Her fitted skirt extended just past her knees but there was a slit in the back, revealing the smallest glimpse of her thigh as she walked. And she walked like a company woman, which is to say, hard footed, assured, the kind of woman you did not want living above you in an apartment building.

As she moved away from me, I had a premonition: Pamela Randolph Walsh would be a captain of industry one day.

In fact, she would eventually become the CFO of the fourth-largest investment bank in the United States. On her ascent, her name would not only catch up with her but propel her forward. The daughter of a book-maker would be branded Wall Street's moral compass. She'd rub elbows with senators and congressmen, and she would be adored not in spite of her story, but because of it. Tough dad; tougher daughter.

Observing Pamela walk away down the hall threw me back into myself, my slouched posture, the way I was touching my face, picking a piece of loose skin from my lip, the position of my leather bag on the floor, hastily dropped. Pamela and I had come from the same neighborhood and gone to the same business school but we were creatures of a different kind. As fate granted, I had arrived at her house. I'd put on the clothes and taken the subway and sucked down the coffee, but I didn't have her middle name and I didn't have her stamina.

Immediately after the meeting, I quit. I simply took the elevator down to the lobby and walked out. It may have been the shortest amount of time anyone has ever lasted on Wall Street: about an hour.

Subway to Ninety-Sixth, three blocks to Ninety-Ninth, trade the heels and nylons for cutoffs and flip-flops, check to make sure soul remains intact, leave boyfriend a note: *Headed upstate, XOXO—Emma.*

Upstate New York seemed like a cross between Brooklyn and Appala-chia, grunge meets hillbilly with a dash of locally sourced food—heirloom tomatoes, foraged mushrooms, free-range everything—to an urbanite, better than the real thing, like oral sex. Back then, I thought I was trapped between towers, not of concrete but of desire, and Upstate seemed like a void, so I was willing to trade one wasteland for another.

I wish I could say I chose this town—the place that would establish my life's trajectory—for a good reason, but I can't. Within a year of moving here, I would fall deeply in love with the man who would become my husband and the father of my son. But I didn't know that then. I moved north to escape. Simple as that. I moved to the middle of nowhere because I didn't want to be anywhere—not New York City, not San Francisco, not Boston. I had one friend here, and some extended family on my dad's side who lived over two hours away, west of Albany, family I didn't know and had no plans to see.

I hopped a train to Poughkeepsie. From there, I called Samantha, who'd grown up with me in Wilton. She worked in admissions at the U., a college that was, at least in my head, so far upstate it might as well have been in Canada. She told me that their business school was hiring a lecturer for business communication and that, with an MBA from Harvard and my father's last name, I was a shoo-in. I bought a one-way ticket on a Greyhound bus.

Perhaps I should have known back then that finance would eventually suck me back in—not the money, not the darling life, but how it feels to succeed in a way that is so immediately and perfectly measurable. *Unrealized gain/loss* in dollars and percent. Right there in black ink on the holdings sheet.

———————

"HAVEN'T SEEN YOU IN here before," I say to a stranger to my left, not with the inflection of a young woman but an old man: friendly, warm.

I take the last sip of whiskey in my glass. Amelia offers me another and I nod.

Whiskey: I like the way it makes me feel. It's obvious to most people that gin and vodka and tequila and whiskey taste different, but drinkers, real drinkers, know that they *feel* different. Gin and vodka feel crisp and cool, operating on the upper fifth, shoulders to head. Tequila and whiskey are diffuse and warm—even if sipped cold—hitting the gut and rising through the stomach to the chest and eventually expanding upward to the head, slow and steady. As far as I can tell, both whiskey and tequila feel this way, but tequila hurts more going down, and people 'round these parts don't like the taste. Sipping tequila is not a thing here at The Final Final. Don Julio is the best on the shelf, and the only time anyone drinks it is when some guy from out of town comes in and wants to do a shot. A few years back, kids from the U. occasionally bought shots of Cuervo, but that's pretty much out of fashion these days. Now they are more inclined to go with the house shot or spin the wheel. Whiskey doesn't need to be top shelf. I like Maker's, but Jim Beam works just the same. Old Charter and Heaven Hill are good, affordable options. Whiskey is like a down comforter on a cold night. Climb in and adjust, let it warm your body as your body warms it. But know: the longer you stay in, the harder it is to get out. It just *feels* good. I really can't describe it any better than that. It's something you need to experience for yourself. Go ahead, have another.

Like breakfast cereal, people begin consuming alcohol at a particular time of life. For cereal, that's when people are kids, when times are simple and failure hasn't yet choked out life's possibilities. This is why you see forty-year-old single men buying Frosted Flakes at the grocery store. They might have lost their taste for it long ago, but they still eat it because nostalgia operates on the brain like a narcotic. Of course, some people turn to liquor during the bad times, but I began ordering whiskey when I moved to Upstate New York. Here, I met Lucas, and he drank whiskey too, and together we drank even more whiskey because we spent more hours at the bar. These were some of the best days of my life. So maybe I like whiskey because of the way it feels, or maybe I like it for the same reason some people like Frosted Flakes.

My fingers touch, tip to tip, forming an igloo. I let them drop into each other and roll my thumbs, once, twice.

If only I could experience my hands with the wonder of an innocent babe. Mesmerizing to watch. Heavenly to feel. Skin soft as silk, grip strong as a vise, holding on and letting go. But I can't. When I look at my hands, I see the story I tell myself again and again.

I'm not married. The woman I used to be, she was.

Everyone always wants to know why relationships fail. It's a spiteful curiosity thing, schadenfreude, but also a self-preservation thing. People want to understand how to avoid the fall.

The answer is complicated. There isn't one reason, one event. It has something to do with smoking cigarettes and drinking all night. It takes into account thousands of hours of labor on a small house, projects finished and unfinished. It is late-night conversations and inside jokes and making love and having a child. The answer is wrapped up, shrouded, and ensconced in prioritization, ambition, and work. Caring about these things is not the problem. Not caring about them is death.

6PM

ADELAIDE IS AT MY apartment now, waiting for me. Her name ricochets in my mind. It sounds ancestral, like it was passed down from a great aunt. I never call her by her formal name. She's a blue heeler, named for the region from which she hails. I call her Addie or Addiecakes or just Cakes, or sometimes Dog when she misbehaves. Lucas used to call her Addie, but when he said it, he'd always emphasize the first syllable and draw out the last—*Ad-deeee*. It had a ring to it. She smells like a dog, but in a good way. She has the hardest head you'll ever touch, designed to withstand the hooves of cattle. I've seen her bash her head into the coffee table and not so much as flinch. I've seen her run straight into a signpost, distracted by a rabbit, and barely break stride. She shows love by pushing her hard head into my head and holding it there—hard dog head against soft human head. Lucas taught her this. When she does it, I always want her to hold the position just a little bit longer because the combination of the hardness of her skull and the warmth of her fur feels so good. She can't help herself, though. She always goes in for the lick when she's close to my face, and I shriek, "No face licks!" and the moment passes by.

Lucas and I maintained a running gag where we'd jot down logical fallacies on scraps of paper. They all related to our lives in some way, topics that were important to us, or random or funny at the time. I wrote the date on each one and collected them in a shoebox. The oldest one is in Lucas's handwriting:

We made some food ∧ *Adelaide ate the food*
∴ *Our food is dog food*

I spend my days at home with Addie, the only thing I love, and my nights here, at The Final Final, the only place that will have me.

———————

BY SIX O'CLOCK, IT'S obvious that The Final Final is a townie bar. The place is full of craggy white guys who drink too much. They all know each other "from the bar." Go ahead—ask them. No one is wearing anything they haven't owned for ten years. An enormous, shimmering Old Style sign hangs to the left of the bar top. It's a mechanical sign with glitches, white lines where there should be blue water. It features a huge mug of beer, as big as the mountains behind it, with a tremendous amount of head. The head alone is greater in volume than the waterfall. The text on it reads, BREWED WITH WATER FROM WHEN THE EARTH WAS PURE. If one of my students wrote this tagline, I would have ripped it to pieces. But I like the sign, especially all that's wrong with it.

When I started teaching Advanced Communications to MBAs at the U., I planned to do it for a year or two, just long enough to get investment banking out of my system, ditch the New York artist boyfriend, and figure out what to do with my life. I designed the course with a focus on storytelling. Students explore how to capture attention, appeal to logic and emotion, and deliver memorable conclusions. The entire class can be summed up in three concepts: beginnings, endings, and transitions. Master these, and *the power and glory are yours, now and forever*! Since my first year of teaching, my conviction in the importance of storytelling has become almost religious in nature. A good story can move a stock! A market! A good story is the difference between a cubicle and the C-suite.

Turns out I like teaching. Having worked in the corporate world for some years—growing up in a world where money and power are fundamental elements like air and water—I recognize that teaching, or more specifically, the decision to teach, is pure stupidity. The fact that there are all these bright, capable people holed up in high schools and universities, making, in some cases, less than a living wage is irrational. It's what people in finance call a *market anomaly*. It's what economists call *behavioral economics*.

The stranger to my left offers to buy me a drink.

My glass is still full, but I've learned to accept these gestures. I offer a simple thank-you. Amelia acknowledges our exchange. My next drink will appear on the correct tab at the end of the night.

Amelia refills my glass once or twice per hour, not too much if I only stay an hour or two. I will probably stay longer tonight.

I flip my phone over. The texts from Grace stopped but I have three missed calls from Samantha. She usually doesn't call in the evenings. She has three kids and a husband to worry about. I check the voicemail: *Can you come over to my house later tonight? Say, nine o'clock?* There's someone she wants me to meet.

I rack my brain for who she could possibly want to introduce me to. She's not trying to set me up again, because she thinks I belong with Lucas. On a regular basis she calls him my soul mate, which drives me crazy, because if I ever had a soul, it's gone dark, incapable of mating.

Samantha and I were like sisters in high school. We'd take the train into Manhattan and spend weekends in my dad's condo. Or we'd crash on the floor at my uncle Nic's place. She went to college at NYU. I assumed she'd stay in the city forever because she always talked so much shit about Wilton. But right out of school, she fell for an oncologist who took a job at a hospital upstate, here at the U. So she left the city for good. In short order, they moved into their big house, and the rest is history.

I think we're the same people we were in high school, but back then we didn't know who those people were yet. Friendship came easy. It's more complicated now. But Samantha got me the job at the business school. Then she sent me Lucas, which is a debt I can never repay.

I text her: *Sorry, conference call with Singapore later tonight.* This is another lie because I have no intention of joining any conference call but I assume it will get Samantha off my back.

This is important, she writes.

Who is it? I ask.

A friend from Boston. Grace is going to Skype in too.

So it was no coincidence that they both wanted me at nine o'clock. Samantha and Grace have met exactly twice. They have no business being on Skype together.

I turn my phone upside down again. I'm not in the mood to go to Samantha's house tonight. By nine, she'll have put her kids down for the night, but the oldest always wakes up and wants something frivolous, like an organic, locally sourced yogurt in a compostable cup.

―――――――

A FEW MONTHS AFTER we met, Lucas took me out to the nicest restaurant in town, a small Italian joint owned by a first-generation immigrant named Angelo Antolini. Offhandedly, I pondered aloud how Antolini found his way here, from Italy to this town, in the middle of nowhere. The question was barely formed. There was nothing behind it. Then Lucas asked me why I was here.

"You asked and I accepted," I said.

"Here in this town, smart-ass."

Antolini's is small, like, twenty-tables small, mostly two-tops. That night, every table was taken, squeezed a bit closer together than usual, only far apart enough to slip a body through sideways. Lucas offered me the better seat, and I took it. I sat with my back to the wall, looking out at the restaurant. Another couple sat to my left, the woman on the inside as well. To serve her, our waitress had to stand between our tables, her butt inches from our water glasses. It was a nice butt, not a small butt but a firm, young butt: a dancer's butt.

Later, I started noticing her around town. She frequented Soul Night at a club so divey I can't really call it a club, more of a bar with a decent-size stage that hosts bands and DJs from out of town. She was, in fact, studying dance at the U. She had long, wavy blond hair, and a quick smile. At the restaurant, I assumed her act was a play for tips, but when we struck up a conversation at Soul Night, I liked her immediately. Her first name was Ellis, which I liked too—I liked it as a girl's first name. I admired her sunny disposition, which was something I never had and always assumed men wanted.

Lucas only had eyes for me, though. He managed to avoid looking at her ass entirely, or if he did, it escaped my notice.

"I moved here because I don't have a high tolerance for pain."

His expression was quixotic.

"There was this woman," I said, "in New York. Her name was Pamela Randolph Walsh. She had a high tolerance for pain. I didn't."

"Who is she?" he asked.

"Nobody, really, just a VP at an investment bank, working her way through the ranks."

"Middle management?"

"I guess. Most of my students would kill to have her job."

"*It is he who is dead and not I!* A classic Ivan Ilyich scenario: your students are destined to clamor for transfers and promotions." Lucas remembered everything he'd ever read.

"It must be agonizing to be you. Truly horrible," I said.

"Why?"

"To have all those books swimming around in your head all the time. What does it all mean? *Das Sein!* Death! The abyss!"

He bit his lower lip.

The kitchen was backed up. We downed an entire bottle of red before Ellis delivered the appetizer. A long, slow meal suited us just fine. Lucas ordered another bottle.

"I mean, how do you even stay hard?" I said. "You'll be having sex and suddenly your brain will flood with thoughts about the basic income experiment and Bertrand Russell—"

The second bottle of wine created a false sense of privacy, even as we eavesdropped on the people around us. The couple next to us was older, a professor and his wife, from the looks of it (wrinkled khakis, shapeless after a couple hundred wash cycles, oversize navy sweater atop a button-down, collar tucked in, rimless suburban-dad glasses, brown comfort shoes, rubber soles, of course—his approach to fashion no different than his approach to God: agnostic). My attention occasionally strayed from Lucas, and I caught wind of their circumstances—he sent his steak back because it was too rare; she said he should slow down on the bread. Even as I observed them, hoping desperately that we would never become them, it didn't occur to me that they probably heard our conversation too. Perhaps if it had, I would have bitten my tongue, curtailing talk of sex and politics. But the great thing about the second bottle of wine is that neither of us cared what they thought, and perhaps that was what separated us and them. We'd never be the kind of people who sent food back to the kitchen.

"Basic income?" This piqued his interest.

"Or whatever. Definitely something socialist. You're a closet socialist."

"So you're worried I won't be able to stay hard when we have sex, because I'll be thinking about basic income?"

"Actually, you're not a closet socialist. You're totally out of the closet," I said.

"Riiight, only bankers can maintain hard-ons these days," he said.

"Yeah, exactly. Their heads are empty—"

"Nothin' in there but mothballs and party drugs," he said.

"Seriously, though. I have no idea how you function on a daily basis."

The man at the next table ordered an espresso. His wife waited until Ellis retreated, and then said, "Do you really need that? It will keep you up." The man insisted espresso didn't affect him. The woman looked at her watch; it was after nine. She was ready to go home. I imagined how the rest of their night would go: He'd put down his espresso in two gulps as he paid the bill. They'd walk to their car, which was parked on the street outside. She'd offer to drive because he'd ordered two glasses of wine, but he'd insist he was fine. They'd listen to NPR on the radio, probably jazz or bluegrass at this time of night, for the duration of their ten-minute drive to the part of town where all the professors lived. He'd pour himself a nightcap and turn on the TV. On the couch, he'd drift off almost immediately. She'd head upstairs and get ready for bed. Maybe she'd read a book for a while. Then she'd go down and rouse him, telling him to come to bed for his own sake, after which she'd lie awake and listen to him snore, deferring her dreams until he left for the office in the early morning.

Lucas grabbed my hand. "Don't worry. I'll be able to keep it up. You're so beautiful. You'll be like that one prostitute Nietzsche had sex with. Three minutes of bliss—he didn't have a care in the world."

"Didn't Nietzsche contract syphilis from that gal?"

"That was a smear campaign. He had regular old brain cancer."

I had only a vague memory of *The Death of Ivan Ilyich* from a Russian lit class I took in college—something about a man's emotional and physical suffering at the very end.

"Ivan Ilyich played the game his whole life," Lucas said. "The best part is when he sees himself in his wife and daughter, *all that for which he had lived*."

"He doesn't like what he sees?"

"He questions whether his life is a deception."

"Maybe he's just having a senior moment. The keys are in the freezer, Ivan!" I held on to Lucas's smile for a beat. "So you think I saw myself in Pamela Randolph Walsh and questioned the authenticity of a life in banking."

"Your words, not mine."

"A true company woman; a total bore?" I said, thinking aloud.

"Is that what you thought of her?" he asked.

"Maybe," I said. "She might figure it out before she lies down to die."

"Have you figured out what you want?"

"Most definitely not." I lifted my glass.

"*Cin cin*," he said.

After the meal, Lucas ordered a port. I ordered a white chocolate martini. This bought us another thirty minutes or so, before the worries of tomorrow set in. I had to teach a class in the morning, and though he didn't say so, Lucas was probably due at a jobsite by seven. These were early days in our relationship, and they were marked by the time we stole—from sleep and from work—so we could be together for one more drink, which was always one drink too many and, at the same time, never enough.

———

THE DOOR SWINGS OPEN fast and hard, yanked by a man on a mission. He walks into the bar, pauses in the entryway, and looks around. He's maybe thirty, forty tops, white, wearing cargo shorts and a camo T-shirt that has been washed so many times the university's wordmark is barely recognizable. His short stature and deformed ears indicate a bygone wrestling career, most likely at the U., which has always had a good team. Glory days, long passed.

I brace myself for the *Damn, girl, looking fine*, for the smell of cigarettes and fast-food breath. None of this happens, though. He makes a beeline for Martin Yagla.

Martin is short too, maybe five foot nine, and he shaves his head because he has started to go bald. Though not nearly as built as the Wrestler, he works out—a tight shirt reveals biceps—but a small gut appeared in his thirties. When he smiles, his teeth take over his face, and it's obvious he has them cosmetically whitened, because they are blue white—too white. Anyone in town would know to find Martin here. Everyone calls him Yag, or Dr. Yag, because he has an MD.

He sits to my right with the latest in a steady stream of twenty-one-year-olds he's brought to the bar. Yag tells the girl to stop crying, which makes her wail louder. He looks around to see if people are listening and catches my eye. He notices the Wrestler, now hovering next to him.

They shake hands but it's a hard shake, not a friendly one.

"Should we take this out to the alley?" Yag's opener, ballsy and panicky all at once.

"Listen to you, cool guy," says the Wrestler.

This is not one of those made-for-TV-movie situations where two guys step outside, each backed by a cadre of buddies: brothers in arms. Martin Yagla is on his own, like the fraternity brother who never sobered up—eventually everyone stops calling.

Whatever is about to happen, Yag probably has it coming. He's always crossing someone. Himself, usually.

Amelia serves his girl another with a steady hand. I can't tell if she's doing it out of compassion, or curiosity, or rote service. The girl moves the straw clockwise in her glass and watches the ice swirl. She is drinking a vodka soda with a splash of pineapple juice, and she's a hot mess. Tousled hair, coarse from bleach, covers half her face. Her shirt slips off her shoulder, revealing the strap of a pink, lacy bra. She's wearing very short cutoff jeans, and her bare thighs are stuck to the stool. She's not bad looking, though, attractive in the same way most college girls are. She is a caricature of youth, and youth counts for everything, especially here.

Two people in this bar are angry at Martin Yagla, and that's if you don't count me, because mine isn't urgent. My anger is like rancid food that's been sitting out too long. No one dares touch it.

Yag owes the guy ten grand. That's the short of it. It's a poker debt from a high-stakes table (high-stakes by Upstate New York standards, which means a little higher than a friendly game, maybe at most a hundred-dollar minimum buy-in). A ten-grand debt must have accumulated over some period. Now it's time to pay up.

He mumbles something under his breath. Under the fear, there's anger, and under the anger, there's indignation.

"What'd you say?" demands the Wrestler.

Cocking his head sideways, looking the Wrestler in the eye for the first time, Yag says, "Your homies cheated. I have proof."

The Wrestler lets out a low-pitched, dopey laugh. "You played with us every week for a year, man. You never once caught a cheat."

"I kept track of hands and did the math. The likelihood everything was legit is 0.13657 percent." The fifth decimal is pretty convincing, but the Wrestler's not buying it. He shakes his head, maintaining a sly half smile—a smirk that asserts, *I have the power here*. "Why should I pay when I know you all cheated?" Yag says.

I can think of a reason: this guy will break his knees with a tire iron.

"You can't calculate your way out of this one, buddy," the Wrestler says. A surprisingly civilized response.

"I don't have the money," Yag says, defeated.

The Wrestler replies, "Borrow the money from your mom."

"I can't ask my mom for ten grand, dude. Just give me a little time."

The guy tells Yag to get up. He complies. They stand there staring at each other, waiting for a waltz to begin.

As the Wrestler rotates his shoulder backward and clenches his fist, a soulful funk melody comes on the jukebox, and by the time the punch lands on Martin's gut, almost everyone in the bar is bobbing and tapping to "You Are the Sunshine of My Life" by Stevie Wonder. It's almost poetic.

Yag crumples into himself.

Amelia points at the Wrestler and says, "Get out now."

He raises both hands into the air, palms open, as if to say, *I mean no harm.* He tells Yag he has one week, and then he'll collect directly from his mom, and he hopes she can take a punch better than her piece-of-shit son. Then he turns and walks toward the door.

At the last second, he looks at Cal and nods. They know each other, which isn't unusual—everyone knows everyone in this town—but the expression on Cal's face betrays that they know each other for a specific reason. My best guess is that it's drug related, and that this guy and others just like him have been out to Cal's ranch many times. Most of them carry weapons and none of them are very nice people, not the types of people good parents allow around their children.

Cal's ten-year-old daughter, Summer, is in her own world, drawing on construction paper, chewing on her tongue. Summer is allowed to hang out at The Final Final before ten o'clock as long as she doesn't sit at the bar. Her little body moves back and forth to the rhythm of the music. She looks happy. I tell myself that I, of all people, have no right to judge, and go back to my drink.

The Wrestler swings the door gently this time. He goes silently into the night.

Outside, there's a storm brewing, one of those big ones that mark the interlude between summer and fall. Everyone knows it's coming because darkness looms, the air is dense, and the insects have stopped rubbing their wings.

Before Yag is back on the stool next to his girl, he looks at me and says, "Mind your own fucking business, Emma."

"Poor little Martin," I say. "Better run home to Mommy."

"You're the reason I started playing poker with those guys in the first place," he says, which is a partial truth, but the broader truth is that Yag's a fuckup, and that's hardly my fault.

———

YAG ATTENDED COLLEGE AT the U. back in the day, along with Lucas and many of their high school buddies, but took several years to graduate because he lost his mind—a result of, as the story goes, a bad trip on LSD.

He claimed he and Marshall Mathers were going in together to buy a city block in Detroit, which they planned to develop into a luxury high-rise condo building. He lied about other things too—little things, things no one would ever lie about because they could be disproven with a single phone call or internet search. Once, he insisted Jimmy was over at his place smoking a bowl when Jimmy was three thousand miles away backpacking in the Sierras. Lucas pulled up a picture Jimmy had sent him but Yag insisted the picture was taken weeks or months earlier. Arguing with him was futile. His mind played tricks on him. Signals got crossed and he believed in these falsehoods with total, blind conviction.

According to Lucas, back when they were in college, Yag would walk into the bar talking about a big math problem he was working on. He talked about it as if he could solve one problem and it would change the world. He didn't, or it didn't. But he did eventually get a degree in math from the U. He bummed around for a few more years, working in restaurants and bars, dipping in and out of Lucas's life. Yag never left town. I think, even in adulthood, he needed the stability his parents provided.

One day he told Lucas he wanted to prove he could finish something: his own life. Lucas thought he should finish something else instead. They stayed up chain-smoking cigarettes on the stoop until four o'clock in the morning, and Yag walked away knowing he would apply to medical school and study psychiatry. He entered med school at the U. around the time Lucas started working for his dad's drywall business—they were both twenty-eight—and he graduated five years later, having to take one off because he had another psychotic break. He practiced medicine for three months as a resident physician before walking out, telling everyone that it wasn't for him and that nurses "could be real bitches." Through the grapevine I heard that an older nurse, someone with seniority, asked Dr. Yagla to go get the newspaper for her, which was left at the front desk of the hospital. Yag refused to do it, asserting *Nurses do not tell doctors what to do*. Word got back to his attending physician, who immediately put him on permanent paperboy duty. Yag quit.

———

I ADJUST MY BODY on the stool. Yag and his teary-eyed girl have picked up where they left off, rudely interrupted by the Wrestler. He slumps over his beer. They both look down at his phone.

The girl is preoccupied by Yag's cheating ways. She doesn't get hung up on the fact that he was just punched in the gut by some guy he's into for ten grand. For a reasonable person, this would be a huge red flag, a reason to run the other direction. If I cared, even a little bit, I'd shake some sense in to her.

Martin Yagla skulks behind his girl—*was it Carol, Sheryl?*—as if he can use his body to muffle the sound of her tears. She braces herself, holding on to the bar with two hands.

He takes a breath so deep I can see his chest rise and fall. "People are looking, Caroline. Can we talk about this some other time?"

It's hot and muggy outside, and in an hour, it will probably storm. I check the forecast on my phone. By eight o'clock there is a 96 percent chance of rain, which is the equivalent of certainty. Meteorologists just don't have the balls to call it.

Yag doesn't have a car. His license is currently suspended, a result of his second DUI. And he isn't about to invite her back to his parents' house, where he lives in the basement. The girl probably lives with four roommates who haven't yet graduated from the U. There's no place for them to fight privately. Also, they're shameless.

The girl turns and grabs at Yag. She demands, "Let me see your phone."

I stare but neither of them seems aware of me anymore.

He says no, but when she asks why, he can't come up with an excuse. He's too drunk to persuade her with an argument about his right to privacy. On some level, he seems to understand he has already shown his hand. She's seen something, and she can't unsee it. He thrusts the phone in her direction, and she begins scrolling silently.

"I told you I'm not interested in her romantically." His words slur. His voice is loud and abrasive.

"But you hooked up?" Caroline lacks confidence. She knows this to be true already but she asks the question anyway.

"We were drunk," Yag blurts out. He reaches over and asks Amelia for another stein of beer. "I wasn't thinking straight."

"Did you have sex?" The girl sucks compulsively from the little straw in her drink.

He throws up his hands, *What do you want me to say?* He looks up at the TV. I follow his lead. The pitcher throws the ball to first base to hold back a runner boldly tagging up, way off the bag. He dives back to first. Safe.

"Why do you owe that guy ten thousand dollars, anyway?" she asks as she scrolls. *You go girl*—ask the serious question.

"It's nothing," he says. "Don't worry about it."

"Ten thousand is a lot of money," she says.

I think about the Wrestler, how wrestling is the thing that defines him, even though he probably hasn't been on the mat in years.

"I'll handle it. Are you done?" Yag reaches for his phone. She's not done.

"Look at me," the girl says.

Yag turns his head toward her. His left hand is on the bar and his right foot is on the base of her stool.

"How many times did you put your dick in her?"

"I don't know. Less than three. We were drunk. We're just friends."

"You are always drunk." If the girl ever took my class, we'd have a serious conversation about up-talk.

Yag shakes his head, not in protest or denial, more like, *So shoot me*.

The pitcher has not yet thrown a single pitch to the batter. He's in a standoff with the guy on first.

"You take zero responsibility?"

"It's a Gen X thing," Yag says.

"A *Gen X* thing?" I'm not sure if the girl isn't familiar with Gen X as a category or if she's questioning Yag's moronic excuse. For her sake, I hope it's the latter.

"We invented hookup culture in college," Yag says. "Four years of popping pills and getting laid—that's pretty hard to turn off." It took Yag more than four years to graduate, but I don't want to split hairs.

Every time Yag opens his mouth, I detest him more. He is brilliant—a mathematician, a doctor for Chrissake—but he will never leave this town. He'll drink every day at this bar for the rest of his life. He won't stop banging twenty-one-year-olds until they stop saying yes, and they might not stop saying yes for another ten years. They seem to be getting stupider by the year, less discriminating.

And maybe it is just a bad night, but I find myself disliking the girl too, though I have no cause. I find her pain distasteful because it isn't real pain. Together with Yag. Not together with Yag. It means nothing, thin as the air at twenty thousand feet.

None of the other regulars are listening. Cal is at the other end of the bar talking shop with a young man who looks about twenty-one or twenty-two. Short Pete and Fancy Pete are chewing the fat about local politics. Summer is at the front table sucking down Cherry Cokes.

Yag puts his arm around Caroline, pulling her toward his chest. She pushes him away, kicks his foot off the base of her stool, and scoots in the opposite direction. He looks at her as if they've been talking about the weather or what they had for lunch, and says flatly, "I'm gonna go play pool. See ya later." His tone reminds me of my father. It rings with superiority. It implies, *I'm done with this now*.

A GLIMMER SQUEEZES THROUGH the door, daylight finding its way in. Jimmy comes in from the heat, wiping the sweat from his forehead, making his way to the bar. He's wearing a dark-blue T-shirt, a size too small. A band name, DIGISAURUS, is inscribed across a boom box with lightning bolts shooting out. The letters are stretched over his pecs, and the bolts curve over his gut, not quite reaching his belly button. This shirt is paired with old Levi's and black-and-white Sambas—the same shoes kids wore for indoor soccer back in the nineties.

Sometimes I feel like I'm straddling where I came from—Wilton, Cambridge, San Francisco, New York—and where I am, this town, like they are two different worlds. Then the whiskey touches my lips and I realize no matter where I am it tastes just the same.

In towns like ours, there's a fine line between rustic and run-down. There are still a few cows in the fields. There are refurbished barns where kids from the U. have wedding receptions. There is a nearby swimming hole maintained as a state park. There's a burger place where you can get your name on the wall and a free T-shirt for eating four burgers in under an hour. There's also an opioid epidemic. And family farms in foreclosure. And historic houses so dilapidated even the frat bros won't live in them. Our town is like a woman who looks good from fifty yards.

Amelia tosses a coaster in his direction and says, "What'll it be?" She says it just like that, the way the bartenders in the movies say it. Jimmy orders a stein of beer, which costs three dollars on Wednesday. Glasses clank as Amelia pulls a frosty mug out of the freezer. A little bit of beer swooshes out as she sets it down in front of Jimmy. She grabs a towel to wipe off the glass, but he is already halfway across the bar, saying hello to one of the other regulars.

Amelia lives in a room above the bar. I've been upstairs only once. Before Amelia moved in, Lucas's friend Jacob had her room. One night, he sent us up to do a line of coke off his empty dresser. His bed was unmade, bare, no sheets, not even a mattress cover. The room had no kitchen, only a small microwave on the floor in the corner. There was one shared bathroom in the hallway. The experience of his room was so depressing that I never followed Lucas up there again. I imagine Amelia has fixed it up a little, maybe painted the walls a deep purple or red, hung a painting purchased from the antique shop up the street.

Jimmy walks toward me. He's put on a few pounds. Jimmy only played soccer, never football, because his parents are scientists and thus take issue with repeated trauma to the brain. He has the anatomy of a football player, though, six foot four with broad shoulders and big hands.

I motion for him to take the empty seat to my left. He smells like a combination of hamburger and fries, greasy and stale. *Not a whiff of tapioca*, I think to myself.

"How ya doin', old friend?" I ask.

It's doubtful that Jimmy thinks of me as a friend—he's Lucas's friend— but the greeting seems to please him nonetheless.

I gesture toward Yag. "How do you stand him?"

He takes a long drink from his beer. "I've learned to compartmentalize. We're only friends at the bar."

"He's being rude to that girl," I say.

If Jimmy cares, he doesn't let on. He shrugs, as if to say, *Tell me something I don't already know.*

A jolt of worry strikes. Or is it hope? I can't tell the difference. Lucas might meet Jimmy here. My mind says, *He never comes to the bar anymore.* He avoids me. But my heart asks, *Maybe tonight is different?*

I decide to fish. "Meeting anyone?"

"Not tonight," Jimmy says. "It's a slow one, so I dipped out for a drink."

He puts a coaster on top of his beer and steps out front for a smoke.

Before Jimmy took that job at the diner up the street, he worked as an aerospace engineer. As kids, he and Lucas set off rockets in his backyard, and Jimmy talked about wanting to be an astronaut. By the time he left for college, he had a private pilot's certificate. After college, he lived out west for several years, designing commercial aircraft for Boeing. He moved back home when the doctors announced the cancer had spread to his sister's lymph nodes, lungs, and liver. He was here to say goodbye and to help his parents, and we all expected him to leave again when she died. He never did.

He's going on five years at the diner. Every year, on the anniversary of his sister's death, Jimmy wraps up two burgers to go and brings them over to his dad's house. They sit on the porch together and eat. He told me once that they don't say much but it's not the talking that matters. It's the being here. Sometimes it's hard for me to reconcile the fact that this Jimmy—the Jimmy who sticks around this town so he can sit on the porch with his dad—is the same Jimmy who lives to party, the Jimmy who used to do lines of coke off the kitchen counter with Lucas and take all our money at the poker table.

Amelia reads my mind. She says, "Lucas hasn't set foot in here in months. He came in on Thanksgiving Day and then again on Christmas Eve. I remember because the second time he came in, he gave me a huge tip—called it a Christmas bonus."

Our divorce was finalized a week before Thanksgiving, three quarters of a year ago, which feels like both an eternity and a flash, like tacky wet paint that's already started to peel from weather. Thanksgiving and Christmas are the only two days that Lucas could be absolutely certain I would be in Connecticut with my mom.

Thanksgiving is Lucas's favorite holiday. He likes cooking all day and walking around in socks and a flannel. But his family never celebrates it on actual Thanksgiving. His mom puts the holiday on hold until his brother, the prodigal son, makes it up from New York City with his wife and two kids. So, for Lucas, Thanksgiving falls on a random Saturday, sometime in November or December, when the big shot litigator, hair combed back and gelled, piles into his Mercedes SUV with his Barbie-doll wife and Norman Rockwell kids, drives four hours, and graces Upstate New York with his indomitable presence. It doesn't surprise me that Lucas spends actual Thanksgiving and Christmas here at The Final Final.

"Got it," I say to Amelia. "Thanks." I'm not sure why I'm thanking her—I suppose for the information. Her intonation suggests disapproval. She prefers Lucas as a customer. He tips better.

ABOUT A YEAR AFTER I met Pamela Randolph Walsh and left Manhattan behind, I read an article in the *Wall Street Journal* about her. The headline was "Daughter of a Bookmaker Becomes Darling of Wall Street."

I showed it to Lucas. "Not Ivan Ilyich after all," he said.

Pamela would never look back on her career and point to this article as a seminal moment. Having met her, however briefly, I understood the publicity was most likely a source of embarrassment, or perhaps not embarrassment exactly, but diminishment. Her success was not intrinsic. It wasn't attributable to anything she did.

Maybe she wasn't Ivan Ilyich. But what was the alternative? I pictured her stick-straight, cropped hair, the perfect arc of her back, the heaviness of her steps as she walked away from me.

If Pamela fell suddenly ill in her forties, she might suffer physical pain, but no mental anguish—and even if she did suffer mental anguish, it would not be the subject of Tolstoy. There would be more salacious points of inquiry. No one would care if her interior décor was exactly the same as every other banker—modern leather chairs, white walls, stainless steel appliances: clean and crisp. No one would question her early maneuvers, the climb from researcher to analyst to VP. No one would examine her family life and consider that time spent at the office might have been an evasion. No one, finally, would take notice of spouse and child, the former a ham-fisted kept man, the latter a private school brat, *all that for which she had lived*, and see, in them, Pamela: a deception.

Lucas paused, processing what he'd read, thinking, no doubt, about the writings of historians and philosophers, charting ideas in his brain. Finally, he said, "Daniel was a nobody too. Then the king threw him to the lions."

Imagine: Wilton, Connecticut, is a modern-day Babylon. The kings of men wear blue blazers and starched button-downs. They live in six-bedroom, eight-bathroom mansions, made of stone and brick. Most of the rooms are vacant because they have only one-point-five kids. One will go to Harvard. The point-five will probably go to Brown.

If you are Pamela Randolph Walsh, this is your station in life. Your life in Babylon is the result of a series of events that transpire because of one predominant motivation: the acquisition of wealth. You have talent; you have ambition; and, if you're like Daniel, you have piety. His Jerusalem is your Wall Street. His God, your Economy. He prays daily. You trade daily. Either way, life is a series of transactions.

You refuse the food and wine of the new money elites. You avoid their yoga studios and coffee shops. You don't set foot in a Whole Foods. And when you take that job at a Wall Street bank, you ditch the Audi your dad bought you with his bookmaking profits, and you take the subway because it keeps you humble.

Sitting in your tower, high above the concrete jungle, you look at your tickers and study your reports, and you begin to understand visions and dreams of all kinds. Management asks you to interpret a series of disclosures, after their wisest men have failed, and you deliver a prophecy about the end of a long reign and all the ways leadership is found wanting.

The bank transitions through a series of kings—one goes crazy and moves to Brooklyn; one is overthrown in a coup. You persevere. You rise through the ranks, first, an underling in the royal court; then, having distinguished yourself among analysts, you are given the title of VP, above the satraps. You are neither corrupt nor negligent, and best of all, you have a high tolerance for pain.

Do you question your piety? Do you cry out in the night? Do you distract yourself with Prada handbags and Jimmy Choo heels and powder-white cocaine? Or, like Daniel, do you stay true to your God?

Daniel, Ivan Ilyich, Pamela Randolph Walsh: each nothing more than a subordinate leader, a talented middle manager subject to the whim of a king. They are barely distinguishable but for the stuff of legends: Daniel is thrown to the lions! Pamela is the daughter of a bookmaker! And what becomes of them? Only Ivan Ilyich dies a nobody.

Pamela's story may never have come to light, or it may have surfaced much later—too late to have an impact on her career—if not for her father's early death and for his obituary in a local Wilton newspaper. As luck would have it, the obit guy at the *Wilton Weekly* actually did his homework, and her name, occupation, and Harvard pedigree were mentioned in an unusually lengthy chronicle of the life and times of a bookmaker some twenty years prior. Apparently, after his release from prison, Walter Randolph lived a reclusive life without incident.

No one would have seen this local obit, except for the fact that a student reporter at the *Harvard Crimson* scoured internet news sites for obituaries of noteworthy alums. While Pamela's father was not an alumnus, his obituary came up in the search because the school was mentioned alongside Pamela's name.

It was this kid at Harvard who realized there was a story here, although there's no way he would have had the slightest idea how it would all spin out. He had been working on a series of articles about Wall Street influencers after the financial crisis, which profiled a number of Harvard graduates. I read some of the articles in the series.

A fellow Harvard alum who worked at the *New York Times* read the one on Pamela and concluded, *Who better than the daughter of a bookmaker to clean up Wall Street?* That article led to the article I happened upon in the *Journal*.

Pamela Randolph Walsh was a nobody before she had a story. She survived on Wall Street because she had a high tolerance for pain. Then the press threw her in with the lions, their jaws locked shut by angels, and she emerged untouched and altogether more spectacular, the talk of the town, a legend.

In short order, she was head of global compliance, and then CFO.

Lucas said, "You should write a book."

LATER, I WOULD CALL the book *The Breakout Effect: How Stories Make Leaders*; it would become a best seller.

The breakout effect is the phenomenon whereby a person pushes through a predetermined ceiling as a result of some extrinsic factor (i.e., not hard work or a brilliant idea). I co-opted it for my own purposes, but *breakout* is a common term in finance. Securities—stocks and bonds—typically move within certain thresholds. The upper limit of these thresholds is the level of resistance. Imagine a chart that shows the movement of the stock. It has peaks and troughs and jagged edges, but for a period of time, the line does not go above a certain ceiling or below a certain floor. Investors look for a breakout point—the point at which the security will climb past the level of resistance. There are many factors that might lead to a breakout: an abrupt shift in supply and demand, which is sometimes predictable; a major news event, the effects of which are often unpredictable. The goal is to take a long position when the price of the security approaches the resistance line.

When you graph the success curves of human beings, adjusting for people who have major health problems and people who are so poor that upward mobility is an American myth, you find that they look exactly like stocks. Everyone has peaks and troughs and resistance levels, and just like the market always goes up in the long run, people, collectively, trend upward. This begs the question: *How do people break through their resistance levels and become leaders?* This is the central concern of the book.

The key insight of *The Breakout Effect* is that it's not who you are that makes you a leader; it's the story about who you are. Because the story is what allows you to break out. The story is what matters, not the reality. Furthermore, telling a good story is like beating a polygraph: anyone can do it with a little training, or the help of a good book. Hence, the appeal.

Beyond principles of storytelling, the book espouses one idea above all else: the story, regardless of subject, must be humanizing, not humbling, necessarily, though it could be, just humanizing.

———————

A COUNTRY SONG PLAYS on the jukebox. It's Cal's pick.

> Ridin' gravel to the jobsite
> Smokin' cigarettes on the morning road
> Everything's gonna be alright
> While my baby dreams at home

The tune takes me back. It was playing when I brought my mother to The Final Final for the first time. The only time. She'd never spent much time on country roads. Wilton wasn't exactly a walking community unless you count the arduous journey from master bedroom to three-car garage. Before she drove up, Mom called and asked if she should bring her boots. I closed my eyes and imagined her high-heeled, pointy-toe Ferragamos and promptly said, "Sure, Mom, bring your boots."

> Only city boys sleep through the morning
> Only royals eat bacon and eggs
> Only bourgeois read the newspaper
> Drivin' to work while my baby dreams at home

When she rolled into town, she said she wanted a martini so we stopped at The Final Final. Upon entry, her nose crinkled up and her body collapsed into itself. She refused to sit down or touch anything. She did not use the bathroom. So I was surprised when she ordered a second martini. She lost herself in thought for a moment as Amelia drained the shaker into her glass.

"You know," she said, "I met your dad in a bar just like this one. It was the late seventies, right after the blackout. Hot as hell in July. The bars had opened their doors again, so I ventured out to meet some friends in the West Village. The place was a filthy dive but that night it felt like a sanctuary. Everyone just seemed so kind, willing to help out however they could."

"Small-town kindness," I said.

"Nico walked in off the street, glasses fogged up from the humidity. He was there to meet this gorgeous girl. She was so bohemian, so free. Just sexy. Nico was all over her. It was the girl who struck up a conversation with me first. She asked me what I did to maintain such beautiful skin." Mom paused, searching my face. "What? You don't believe me? I was young once too, Emma. You get your looks from me, not your dad."

I believed her. She never talked about those days. New York in the gritty seventies. It was such a departure from the way I saw her: a stay-at-home mom in Wilton.

"Nico looked me up and down, head to toe, and gently pushed that beautiful girl off his lap. He told us he was going to call his brother. In those days, bars had pay phones in the back. Then he looked me in the eye and said, 'I promise you'll like him if you give him a chance.'"

> Ridin' gravel to the jobsite
> Smokin' cigarettes on the morning road
> Everything's gonna be alright
> While my baby dreams at home

"Your father showed up thirty minutes later. He'd been at the public library, his office at the time. Apparently, when the librarian handed your dad the phone, she said, 'I'm not your secretary.' Nico thought that was hilarious. I'm quite certain he called him at the library all the time. Your dad introduced himself as a developer, even though he hadn't developed anything yet. He said he had his eye on a six hundred thousand–square-foot office building on a side street in Midtown that was underpriced but no one wanted. There was so much trepidation back then. Unemployment was off the charts. Wall Street was taking a beating."

Mom laughed to herself like she was in the middle of a daydream and forgot anyone was listening.

"What's so funny?" I asked.

"Your dad was just so out of place in that bar. Everyone else, myself included, tried hard to be cool. He rambled on and on about buildings. I'd never met anyone so ambitious. The way he carried himself. He was bigger than himself."

"Sounds like a real catch," I said. She ignored my sarcasm.

"That blond beauty was back on Nico's lap, kissing him. He pulled back, pointed at me, and said, 'Brother, I knew she was your type.' Nico was the handsome one, but I was enamored with your father. I knew he'd do everything he said he would and more. It took him ten years to buy his first building. You were in grade school by then. It seems like it happened overnight but it didn't. Those were the hardest years but they were the best. That's usually how it is. You think you'll never get through them, and then you spend the rest of your life missing their intensity, those beautiful years."

When she finished her martini, she licked her lips and said, "Perfect martini, but please tell me you have a decent restaurant in this town for dinner."

THERE IS SOMETHING EXOTIC about small-town life. Though some people (people who say things like, *This is a gorgeous wine*) can't see it, and even if they do, they are unwilling or unable to tap into it. I'm not sure exactly what to call it, but it has something to do with joy.

After the relationship grew serious, Lucas invited me to join his coed softball team, sponsored by The Final Final. After my first game (I caught a fly ball in right field and hit an RBI double), we stopped for a drink in a part of town infested by strip malls. The closest place to the field was a LongHorn Steakhouse on Route 1.

Lucas inspected the menu. From across the table, I could see him scan through little pictures of various cuts of meat, filet down to porterhouse. The graphics were not to scale because the porterhouse should have been like four times bigger. The guy sitting to our left was eating one that was the size of a large plate, leaving little room for the side of limp asparagus threatening to fall off onto the table. He didn't give a rip; he wasn't there for the asparagus. "I wonder where they get their beef," Lucas said.

In lieu of becoming a vegan, Lucas had gone on a whole-animal buying spree. First he bought a cow, then later a pig. His freezer and a second freezer in his parents' garage were stacked chockablock with butchered animal parts, including pork hocks, cow tongue, and a heart that may have belonged to the pig or the cow—he wasn't sure which. In Lucas's mind, the zealous consumption of whole animals was the moral equivalent of a juice cleanse. Animals were sacred.

"This is a LongHorn, Lucas. Where do you think they get their beef?"

"There are a lot of cows in Upstate New York. It could make sense to source locally." A Canadian-at-heart with the soul of a dad. He was born to hold a clipboard and deliver a slow clap. He would definitely drive a minivan. His greatest, existential question would one day be, *How do I get these squirts to stop clustering on one side of the field? Bring it in, kids! One, two, three, fun!* Way back then, I could picture it.

"Are you kidding? The meat probably comes from China," I said.

"I'm going to ask the waiter."

I rolled my eyes. "Please don't."

"Why not?"

"Fremdscham."

He laughed.

"Everyone will know you're a thirtysomething white dude with disposable income," I said.

He motioned with his hand at my entire body, head to toe: *Look at yourself.*

I wore Lululemon yoga pants, a loose racer-back tank with the insignia of the U. on the front, and a hot-pink sports bra. Two thin gold necklaces, different lengths, which I'd forgotten to remove, glimmered on my neck. I twisted and untwisted them half-consciously. So yeah: a sporty yuppie.

"What else would I wear to softball?" I snapped.

"Exactly," he said. "Look at what you've become. One of those women."

"Those women?"

"Oh, you know, one who talks about the dog all the time. Pretty soon, you'll trade whiskey for chardonnay."

"Whoa whoa whoa. It's not like I have a pair of corgis named Princess and Muffin. Addie is a badass dog. She's my best friend."

He gave me that look: *Case in point.*

"I don't post about her on the internet," I said.

"You talk about her so much you don't have time to post stuff on the internet," he said.

"I do not."

"You're just like Sienna, going on and on about how her kid won a leadership award."

Ugh, Sienna: Samantha's friend and my nemesis. The leadership award Lucas referred to was handed out by her daughter's new-age preschool. It was called the Hungry Spirit Award, and it was trending on Facebook. What constitutes leadership for a four-year-old? Not peeing on the carpet?

Sienna orders oatmeal at brunch. Sometimes she deviates and orders an egg-white, no-cheese omelet with a side of leafy greens. Her enthusiasm for charity bake sales is both gluten-free and social-media smart. She drinks herbal tea, never coffee. She uses a straw so the tea doesn't stain her teeth. She carries compostable straws in her purse because her image would suffer if associated with plastic. The compostable straw is a natural talking point: a personal crusade to reduce her impact on fish and marine mammals. Meanwhile, her AC runs 24/7, her snow removal guy uses a blower, not a shovel, and a giant propane tank is refilled regularly to heat a massive backyard pool she had installed on the off chance her hungry-spirit kid is the next Katie Ledecky. I've never liked oatmeal. Or tea. Amelia knows I don't take straws, but I don't brag about it, because a bartender knowing my every whim is not exactly a point of pride. It's certainly not Facebook material.

The waitress came by to refill our waters.

"Where do you get your beef?" Lucas asked. His tone was very serious, almost scholarly.

"I dunno," she said, sweet as apple pie. "I can get a manager for you."

"That won't be necessary," I said. "We're just having a drink."

"Really," she said. "It's no problem at all." LongHorn trained servers to be very accommodating.

Porterhouse Guy pulled his face out of his steak and glanced over at us.

"People are going to think we're from the city, Lucas."

"You're from Connecticut."

The manager was maybe thirty or thirty-five—our age—with the hair and body of John Daly before his gastric-band surgery. Too much imported beef from China.

"We get most of our meat from the Panhandle." As he spoke, I pictured him swinging a golf club, gut square with the ground, a cigarette hanging from his lips.

"Thank you very much," Lucas said. "We don't have time for food today. Maybe next time, though."

"Sure thing," he said.

As soon as he was out of earshot, we said in unison, "The Panhandle?"

"The Florida Panhandle?" I suggested. I went to grad school with a girl from Tallahassee so I had a vague sense that Florida had a panhandle, in addition to various oddities I associated with the region. "Holy shit, that guy looked a lot like John Daly. Do you think he took a job here at the LongHorn to pay off his gambling debts?"

"I'm pretty sure John Daly owns a steakhouse in Arkansas, so if he's wandering around anywhere answering questions about where the beef comes from, it's probably there," Lucas said.

"That might be true, but you see the resemblance, right? He certainly looks familiar. Maybe I recognize him from your high school reunion. Any chance he went to Horace Mann?"

"Why do you think everyone in town went to high school with me?" He gave me a little shove. I tipped off my stool, catching myself with my foot.

"Where else would they have gone?" I smiled.

"I think he's talking about Texas. The Texas/Oklahoma Panhandle," Lucas said.

"I'm pretty sure there's a panhandle in China," I said, and we both had a good chuckle.

Of course, this is how I witnessed the LongHorn *before*. Light, humorous, exotic. Home of John Daly's doppelgänger. Place where love existed. Now, *after*, I see it differently.

———

I TEXT SAMANTHA BACK. *Who's at your house tonight and why is Grace involved?*

Party emoji, smiley tongue–face emoji, thumbs-up emoji, followed by the words *GIRLS NIGHT* in all caps. Samantha uses emojis gratuitously either to look cool or to inspire people to come over to her house, where she is a prisoner of circumstance (three kids).

Will Sienna be there? I ask.

No, not tonight.

When I don't respond, she types that Grace's friend Elisa Monfils is *passing through town.* She goes on to say that Grace asked her to host Elisa for the night because she *has the space.* Samantha lives in an unreasonably large house, a three-thousand-square-foot McMansion. So her claim is true on one level but it's also a lie. No one passes through this town unless they have a reason. Samantha must realize this is suspicious because without prompting, she writes, *I think she's giving a talk at the U. tomorrow.*

My whiskey is gone. I tilt back my head and use my tongue to separate a piece of ice, dropping it into my mouth. I suck on it, push the cube upward against my palate until the cold hurts, and then move the ice from one cheek to the other, crunching down to feel an uncomfortable but oddly pleasant sensation in my molar. The ice is part of the ritual—its melting away acting as a coded message to my brain: *It's time for another.*

A GUY TAPS ME on the shoulder. "Did I sell you a house?"

"You must be thinking of someone else." I recognize him right away: Aldrich Gilfillan, real estate agent. His signs say, CALL GIL. They do not say, CALL ALDRICH, because Aldrich is the kind of name that doesn't go over well in a town like ours. Aldrich plays golf at the private club. Aldrich drinks top-shelf liquor. Aldrich takes his family on vacation to Kiawah. Gil enjoys fishing on the Finger Lakes. Gil buys thirty-packs of Bud Light for his annual backyard barbeque, and he invites the whole town.

Gil is on his second wife because, for one thing, he cheated on his first wife with some college girl, a friend of his son. His second wife, who's with him now, stands patiently but doesn't say a word.

"Where do I recognize you from?" Gil asks.

"Lucas," I say. "Lucas Murphy."

I doubt he picks up on the fact that he has just opened a wound. Real estate agents don't know when to keep their mouths shut and pretend like they don't know you. I live in a small town. I pretend like I don't recognize people all the time—Lucas's ex-girlfriend, for example. I just walk on by. I silently judge her because she has a tramp stamp and smokes cigarettes even though she has a toddler, et cetera, but I definitely don't smile and ask where we've met. Aldrich Gilfillan: of all people, he should know a house is a sacred place.

He continues to talk. "That's right! I never forget a house. That's what I always say. I might forget a face but not a house. I sold him that little place on Catherine Street, a fine house. I knew Lucas was going to take it when we were halfway up the walk."

"Uh-huh," I say, and the name of my old street brings back another rush of memories. My eyes are looking at the glass in my hands but my mind is watching Lucas roll up on his bike, dismounting while still moving. I'm having a glass of wine on the porch, and Addie's entire body is shaking with joy. She hangs back for a second until I say, "Go ahead," and she bolts toward him.

A FEW WEEKS AFTER I moved in, Lucas said, "Come with me to the hardware store." The small store was just a five-minute walk from the house, its proximity a pleasant legacy of the way people used to shop, before they started driving to megastores in the suburbs. We paid a premium for all sorts of things there—tools, coffee filters, even kitchen equipment. We wanted the place to stay in business.

"Okay," I said, not bothering to ask what we needed. I grabbed Addie's leash. The hardware store is one of her favorite places. The cashier always gives her a treat.

On our way out the door, Lucas pulled up a picture on his phone. "I made something for you," he said. "I want you to pick the stain."

The picture was of a traditional porch swing, propped up on sawhorses in his dad's shop. I pinched out the screen to zoom in for a closer look, examining the grain of red cedar on evenly spaced slats.

"After we stain it, I'll drill holes in each side and add the chain to hang it," Lucas said.

"It's perfect," I said.

"I know how much you love the porch," he said. "Just figured it needs a swing."

Our house had a traditional porch with a haint-blue ceiling, a color chosen by the previous owner, a Southerner, who believed the pale blue would keep the spirits away. I'd never had a proper porch before. Where I came from, no one wanted to sit outside and look at their neighbors.

Lucas helped me pick a light stain that would show off the grain and knots of the cedar. I insisted we take our can of stain and walk straight to his dad's shop because I couldn't wait another day for something that until that moment I didn't even know I wanted.

Lucas showed me how to stain wood, applying it with a brush and wiping it off with a rag. He told me not to leave it on too thick or the qualities of the wood wouldn't show through. Then he just let me go, like he trusted me, or he didn't care if my method deviated from his. The staining didn't take long. That swing was a thing of beauty.

Before we took off, Lucas's mother, Joan, invited us into the house for iced tea. She could see how happy we were. She said, "All I ever wanted for Lucas was for him to find somebody like you."

Lucas and his dad loaded the swing in the truck and we drove it home to Catherine Street.

ALL THE HOUSES ON our block were turn of the century, lovely houses in varying states of disrepair: peeling paint, wild ivy, broken fences. Ours was white with black shutters, classic and stately. Lucas put in a red-brick path with three steps leading to the front porch. The red brick was my suggestion. As an accent to our white house, it reminded me of New England. Lucas had more visual intelligence than I did. He was better at making these types of decisions. But he always listened to me anyway because he wanted his home to be my home. In the evenings, Addie sat on the brick dangling her feet off the top step while we rocked on the porch swing, talking about our days and the lives we dreamed up.

From the inside, the house felt like a bungalow but wasn't really, because it had a weirdly tall body—tall for its girth. From the open kitchen, you could see the entire first floor, just a small living room and a dining room littered with toys—first the dog's, then later, Lionel's. No one was ever more than thirty feet away from anyone else on the first floor of that house, which satisfied Addie's herding instinct, to have the entire family together at all times.

The view from the front window was framed by a big old tree, surrounded by hostas, which would bloom in the heat of July. Next to the window, there was a ratty, old leather chair that Addie had scratched up many times over as she clawed her way to the top. From that vantage, she could see all the neighborhood activity—the old lady who walked home with a book in her face, the guy who always wore jeans tucked into cowboy boots, a cigarette hanging from his lips, the girl next door with a boyfriend who climbed in through her window. Addie watched over the house, and if anyone walked up that redbrick path toward the front steps, she barked like crazy. The castle is under attack! It's the mailman!

In my head, our house on Catherine Street was a palace fit for a princess, a delusion only apparent to me in the occasional glare or grimace of a visitor. When I gave Samantha the grand tour, her face read, *Did I just walk into a South Bronx crack house?* A family of bats had recently taken up residence in the north wall, and they squeaked mercilessly after dark. Lucas bought one of those ultrasonic devices but they took to it like a white noise machine and extended their stay. Samantha said only, "I can't stay long. I have to pick up the kids."

———————————

LUCAS AND I DECIDED we needed to add on to our kitchen. This required tearing down an exterior wall. (No bats were harmed in the process.) We planned a one-month job, which we knew meant three months, and we started in June to take advantage of the warm weather.

In retrospect, living without a wall on the back of our house was risky.

The lower floor was sealed off from the backyard only by a thin nylon tarp. We'd heard about occasional break-ins in the neighborhood but blindly believed nothing bad would happen to us. We had a dog! Also, we owned nothing worth stealing.

Our summer project bulged into fall, finding ways to expand, like a fat body in a small wooden chair. Lucas had a football game on TV and a beer in hand. Papers strewn across the coffee table, I complained about grading—the most tedious part of my job—lopping off points for poorly structured arguments, boring first lines, weak linkages, the absence of conclusions. Beginnings, endings, and transitions! Students never learn!

When Addie's tail knocked what was left of Lucas's beer over onto one of my student's papers, it was hard to place blame: Lucas's beer, my mess, Addie's tail? Lucas took the green pen out of my hand, drew an arrow pointing at the beer splotch, and wrote *butt fumble* on the paper, referring to an incident the Jets would never live down, a real low point, when your own lineman's ass jars the ball loose. Lucas thought it was a good metaphor for our relationship. Fortunately, my student appreciated the joke. And the beer.

We were enjoying this peaceful Sunday, when Addie went nuts because she heard a squirrel. The creature had entered our home through the tarp, probably in search of food, and the second he saw Addie bolt toward him, he knew he'd made a mistake.

Barking, Addie chased him up onto the counter. Lucas and I sat dumbstruck for a beat. The squirrel scurried all the way up to the top of the kitchen cabinets, which dropped about six inches below the ceiling. He paced back and forth. Addie followed him from the floor, jumping and barking, her front paws on the counter and then down again.

The squirrel was safe as long as he held his position, but he was increasingly agitated. Lucas stood up, inched toward the kitchen, and called Addie to back down. A terrible listener, especially when excited, she continued to jump and bark. Then the squirrel made a run for it, down the side of the cabinet and toward the center of the house. That's when Addie caught him in her mouth.

I'd never heard a squirrel make so much noise. That little guy let out a horrible, fearful squeal: the sound of helplessness. It must have been the first time Addie ever caught anything because the look on her face was of complete bewilderment. She didn't want to clamp down. She didn't want to toy with the squirrel. She didn't want to kill him. But she didn't want to let him go. This was her house. It was her job to watch over it. And she'd done that job. She'd caught the intruder. So what now? She froze.

Addie's fangs reminded me of Lucas's mind. She had this God-given feature that enabled her to rip another living thing to pieces, but she wasn't psychologically capable of it. She could chase and bark and provoke but she didn't know how to snap her jaw or sink her teeth in. An Australian cattle dog with the heart of a Canadian, just like her master!

When Lucas spoke to her—*How was your day, Ruffers? Rufferstiltskin. Ruffers have ridges*—I couldn't help but wonder how much of her personality was her nature and how much she'd picked up from him. Certainly, the way he horsed around with her, putting his hand in her mouth, shaking her by the teeth, taught her never to bite down.

Slowly, she opened her mouth and the poor squirrel was released into the house. Lucas lifted the tarp and exposed the back side of the kitchen to the yard, an enormous gap. Even in shock, the squirrel found his own way out.

———————

TOWARD THE END OF the kitchen project, Lucas asked his father to come over to help with the drywall. For most of my life, I never thought much about walls. They were flat. They were covered in paint. Then I fell in love with a guy who hangs drywall for a living, and I began to see walls for what they really are: a thin façade covering up ducts and electrical wiring and insulation. The process of drywalling a room is patchwork, filling in gaps, taping joints, mudding over everything, layer after layer, until the surface is smooth. Now, when I see a beautiful human with a perfect child and a thriving vegetable garden and a clean car, I imagine her as drywall. I think about all the seams and joints and layers of mud. I think about everything it takes to make the surface appear smooth.

To watch Lucas's father hang and finish drywall was to experience virtuosity. He made it look so easy, so fluid, so precise. His pace was about one and a half times Lucas's pace. The old man had been handsome once, like Lucas. In old age, he had wiry gray hair that stuck straight up in the humid months, and a smoker's face, leathery and lined. When he ran into other old-timers, he'd say, "How you doin', my brother?" He claimed to run two miles every morning and then drink two beers to start his day.

He encouraged me to try the finishing once and only once. I ended up with a layer of mud on the wall, and also a layer on the floor and on my ripped jeans, which were, incidentally, not work pants. My pace I need not record.

Lucas may have been aware that there would be a time when his father could not so easily lift his arms over his head for long intervals, or climb a ladder without a second thought, but the notion that a father's physical decline is the only thing that will allow his son to surpass him is not a comforting one.

Sometime before I'd ever seen him work, Lucas and I were in a conversation with two guys—one had just remodeled his master bathroom and the other was adding on a sunroom. One guy said, "Well, Murphy sure did a fantastic job on my drywall. Good price too," and the other guy said, "Did you now, Lucas?" and then the first guy said, "No, no, I mean the *real Murphy*," and I could see something in Lucas's eyes but he just smiled and said, "Dad's the best, no doubt about that."

I'd like to think the reason Lucas delayed joining the family business for so long was because he had other ambitions, but I wouldn't doubt it was also because he wanted to be a *real Murphy*, as opposed to some less real version of his dad. It could also be the case that I'm projecting—that I've spent a lifetime avoiding measuring up to my own father's success, albeit a different kind of success.

These memories of our old home float through my mind like the ghost that comes with the house.

7PM

THE LOST-AND-FOUND BOX IS out on top of the bar. A guy is looking for his hoodie. He's not a regular here but he's a barfly. I run into him here and there around town. If I recall correctly, he works as a delivery guy, not a UPS guy—he doesn't wear a uniform—more like a guy who moves medical equipment for some no-name company that operates in New York and New Jersey. He has bought me a drink before but I don't remember his name.

He digs through the box. I can see from where I'm sitting: there's no hoodie in there. Amelia knows this. So why pull out the box at all?

Finally, the guy announces, "My hoodie's not in here."

Amelia nods, leaving the box on the bar. The guy fishes around a little more.

Cal says, "Take something else to replace it, if you want."

The regulars collectively look down into their drinks, watching the guy peripherally. He pulls out a pair of cheap, black plastic sunglasses and inspects them. He puts them back. The box also holds men's black leather gloves, a red-and-yellow polka-dot umbrella, a single hoop earring, and several other items that aren't worth claiming.

The guy tries on one of the gloves. He puts it back in the box and returns to his beer.

Amelia says, "Go ahead—take it if you want it."

He reaches back into the box and takes both gloves this time, holding them up in front of his face. "What if someone comes for them?"

"It's hot as hell out there," Cal says. "No one's gonna come lookin' for gloves this time of year."

The guy catches my eye.

Suddenly, I feel bad for him, maybe because he bought me that drink a while back, but more likely because I can see he's a nice guy. It's not a complicated analysis—I don't know anything about him—he just has a nice-guy disposition: sunny, a little distant, the opposite of exacting. He's one of those people who doesn't recycle, doesn't vote, doesn't buy local, doesn't care if produce is non-GMO, and he's also not an asshole. There's a correlation there, I'm sure.

I shake my head: *No.* I try to do it subtly, but Cal sees me. The guy drops the gloves back in the box and says, "I'm good; thanks, though."

"Fuck, Em. Why'd you have to ruin it?"

"That's entrapment," I say. "You wanna put the box out, fine, but you can't keep telling him to take something."

"That's the test—the Willy Wonka test," Cal says. "Gotta be able to say no to temptation."

"If I remember correctly, Willy Wonka didn't run around insisting the kids steal the Gobstopper. You gotta just put out the box and see what happens."

If you pass the test, it doesn't make you a regular. Regulars are people who come by two or more nights a week, every week, for at least three drinks. It takes time and money to become a regular. And beyond time and money, the guys have to like you. I came in through the back door because of Lucas, but it doesn't work that way for everyone. And if you fail the test, there are no consequences. You catch hell for about ten minutes for being a no-good thief, and maybe, if you look like you have the money, you are goaded into buying a round. Then everyone forgets the thing ever happened. The test doesn't work, anyway. All the good items are taken before they make it to the box, like those Tom Ford aviators I left behind six months ago that I'm still bitter about.

The guys decide they need to plant some better items in the box to raise the stakes. I agree that's reasonable. They tell me to bring in some "female items." I'll never get around to it.

———————

WHEN LUCAS AND I got married, my father insisted on speaking at the wedding. He was picking up the tab so it was his moral right. Against my better judgment, I allowed it. This was my only concession. I had not permitted him to bring his girlfriend—the woman with whom he had cheated on my mother. Something about saying no to the first request softened me to the second.

Our wedding was rustic, a euphemism for paying a ton of money to recreate a down-home atmosphere with a veneer of elitism apparent in the quality of the solid wood cross-back chairs and top-shelf liquor. The soirée unironically involved a Catholic priest and a country church, a restored hundred-year-old barn and a whole hog, cake *and* pie, pictures of our dog even though the dog wasn't present because she'd have eaten the pig, a hayrack ride to nowhere, a DJ in a skinny tie with a torso-length beard, mint juleps, gin and tonics, whiskey neat or on the rocks, kegs of Bud Light (townies prefer beer that tastes like piss), and a slew of family dysfunction that we choked down with the pork like a side of corn bread.

Dad's speech started with the smell of our town.

"When the wind blows from the northeast, there is an unmistakable stink of manure in this country town. I smelled it immediately upon my arrival."

My father was a great speaker, his vocal and physical delivery: impeccable. He used no notes. He didn't merely gaze around the audience, as a lighthouse presenter rotates systematically around the room. He made eye contact with individuals in the crowd, our guests, lingering on the important ones—my mother, my in-laws, Lucas, our best friends whom he'd met earlier in the night. His style of elocution was flawless. His voice rose and fell, volume creating suspense. He was also the best-dressed man in Upstate New York, which alone commanded a certain authority.

Dad paused for a second, a perfected technique, and I thought maybe he'd reflect on the smells of his childhood, floating across his hilltop town—smells of olive oil production and burning wood.

"It took me back in time in a powerful way, and I was with my little girl again. She liked to arrange my pens and pencils in my briefcase and listen to me on the phone on Saturday mornings, when I took care of odds and ends from the kitchen table.

"She asked me, 'Daddy, what is *a manure*?' She drew out the end of the word into distinct syllables, *ooo-er*. I had no idea what she was talking about. I racked my brain. I repeated *a manure* aloud. Then I realized she had been listening intently to my conversation from earlier that morning. I couldn't help but laugh to myself. I told her Daddy was an *entrepreneur* and explained that meant building something from nothing. I told her with initiative and hard work, she could be one too someday. Then she would be somebody special."

Why this memory? I thought. Why not talk about the only trip we ever took together, just the two of us? A father-daughter journey to the homeland to meet my grandfather. I was so young; the details were fuzzy. The TWA flight attendant gave me a little pair of wings and led me by the hand to the cockpit, where I met the pilots. The plane seemed enormous, four seats in the middle and three on either side. The trip was long—we had to fly to Rome, rent a car, and drive to the toe of the boot. I wanted to remember my grandfather; I wanted to know if his eyes were my father's eyes, *my eyes*. I wanted to understand what his life was like in the old country: ancient, rural, and slow. I wanted to ask him about my grandmother, who died when my dad was just a child, not so much older than I was at the time. I was too young for these questions—these *wants*—but my father wasn't. He must have remembered that trip like it was yesterday, and I couldn't figure out why a story about manure was more important to him.

Then he delivered his punch line: "And here we are. My little entrepreneur now lives in a town that smells like manure."

Dad had made a mistake, a cardinal sin. He'd forgotten the fundamental principle of communication: know your audience. *Had my father forgotten where he came from?* He, of all people, should have remembered small-town pride. He spent his adolescence in a town in Albany County, New York, population 792, at a time when people still put on their finest for church and took their kids to the town center to watch the parade on the Fourth of July. But then, he was the kid who left the place he came from, who never set foot in that hick town again, and, for the life of him, he couldn't fathom why anyone with a modicum of talent would stay.

Head tilted back, he chuckled at his own story. Then he looked at me. He must have noticed my dropped jaw, my mind fixed on the question he asked me when I told him my plan to live upstate and teach: *Why?*

Of course, there was no mention of Lucas in this story. A family drywall business was far removed from my dad's definition of entrepreneurship, from what he deemed worthy of his time. I wasn't entirely sure whether my father knew what Lucas did for a living. I'd never spoken to him about it because he'd never asked, and he'd shown no interest in spending time with Lucas.

He rambled on. I heard the words "She had a lot of spunk."

I thought, *I'll show you spunk*. I wanted to interrupt with a few choice words about how I'd found a man who was nothing like my father. But neither Lucas nor I had enough money in our name at the time to even cover the bar tab.

It made sense that he would tell a story that occurred when I was a child. He probably had the image of a third grader burned into his mind because that was the only time he knew me. Back then, we talked. I wanted a briefcase and a gold watch and a suit that smelled of cigar smoke. I wanted people to call me on Saturday morning because whatever it was couldn't wait 'til Monday. I wanted to be important so I would be important to him.

Eventually, he began spending Saturday mornings at his condo in Manhattan rather than at home in Wilton. I figured out I couldn't impress him if he wasn't there, so I stopped trying.

When he concluded his remarks, some of our friends offered a subdued, polite applause. Others remained notably, understandably, silent. I froze in shame. Lucas's father took the mic after him. His hair stuck straight up in the humidity. His black suit hung loose on his body, the shoulders just off, the sleeves half an inch too long—a funeral suit—and his shirt had come untucked. He cursed several times as he told a story about Lucas falling off a stepladder on a drywall job. He made fun of the way I drank beer, using my tongue to regulate the flow of liquid into my mouth, joking that every time he caught me sticking my tongue in my glass he wondered how a smart person could look so *retarded*. When I looked around, only Samantha registered any offense at his vulgarity. Everyone else was too busy laughing, or crying because the subtext was so full of love.

My father cornered me before he left our wedding reception, and I could see by the way he looked at me that he wanted me to thank him.

"I'll take my upstate manure over your city shit any day," I said.

And then, as if it were a serious comparison, he said, "Yes, you would."

Dad reached into his lapel pocket. He pulled out an envelope and a set of two keys attached to an *I ♥ NY* key chain.

"Dad, I don't have any pockets."

"Just open the envelope," he said.

It contained a slip of paper with an address in Brooklyn scribbled in his handwriting—all caps.

"It's yours," he said. "Well, technically it's the trust's. In fifteen years, you can do whatever you want with it." The trust was just a rich-person way to circumvent estate tax. I'd spent enough time around my father to know that.

The gift caught me completely off guard. My dad usually went out of his way to avoid giving me anything because he worried a free lunch would thwart his only child's ambition.

"Think of it as an investment," he said. "A town house in Cobble Hill. You'll need a place to land when this country quiet gets under your skin. And it'll be worth a fortune should you ever sell it."

I think he expected me to throw my arms around his neck and thank him but I was stunned.

As if he could read my mind, he said, "You should appoint it to your taste so you and Lucas have a place to stay when you come to the city."

"We really don't come down to the city that much, Dad," I said. "Maybe you should rent the place out."

"There's a small yard for the dog in the back."

"For Addie? You just said it was an investment property."

"That doesn't mean you can't live in it," he said.

"We live here."

"Lucas can hang drywall in the city."

"So you *do* know what Lucas does for a living!"

"Of course I know. He's my son-in-law."

"I just assumed you didn't care."

Loving my father never felt like a choice. He was a good dad, insofar as that distinction only required his presence and not being verbally or physically abusive. In other words, if you're a man, all you have to do is *not do* a few things and *Congratulations! Dad of the year!* Being a good mom requires perfection, in public and in private, without end.

"What are you going to do when you get bored with teaching?" Dad asked.

"Let's not do this now," I said. "Thank you for the town house."

I had a sudden urge to unload the *I ♥ NY* key ring into Lucas's pocket. My slinky silk gown was not designed to hold much of anything. He was across the dance floor talking to the DJ, his buddy from high school with a penchant for funk.

Then my dad said something that struck me, even on that happy occasion, as an omen of what was to come. "Think of it as a contingency. If things don't work out as you expect, you'll have a place to go, and down the road, if you need to, you can sell it." Maybe the notion of it—a contingency on my wedding day—should have pissed me off. But he was so sincere—the look in his eyes so paternal—I understood, maybe for the first time, what fatherhood meant to him.

———

JIMMY GRABS HIS BEER and heads back to the pool table on the other side of the bar.

Another thing about The Final Final: it's a sound tunnel. If you aren't focusing on your own thing, you can hear every word of someone else's thing. A couple of young girls who came in pretty frequently spoke on more than one occasion about Amelia's body. They noticed when she gained five pounds and lost five pounds. They thought they could tell if she'd been working out. They always huddled together and whispered. Amelia never said anything. She continued to serve the girls their drinks. Only her eyes, piercing as she shot soda water into their vodkas, showed that these conversations affected her. Finally, one of the girls loud-whispered, "Saggy boobs: strapless is not for everyone." I leaned over and said, "You realize everyone in the fucking bar can hear you, right?" They were mortified. Maybe they figured Amelia had been slowly poisoning their drinks. They never came back.

That's a long way of explaining that even though Jimmy and Yag are in the back, Amelia and I can hear every word of their conversation.

"Dude, I had this dream last night," Jimmy says. Yag misses his shot. "We were getting hammered at the bar." They both laugh. Jimmy is unusually spirited tonight, a departure for a guy who almost always has bags under his eyes from early mornings at the diner.

"Remember when you clocked in for an entire week at Bageltown and didn't serve a single customer?" Yag laughs. "How the fuck did you manage that?"

Lucas also worked at the bagel shop back in the day. Apparently, at one time or another, the manager hired every sixteen-year-old dumbass in town. For some period of time, these young guys all worked there together, until, one by one, they were all fired. One guy, for standing in the parking lot throwing bagels at anyone riding by on a bike, until a woman fell and broke her wrist; one guy, for making sandwiches so slowly that a customer complained she watched another worker make five before hers was complete, each lettuce leaf placed with craftsmanlike precision; Jimmy, for smoking weed in the supply closet.

"I hid out in the supply closet," Jimmy says. "Krista knew where I was but she had the hots for me." Krista was the manager. Jimmy sinks a shot and looks over at the bar. "Speaking of girls, what happened over there?"

"Who, Caroline? She's young," Yag says. "Doesn't understand that evolved men can have female friends."

"Girls are weird about their boyfriends sleeping with other girls— sometimes you just gotta listen to them."

"Sometimes I think it'd be easier to just have sex with myself." Yag gestures with his hand, making a loose fist, pulling up and down. He grabs the cue and squares up to take a shot. "Tonight is not my night."

HANGING OUT AT THE bar one night, trying to mind our own business, Lucas and I overheard Yag break up with his girlfriend of one year. Most of Martin's girls only stuck around for a matter of weeks, a few months tops, so this girl was the exception.

Tears streaming down her face, she asked why he wanted to break it off. He told her she wasn't attractive to him because she had put on weight. She asked why he called her beautiful so many times. He told her he only said those things because that's what good boyfriends did; he didn't really mean them. The girl believed him.

I knew how Yag's crazy mind worked, how it played tricks, and I was quite certain he did find her beautiful at one time, but, as a result of years of watching porn and jerking off, perception was fickle and he couldn't hold on to one idea for very long, so his mind turned on him and somehow morphed this beautiful thing into an ugly thing, and the only way he could rationalize it was to insist the beauty never existed in the first place. The girl didn't know any of this, though. She just thought she was unattractive. He added that she was perfect from the waist up but he was a "hips-and-ass guy." He paused like he wanted to suggest something but knew he shouldn't. Finally, he said maybe it was something she could work on. That's when she told him she was pregnant.

He told her to get an abortion. Then he swiveled around on his stool, stood up, and walked out of the bar.

Lucas turned to the girl and said, "He's crazy, you know—you are beautiful," which was exactly what she needed to hear at the time.

From that point on, Martin Yagla was no longer welcome in our house. I couldn't stand the sight of him. When Lucas hosted a poker night, Yag showed up with Jimmy and a couple of other guys. I stood on the front porch and pointed, my finger inches from his chest, and said, "Not him." Lucas looked at me, surprised, and then at Yag and then back at me, and then said to him, "Sorry, man; she's serious." And Yag said, "It's your house too." Lucas put his arm around him and walked him down the front path to the sidewalk. I don't know what he said to him. Yag didn't come back for as long as I lived there.

Lucas was always softer than I was, kinder, and I know he found my stance overly harsh. On his own, he would have given him a pass, but living with me, I think he agreed that understanding Yag's behavior and excusing it were two very different things.

As much as I dislike Yag, he probably hates me more. I took more away from him than he ever took from me. When he spoke of me to Lucas, he always referred to me as *The Mrs.*, even before we were married.

I'm sure he thinks I ought to be embarrassed by the ways Lucas changed after he met me, the fact that he gave up cigarettes and stopped texting some girl who had been in love with him for years. Somehow, knowing Yag believes this makes me self-conscious. I never wanted to be *that woman*, the woman Yag sees me as, but I had to be that woman because Lucas was better off. Still, something about Yag makes me feel ashamed about myself, as if commitment is for losers—conventionality, a sucker's burden. I am weirdly intimidated by him, though I can't say exactly why.

Lucas told me once, unprompted, that he was glad Martin Yagla was not prominently in his life anymore, which was his way of admitting that I had been right. That should have been the end of it. We should have all moved on with our lives. But it's a small town, and that's not what happened.

———

A GUY APPROACHES THE pool table and asks if they want to play Cut Throat when they finish their game. Jimmy says, "Sure, man, put down your quarters."

"Man, we never do crazy shit anymore," Yag says. "Like the pumpkin."

I've heard the pumpkin story at least five times, but I'm about to hear Yagla retell it for the benefit of the new guy.

Jimmy racks the balls for their game of Cut Throat. Yag breaks because he won last.

"We stole this pumpkin from the ShopRite. That's how it started. It was, like, a week before Halloween so we wanted a pumpkin. And then I remembered I had a bunch of illegal fireworks in my trunk. The kind that really explode." At a young age, Yag had a propensity for pyrotechnics. "Whose idea was the bowling alley?"

In high school, the guys referred to nights like this one as "High Quality Nights," a euphemism for nights when they didn't drink. On these nights, they occupied themselves in other ways.

"The bowling alley had those automatic doors, so we figured we could wait until someone walked through, triggering them to open, then we'd roll in the pumpkin." Their adolescent plan was to fill the pumpkin with lit fireworks before rolling it into the bowling alley. "After the pumpkin exploded we were gonna floor it outa there. I drove the getaway car," Yag says.

Mind you, this happened in the nineties, pre-9/11. These were the halcyon days of pranks. Still, these kids had no idea what kind of firepower they were packing into this pumpkin, and I can see by Jimmy's body language, the way he shakes his head and looks at the floor, that he now understands how reckless they were back then.

Yag continues. "I was behind the wheel. Jimmy was in the passenger seat cutting that pumpkin open with my hunting knife and packing it full. Our boy Lucas was in the back seat doing nothing, along for the ride. It's so typical that Lucas would take the back seat. He's a classic accomplice, sittin' back there smoking American Spirits."

"It's not like he tried to stop us."

"Hell, no. Lucas wanted us to do it. What the fuck else was he gonna do on a Friday night?"

The best part of the story is coming up. Depending on who's telling it, you either get what happened up front, like one of those movies that starts where the sequence ends, usually with a bunch of dead bodies, and jumps back to the beginning, or you have to wait to find out what happens, sometimes for a long time, while the storyteller describes the rising action—the stealing of the pumpkin, the loading of explosives, the chugging engine of Yag's Chevy Lumina, dubbed, affectionately, Luminus Maximus—as well as a hefty backstory, where Yag got the illegal fireworks (New Hampshire—*Live Free or Die*), the fact that the car was on empty because Yag's mom canceled his gas card for reasons that escape me now.

There's no right way to tell a story. I teach my students that the content and an understanding of the audience should dictate these choices. I have to admit Martin Yagla is good at telling stories. I want to know what is going to happen with the exploding pumpkin. In fact, I already know what happened because I've heard the story before, and I still want to hear it again.

He continues. "We idled in front. There was about twenty feet of sidewalk between the car and the door. And the door stayed open for about thirty seconds after a person cleared the motion sensor. I did a quick calculation in my head. We figured that was enough time to light it and roll it in."

"You calculated how long it would take the pumpkin to roll in through the door," Jimmy says. "Not how long it would take the pumpkin to explode."

"We just assumed—"

"Bad assumption—"

Yagla laughs. "Boom! The car filled with smoke. Pumpkin seeds went everywhere. Who would've thought it would explode immediately? We rolled all the windows down. I hit the gas just as soon as I could see out the windshield."

"That thick pumpkin skin saved my life," Jimmy says.

"Well, it saved your eyebrows, at least—maybe a couple fingers. I was picking pumpkin guts off the ceiling of Luminus Maximus for months. Seeds were stuck everywhere—"

Yag has a million stories like this one. He continues to talk, loudly and condescendingly, even as the details become more and more embarrassing. Martin Yagla: King of the Bar! I shake my head, though no one is looking at me.

The game drags on, and I can tell the new guy has had enough. He might as well be from another planet—an outsider looking in. He doesn't share their constitution.

They finally finish their game. By their body language, I can tell the outsider won. Yag asks him if he wants to play again. He says not tonight, puts his cue on the rack, and walks out the back door.

There are two types of people in the world: people who are glad high school is behind them, seen only through a tiny rearview mirror, and those who want to relive it as a state of constant present, glory days remembered as if they were only yesterday. Yag falls squarely in the latter camp.

Nostalgia makes me want to bury the hatchet with him. Nostalgia: memory's rosy-cheeked sister. If memory is a state of fractional loss, a slipping away, nostalgia is a state of fictional gain, an imaginative expansion. I allow it to take hold, partly because all the whiskey has softened me but also because, without Lucas around, Yag's impishness doesn't matter anymore. He's someone else's problem.

I ask Amelia for three house shots. The Final Final house shot is something called the blood orange, at least when Amelia's bartending. She invented it. It doesn't taste like orange but it is reddish orange in color. I have no idea what's in it, but it's quite boozy and it goes down easy. The college girls love it.

I bring the shots over to the pool table. Yag appears delighted by the gesture. He says, "You're not so bad, Em," then, pulling the glass toward his lips, he looks at Jimmy and says, "Here's to being free men." He shoots it down.

At first I think he's referring to the girl he said goodbye to earlier in the night, but he gives me a sly smile and pulls a cigarette out of the pack and puts it behind his ear. I realize he's talking about Lucas.

"Woohoo," I say. "Congratulations, Martin, no one cares about you. You cheat on your girlfriend. You owe ten grand to some over-the-hill wrestler, who may or may not collect the debt from your mother, scaring the life out of her for no other reason than her loser grown son still lives at home. Go ahead. Smoke your lungs out."

"You know what I can't figure out?" Yag says. Spit flies out of his mouth onto my face. "Why do you come here? Look around, Emma. You don't belong. No one wants you here. You are a sad, uptight bitch. You think you're better than us because you don't smoke and your daddy has money. You think we're a bunch of loser drunks. News flash, Emma— you're a drunk too! Three years ago, you were hot. We let you hang around with us because Lucas is our friend, but then you walked out on him. No one said anything because we all felt bad for you. No one had the balls. Well, I'll say it now. I'll be the asshole. Find your own fucking bar. Find your own fucking town. Why the fuck do you stay here?"

Jimmy ushers Yag out back for another smoke, sparing me a retort. I return to my bar stool, the spell of nostalgia now broken. My hands are shaking, all the rage manifest in my extremities.

Cal touches my right shoulder. He mumbles, "Don't listen to him. You belong here as much as any of us." He rambles on about friendship. He says something kind. I'm not really listening, though. I can't shake Yag's question: *Why the fuck do you stay?* The answer is obvious, isn't it? I stay to live in the past, the *before*.

"LUCAS," I SAID. "I'M sorry but I have to confess something to you."

Lucas was behind the stove, making pasta sauce. Since he took out the wall between the kitchen and the living room, he could stand over the stove, watch TV, and talk to me, all at the same time. He had several balls in the air, but he managed everything gracefully: chopping, sautéing, cleaning. Somehow he found time to pour himself a whiskey.

"Something serious?"

"Serious as a heart attack."

Addie was up on the back of the couch. I leaned back and rested my head on her warm, furry body and crossed my legs on the coffee table.

"Only a sociopath could make a confession and appear so relaxed," Lucas said.

"I was raised Catholic," I said. "Confessing is a part-time job."

"Lay it on me, baby," he said.

"I think maybe I love Addie more than you." She perked up at the sound of her name. When Lucas cooked, Addie was ultra-attuned to any clue that a food scrap had been accidentally dropped or a piece of gristle was there for the taking.

"Why do you think that?"

"Well, it's just that she occupies most of my idle thought."

He opened a can of tomatoes and added the contents to the sauce, while turning down the flame with his other hand.

"It's not you," I said. "It's Addie. She's too cute. I love her dog body. I love when she opens her mouth just a little and her tongue pokes out."

"So, let's say our house is burning down—"

"The ol' house-is-on-fire scenario."

"You wake up and realize you only have time to save one of us."

I got up from the couch and joined him behind the stove. Addie followed. The sauce simmered and the water was just coming to a boil. I had dallied on the couch just long enough—there was very little left to do. The cutting board and knife needed washing. I turned on the faucet.

"Well," I said. "The three of us sleep in the same bed. So how would I only have time to save one of you?"

"Let's say I'm passed out cold."

"Too many whiskeys?"

"Yeah, let's say I had too many whiskeys and I passed out."

"Want me to make a salad?" We had a bag of super greens in the keeper that I had purchased at the farmer's market. Kale and chard were the kinds of greens we forced ourselves to choke down because I insisted on a nutrient-rich diet while we were trying to get pregnant. "I'd just throw you over my shoulder and run out. Addie follows us wherever we go."

"You do know I weigh more than a sack of potatoes, right?" He shook his head. "Sometimes I wonder how I ever fell for you in the first place."

I crouched down next to him. Addie stood next to me, ready to play. I bent his body over my shoulder. The front half of Addie's body bounced up and down. She positioned her face as close to mine as possible and then inched closer, trying to steal a lick. Lifting Lucas's feet about two inches off the floor, I attempted to stand upright from my squatting position so I could make a move for the door. "Damn, Lucas, packing on some extra pounds, eh? Well, I'd have adrenaline pumping through me. Or! Addie and I could roll you out together."

"Down the stairs?"

"Bruises beat death." For salad dressing, I mixed mustard, fresh lemon, and a little bit of olive oil in a jar.

"Let's just say you are forced to choose," he said. "Me or Addie. Who will it be?"

"Furry love bug or chiseled hunk?"

"You just said I put on some pounds."

"Yeah, pounds of muscle." I squeezed his arm. He grabbed my ass.

"I'd have a moral obligation to save you," I said.

"Classic speciesism," he said.

Our whole house smelled of olive oil, onions, and garlic. It was the smell of *hygge*. "Also, Addie can't cook. Point, Lucas," I said.

"But she can lick the dishes," he said.

"True. She definitely does her part cleaning dishes."

"But she sheds everywhere."

"That's why I need you both." I pointed at her and then at him. "She sheds and you love to vacuum."

"I do not love to vacuum." He poured salt into the boiling water and added the noodles. Lucas would have just winged it, waiting about as long as he thought the noodles would take and then scooping one out with a spoon to test its consistency, but I read the package and set the timer on the oven: eight minutes.

"Then why are you always vacuuming?"

Lucas had this enormous, industrial Shop-Vac with a long nozzle. He stuck it in nooks and crevices and sucked up dog hair.

"Okay, I'll admit I find it satisfying."

"I'm going to tell everyone at the bar," I said. "You'll catch hell."

Making fun of the guys at the bar was Lucas's favorite pastime. Most times the jokes were spontaneous but I suspected they planned the particularly biting repartee in advance.

"Maybe I love vacuuming more than I love you."

"It's me or the vacuum. You have to choose."

"The vacuum doesn't put out."

"You could try putting your dick in the nozzle?"

"Suction, no friction," he said.

"Gross," I said. "Point, Addie. She can't talk."

We had a case of red wine in the dining room, left over from the wedding. I took out a bottle, opened it, and poured two glasses. This was my primary responsibility for the evening. Lucas still had whiskey left in his glass, but he took a sip of wine anyway.

"Take it easy, man," I said. "You can let it breathe for a minute." I took a huge swig from my glass. "How'd the fire start, anyway?"

"What's that got to do with anything?"

"I just need to know if it was your fault or Addie's. Was it your faulty electrical wiring? Or did Addie turn on the gas stove with her paw when she tried to reach an old pizza box so she could lick it?"

"My wiring is not faulty," he protested.

"I'm pretty sure it's illegal to do it yourself, though. Maybe I should call the inspector."

"No one calls the inspector on themselves," Lucas said.

I can't remember what the pasta tasted like. When I imagine this night, my mind inserts a facsimile of taste but I am aware it is an amalgamation of all the pasta that has touched my lips over many years—Uncle Nic's spaghetti, Antolini's fettuccini, the sauces Lucas and I made together, and some he made on his own. This bothers me—the fact that I cannot remember the specific pasta that Lucas made on this specific occasion. I recall the exact way he cut the onion: starting with the knife pointed toward the root, using the top knuckle on his left middle finger to guide it, slicing, then rotating the onion and dicing. I can close my eyes and smell the aroma in the house. But I cannot taste the true flavor in my mouth, try as I might. This inability to taste my memory is the thing that always tips me off to its falseness, the idea that I may have made some of it up, that my reporting of the words that passed between us may not be entirely accurate, that the way he looked at me might have been less passionate and more world-weary, that Addie might not have put her nose to my face as I stooped down to lift Lucas from the floor. Knowing this act of remembering is, at the same time, an act of misremembering is the reason every time I imagine this moment, I experience loss—not a single loss but an infinite series of fractional losses, invisible in their minuteness but known entirely to me—a side effect of my addiction to these memories, my need to relive them. Each time I return, I rub away a bit more, but I still must return, again and again, out of fear that losing them is losing everything.

If memory serves, the conversation ended like this:

"I'll wait 'til we break up, and I'm a jilted lover. That's how I'll get back at you. I'll call the town and tell them you put in faulty wiring."

"We're married," he said. "You can't break up with me."

CAL IS RUMMAGING THROUGH his wallet. He's only a few feet away from me, and I can see he's carrying a big wad of cash, maybe a thousand bucks, by the looks of it.

He hands me a new business card: *FINGER LAKES CONSTRUCTION*. Under his name his title reads *GENERAL CONTRACTOR*, followed by his cell phone number.

"Can I keep this?" I ask.

"Today I did some work for Veronica Lewis," Cal says.

"Old Lady Lewis?" Jimmy says. Veronica Lewis is a widow in her seventies.

When Cal isn't pulling in fifty or sixty K for a kitchen remodel or home addition, he moonlights as a handyman, helping out people around town whenever he can. If he knows the person is hard up and can't pay, he does work for free. Most of the time, people throw him cash. There are a couple of old ladies in town who enjoy his friendship in addition to his handiwork, and I have it on good authority that on multiple occasions he's been offered a hundred dollars for an hour of light work.

"Whooeee, I bet she wanted some of this." Short Pete reaches out and tugs Cal's beard.

"Don't touch my beard, man. If you must know, her hot water wasn't working. She asked me to take a look." He strokes his beard into place with his thumb and forefinger. He can't think of a snappy comeback. Everything's a competition of no consequence for these guys—who can get in the sharper dig? Who is right? Most important, who's funnier?

"Lemme guess," Yag says. "The pilot light was out."

Cal tilts his head and smiles. "No, guy. The control panel was melted out. I replaced it. Then I hung a mirror for her."

"You hung a mirror for her?"

"A heavy mirror."

"Did you charge her for that?"

"She tips real well but I don't need the money. That's not why I do it. She lives alone. Needs the help."

Just about everyone in town has been on the receiving end of Cal's kindheartedness at one time or another. He'd spend half a day helping any regular at this bar move furniture for a six-pack of beer. Before he left Veronica's house, she probably offered him something to eat, and regardless of whether he was hungry, I have no doubt he sat with her for a while and asked her how she was getting along.

I'm glad to have his business card.

"You really know how to hang a mirror," Short Pete says.

"Cal sure can hang," Fancy Pete says.

"That's why the old ladies pay him the big bucks," Yag says. "Did ya hammer the nail in the wall with your big dick?"

Cal turns his back and walks to the front to check on Summer. His rain jacket hangs over the chair across from her—the only other seat at the table—as if he's reserving it, though I doubt he will sit down. He slides his bulky wallet into the pocket of the jacket before rubbing foreheads with Summer. She rotates gleefully, keeping her head pressed against him—a kiss and an embrace all at once. It strikes me as so personal, so joyous.

Cal is still nursing the same Bud Light. He has to drive Summer home by ten. By then he won't be drunk but he won't be entirely sober either. He'll be just sober enough that no one here, including me, will think he's a piece of shit for getting behind the wheel with his little girl in the car.

"My dick joke would've gotten a laugh three years ago," Yag says. He drops his head and tilts his glass toward his eye to observe the bubbles, disappointed in us all.

Once, sitting outside in the garden at the bakery with Samantha—our entire friendship centers around the bakery (there's only one), the juice bar / broth bar (juice in summer, broth in winter), and the salad place (a chain called Leaf for obvious reasons: Who said the corporate yuppies didn't get their grubby little fingers this far upstate?)—lattes and almond croissants laid before us, Samantha's baby sleeping, snug in her bassinet, I mentioned that Cal brought Summer to the bar. I made some mistake of phrasing, a comparison implicit, something like, "It's cool that you can just bring the kid along." Samantha's nose crinkled and her upper lip turned up: disgust evident. "What kind of parent would bring a child to a bar?" she said. "That's so . . . sad."

MY DAD WAS THE second person I profiled in *The Breakout Effect*, after Pamela Randolph Walsh. His name was the reason the book sold in the first place. I have no delusions about that.

Growing up, I heard bits and pieces of his story. His father, my grandfather, was a tailor from a hilltop town in southern Italy. When my grandmother fell ill, he used all of his savings and all of his time to care for her, and when she died, there was nothing left. Along with my grand-mother, their town had slowly begun to die too—the shops closed one by one, first the cobbler, then the baker, then the tailor. The younger genera-tion moved to Rome; the old lived on government subsistence. My father, then only twelve, and his brother, Nico, were sent to live in America. Dad chose to believe the reasons were economic, but based on old pictures, I think he was sent away because he looked so much like his mother.

He was taken in by his aunt and uncle who owned land near Albany, where he was made to work the farm and rarely permitted to attend school. He might have suffered other abuse, though he never spoke of it. It was on that farm that he started dreaming of city skyscrapers, beautiful women, and Italian suits—suits made of the finest wool and silk, materi-als his father once admired.

At the beginning of his career, my dad purchased a business with warehouse space in New York City's Garment District. To do this, he borrowed money from wealthy investors. Upon consolidating the busi-ness, introducing automation, and laying off well over half the workforce, he realized he had something very valuable: space.

My father's foray into real estate was not especially interesting. The thing that captivated me was how an Italian immigrant from outside of Albany with no college degree convinced a cohort of wealthy investors to back him in the first place. This, I came to learn, had everything to do with a hilltop town in Italy and a love of fine Italian suits.

The warehouse space was converted into residential lofts and sold off at a fantastic premium. The investors were over the moon. They took my dad and all the wives out to celebrate. According to my mom, when one of the investors was good and drunk, he leaned back in his chair and said cheerfully, "Hell, I can't even remember why we agreed to give you the money in the first place."

And the other guy said, "You couldn't figure out how this kid from Albany got his hands on a nicer suit than yours."

And the first guy laughed and said, "I figured it was a Mafia thing."

Then my mom told them my dad's story, about his father, the tailor from Calabria who sent him to live with his aunt in America.

And one of the investors said, "Well, I'll be. Son of a tailor spins gold in the Garment District."

Dad never wanted for capital again. He quickly transitioned from buying buildings, renovating, and managing them, to investing in other people who did all that. Investing in things was a much better gig than actually doing things. He didn't have to get his hands dirty (no more gloves-off fights with general contractors and tenants). And the best part: the benevolent IRS taxed his income at capital gains rates, so while every other loser punched the clock and shelled out their earnings at much higher ordinary income rates, guys like my dad, who had the money to make money, amassed enormous wealth. This was how the son of a tailor became a private equity mogul. God bless America.

I wanted to know how he had acquired that beautiful suit, perfectly tailored, the best suit in Manhattan. When I called to ask him about it, he said, "What do you remember about your grandfather?"

"He was a short man with small shoes. He wore a tweed coat. His eyes filled with tears when he saw me—I couldn't have been older than six. He sat with you in the lobby of our hotel while I played by the fireplace. He spoke mostly Italian, and you, mostly English." That was all I had. "Why didn't Mom go with us on that trip?" I asked.

"She was in one of her blue periods," he said. "She couldn't care for you at the time. I spent our last dollar on airfare for the two of us."

"I wish I could remember more," I said. "My grandfather—"

"I asked him to make me a suit," my dad interrupted. "Before we made the trip to see him, he went to Naples to get the material, the finest in the world. He traded his labor, sewing for a much younger man who had more work than he could handle, making suits for Swiss bankers and German executives, French actors and Italian musicians. Your grandfather worked three months for three meters of material. He'd touched nothing like it before: a luxurious vicuña blend, invented by a French cloth maker. I still say that cheap *Napoletano* got the better trade. A quarter year of labor from one of the best tailors in Italy. Younger men don't stitch with the same skill. But the old man returned with the material he needed. Mine was the last suit he ever made. In all my years, I've never found another that fits to such perfection."

Picturing my father and grandfather in that hotel lobby, I realized there must have been an intimacy between them that I could not understand as a small child. The old man would have pulled out his tape measure and recorded my father's every dimension. The process probably took a long time. I could only imagine the care he put into every stitch.

There was a question on the tip of my tongue, the only question that mattered, the question I could not ask: *Did we go to Italy so your father,* mio nonno, *could meet his only grandchild before he died, or did we travel all that way to pick up a suit?*

My father transitioned the conversation back to me.

"What do you want to write a book for, anyway?" His tone was gruff.

"Because that's what I want to do, write and teach."

"Your little teaching job has been a nice break from the real world." I pictured him in a fine suit as he spoke these words.

"In what way is it little?"

"I'm sorry, your current teaching job."

"Because it pays little?"

"Well, yes, for one thing." He wasn't speaking into the receiver when he said this. His voice began to trail off.

"Because it carries little status?"

"You used to be so ambitious." When he said these words, he spoke directly into the phone, loud, abrupt, with a certain righteousness, which came across almost like anger. There were many things my father said to me over the years that annoyed or offended me, which I have long since forgotten, but these words stayed with me. They were with me when I read my first negative review; they were with me when I moved into my one-bedroom, garden-level apartment; they are with me here, at The Final Final. *You used to be so ambitious.*

"This is ambitious, Dad," I said. "This is the most ambitious thing I've ever done."

"It's not too late to go back to finance. Use those degrees I paid for."

That's what it always came back to with him: a transaction. He'd invested in me and I wasn't paying off.

Dad didn't bother to read the book until it became a best seller. Then he told me it wasn't half-bad.

I HAVE THIS OLD picture of my parents in their twenties: my dad with his carefree coif of thick, black hair, skinny with tan legs, and my mom in a bathing suit and big sunglasses. I use it as a bookmark for whatever I happen to be reading. From time to time, I examine the photo and try to imagine how they were back then. The picture was taken on their honeymoon, before they had any money. They are standing in front of a tiny, rustic cabin, which apparently had no electricity or running water. For a full week, they washed by swimming in the lake. The people in the photo aren't touching but there is an energy between them, apparent in the way they look at the camera while maintaining awareness of each other, and they are at ease with themselves and the world, which anyone would notice in the looseness of their bodies, the way they appear to dance even when still. They look like completely different people—different from the people I know now and different from the people who raised me. I don't recognize these happy people, so to imagine them as they were is a completely speculative act, a construction based partially on the anecdotes of my youth but mostly on pure fantasy. If I could not distinguish my dad's watery, *calabresi* eyes, or my mom's small, celestial nose—features I see in the mirror—it would be easier to assume these people were not my parents at all. Knowing who they are now creates cognitive dissonance that, try as I might, I cannot reconcile. How did the happiness of youth, and, beyond happiness, the characteristics of the self, existing in relation to another human being and to the world, undergo this titanic shift, such that the landscape of being is fundamentally altered and essentially unrecognizable but for a couple of lingering, ancestral features?

In my adolescence, my parents presented a certain reality to me: they were right and I was wrong. That reality is like old skin. It itches a little. It flakes. Yet it still offers a layer of protection from the world. Even with miles between us, I find that skin difficult to shed. Still, I cut the cord a long time ago, which is more than I can say for Lucas.

We argued about this, shortly after we married.

We were in bed by midnight—it was definitely no earlier than eleven thirty—and Lucas's cell rang. The sound jolted me. I could tell who it was immediately by the way he shot up and turned his back to me. I could tell who it was even before he said, "Mom."

My first thought was that something bad had happened, like maybe his dad suddenly fell ill. She had never called at this hour before. Lucas spoke calmly and didn't ask about the old man. He grabbed paper and pen on the nightstand and started jotting something down as she spoke to him. I crawled over to his side of the bed to look over his shoulder. Either my eyes deceived me, or it was exactly what I feared it would be: a grocery list. They had this weird practice of ordering basic grocery items in bulk quantities. She was telling him to order lentils and couscous. He eventually told her he loved her and hung up the phone.

There is something in the water in this town. A mysterious chemical that keeps grown men attached, a castration of independence. Lucas's childhood bedroom was perfectly preserved in his parents' house. We slept there once when the kitchen renovation made our house temporarily unlivable. On the dresser, there was an old Wheaties box from the nineties, featuring the Yankees as the American League Champs. The cereal was still in it.

Really, though, who am I to say what is a healthy relationship and what is not? Most people tell themselves the healthy ones are those that last, but we all know that's not true.

"Lucas," I said. "Your mom cannot call here at this hour."

"We weren't asleep."

"I'd like to be asleep."

"I can't tell her not to call. What if something happens?"

"Does her giving you a grocery list constitute something happening?"

"You know what I mean."

"No, Lucas. Well, yes, I know what you mean, but I completely disagree."

"Fine. I'll tell her not to call so late," he said.

"Why are you ordering her bulk groceries anyway? Seems like she's perfectly capable of using the telephone."

"I'm helping out my mom, Emma. Would you like anything from the health food store?"

"What century are we living in? Can't you just set up a recurring shipment on Amazon? Or would all that cardboard disrupt Joan's vastu shastra?"

"Can we just go to bed?"

"You need to cut the cord. You're a grown man. How does it go again? 'A man shall leave his father and his mother and hold on to his wife.' Something like that?"

He didn't respond. He was on his stomach with his head turned away from me.

"You aren't listening," I said.

"I was listening. For the longest time," he said, and he shoved his face down into the pillow.

Joan told me once that I should meditate. Every morning she sat cross-legged on the floor and stared at the wall for fifteen minutes. She called it *mindfulness*. I told her that every morning I hit snooze and stared at the ceiling for fifteen minutes. I called it *lethargy*.

"I can't do dinner with your parents this weekend, Lucas."

"Why?"

"I have to work on the book. Sorry," I said.

He was still on his stomach but his head was turned toward me, half-sunk into the pillow. From this position, he could look at me with only his left eye. A cyclops dagger.

"You can take a break for dinner," he said.

"It always takes, like, three hours. That's too much time," I said.

"We were at the bar last night for six."

"That's different."

"Time is time," Lucas said.

"Friday night: I needed a drink."

"You can have a drink at my folks' house."

"Your mom judges me."

"Dad drinks beer in the morning, Em. No one is judging you."

"Sorry. Just tell her I'm not feeling well this week."

"I'd prefer it if you just come with me," he said.

I told him I didn't want to eat gluten-free, non-GMO casseroles fortified with flax. I told him I could taste the flax and I didn't like it. I told him I knew his mother made his lunch most days because I saw the Tupperware in the sink. I told him a man in his thirties should make his own lunch.

I told him, "I gave up everything to live in this town; the least you could do is give up your mother's teat."

JIMMY WEDGES HIS BODY next to me at the bar. He orders another stein of beer for himself and tells Amelia to put my next drink on his tab. He's either apologizing for Yag's behavior or paying a debt. Lucas was the same way when people bought him drinks. He never left the bar without returning the favor.

He looks tired now, less spirited. A day of hard drinking and cigarettes and greasy food is finally catching up with him. Amelia pours his beer and he's gone, back at the pool table with Yag.

When Jimmy's sister died, Lucas didn't know what to say to him. For weeks, he fretted about this. He stopped calling. Jimmy had taken a break from the bar—he dabbled with AA for a bit—so they were virtually cut off. Out of the blue, Lucas received a text message from Jimmy that read, *Nostalgia comes from the Greek:* nostos, *homecoming, and* algos, *pain.* Most people wouldn't know how to respond but Lucas understood what Jimmy was after immediately. What's the best way to respond to a fact? More facts. Lucas knew the origin of the word *nostalgia* already. He'd read about it somewhere. He wrote, *Defined as a "cerebral disease of demonic cause that originated from continuous vibrations of animal spirits."* They riffed off this for a while. And with that, they found their way back in.

I'll never forget this exchange for two reasons. First, the idea of the portmanteau, homecoming and pain, is so precisely relevant to Jimmy. His return to our town, his homecoming, made him a witness to pain, and his continual presence here is the enactment of pain. And second, *animal spirits* is a term that has been co-opted by economists and investors to describe psychological factors that drive certain market outcomes, and the fact that it is conceptually connected to pain is, ultimately, what *The Breakout Effect* is about.

A SPARROW IS IN the bar, flying into walls: a bat in the belfry.

Amelia appears from the cellar door, wielding a broom. She points to Fancy Pete. "Hold 'er open!"

The sparrow drops to the floor and begins to hop. Amelia coaxes the bird toward the front door. I think it's working.

As regulars, we believe our presence here is an inalienable right of higher order than the natural world. The bird has no claim to this place. She is an interloper, infringing on our interests, which are to drink, and occasionally to talk, and, in rare instances, to make peace with our lots.

I've decided the bird is female: a *she*. I'm not sure why; I know nothing about birds.

She panics, takes flight again. A few patrons duck down on the bar, like school children playing heads down, thumbs up.

A series of loud, sharp chirps rap, one after another, in quick, uneven intervals. The song has no rhythm; the lyrics are chaos. It isn't the frenetic movement of the sparrow but this unyielding noise, a combination of strange vocalization and flapping wings, that makes her presence alarming. We are under siege.

Because we are still relatively sober—not sober, exactly, but still mindful—both individually and collectively, nothing escapes our notice, no friend or foe, pleasure or annoyance. Everything either adds to or detracts from a great, invisible basin of grievances to which each of us contributed, one by one, upon walking through the front door. Behind the bar, a few photos of bartenders and regulars are tacked up. Among them, there is a single tarot card depicting Lady Justice and her scales. I imagine our basin of grievances rests on one side of the scale, and as the night progresses, it is counterbalanced by inebriation on the other side. The sweet spot is when we are collectively drunk enough to balance the burden but not so drunk that we have tipped the scale in the other direction.

The bird flies directly into the mirror behind the bar: smack! She drops into a line of bottles. Glass shatters on the floor. I cross my arms over my face. She takes flight again, this time in the direction of the pool table.

Somehow this bird, large as sparrows go but small for a creature of the earth, has us all subdued. How many times have I seen a sparrow in a tree outside my window? A little brown friend, about the size of my hand. A welcome guest in my yard. When the bird leaves the tree and enters the bar, she is suddenly different: predatory. Outside she is light and gentle, in search of grain and seeds. Inside, she works herself into a frenzy. The bird hasn't changed; the place has changed. To her, the bar must seem oppressively small, a cage, or alternatively, dangerously large, a labyrinth. Removed from her natural habitat, she is lost and alone, a threat to herself and others. Take away the habitat and the creature scarcely has a chance.

The Final Final is my natural habitat, but it wasn't always. I'm like an animal inured to captivity. I can no longer survive in the wild.

"Call animal control," someone says, but we all know that will take too long.

Cal takes the broom from Amelia, tells her that she's scaring the bird and that she should hit the lights.

"Turn them off?"

"Yep. Do it."

Amelia trusts Cal.

The front and back doors are propped open with bar stools. Amelia hits the lights, and the place turns into a tunnel, black in the middle, light at the ends. This is the first time I've been in The Final Final with all the lights out. I'm surprised by how little light makes its way in. The front window is tinted black, partially covered by a low-hanging awning and a couple of fluorescent beer signs, hung from the outside. There are no back windows and there are solid brick walls on either side of the bar. One side abuts the alley, and the other separates the bar from a late-night take-out spot, called China Star.

The bird's instinct will take it toward the streetlight. This is our collective expectation, as if we are churchgoers awaiting a reckoning.

The darkness lends a special quality to the bar, a false expansiveness: a beautiful emptiness. No one speaks. No one moves. The TV audio is off. The jukebox does not have a queue. Stillness hijacks the room.

The bird is quiet now too. She is resting on the floor in the middle of the bar. Her tiny bird head turns to the back door and then to the front. She decides between the two ends of the tunnel. It occurs to me that the expression *The light at the end of the tunnel* carries with it a false idea of forward progress. In fact, there is light at both ends of the tunnel, which can be reached either by forward movement or by turning back to the place from whence one came.

Four TVs are mounted above, two directly over the bar, and two at either end. The faces of the patrons, men bellied up, are illuminated by their glow and the beer signs hanging behind the bar. Some combination of sunlight from outdoor work, cigarettes, and hard drinking has deepened the lines on their faces, which are exaggerated by the bluish light. To my left, Cal, Short Pete, and Fancy Pete sit, one, two, three.

I want to hold on to this moment a little bit longer.

I think about all those black birds, dead on the shoulder of the 101 near San Francisco. Maybe The Final Final is about to have an earthquake. Or maybe I've just had too many whiskeys already and I need to go home and go to bed.

The bird hops, rotating toward the front door. She flaps her wings a couple of times. She pushes off. Halfway to the door her feet tuck in, like landing gear retracting into the belly of the plane. Then she is gone.

8PM

A GROUP OF COLLEGE girls rolls in. Wet high heels stomping on the doormat, umbrellas jettisoned, they shake off excess water like dogs. They never wear rain slickers or rain boots or anything else that would protect them, regardless of season. They are impervious to weather. It is a superpower of youth.

Huddled together, they shuffle over to the shot wheel, and the queen bee sends it spinning. They'll stay for one drink and then head downtown to join the sea of crop tops and four-inch heels. Amelia half pays attention to them, waiting for them to decide what they want. *No, not that one. That sounds gross.* They spin again and it lands on redheaded slut. *That's offensive.* One of the girls looks up at the line of men watching from their seats at the bar, seats they've been in all night. *This is such a gross townie bar.*

Amelia doesn't do or say anything to the girls. She serves other customers. She asks me if I'm doin' okay.

Martin Yagla and I can't share this space. This much is clear. It's him or me. And though I'm sure he needs The Final Final as much as I do, I decide to step over him when he falls, as if he is nobody, subhuman, a danger to himself and others.

Everyone in the bar knows Yag is hard up for money. He's on thin ice because he brought in trouble, which makes him vulnerable.

Cal is carrying that huge wad of cash in his wallet, money he's accumulated from a week or more of odd jobs, money he'll use to cover his bills, which probably include whatever amount he fronted for parts. I picture the fat wallet in the pocket of his rain jacket slung over the empty chair across from Summer.

She sits in front by the darkened windows, playing with a vintage, plastic Breyer horse on a high-top table, squirming left and right and back again on a low-back swivel chair. There's a small enclave there, a nook to the right of the entrance. Lucas and his friends used to commandeer this space, back when they had a big crew, before people started moving away and having kids. I take my fresh whiskey over and position myself in the chair reserved with Cal's jacket.

I ask Summer if her horse has a name.

"Pony," she says. She makes it gallop toward me on the table. "Want to draw with me?" Summer hands me a piece of orange construction paper and a blue crayon. She keeps a yellow piece and the rest of the crayon box for herself. She asks me what she should draw. I suggest her pony.

She begins. Her ability to focus is impressive. She chews on her tongue as she draws.

Reaching back, I slip my hand into the pocket of Cal's jacket and wrap my fingers around the fat leather wallet. Quickly, I shuffle the wallet from his pocket into my rear waistband, where it fits tightly between my underwear and jeans, just above the crack of my ass. I make sure my tank top is pulled down over the bulge, which is probably still visible but shouldn't draw attention from a bunch of unsuspecting drunks.

I start doodling logical fallacies with my blue crayon:

Cal is a good dad ∧ Good dads spend time with their kids

∴ Cal brings his kid to the bar

Everyone likes Lucas ∧ Lucas likes me

∴ Everyone likes me

The second one nags at me. It's a man's prerogative to be liked. Women are sometimes respected, sometimes admired, sometimes adored, but they aren't liked, not really. I know this because I am a teacher. My course evals don't benefit from the affable-white-guy bump.

My own mother preferred Lucas to me. Once, she steadied herself by pawing his bicep and resting her head on his shoulder. "So firm," she slurred. Lucas was like a funnel. He took all the love in—from his vast network of friends, from people in the town, people he'd known for thirty years, patrons of this bar, Amelia and Jimmy and Yag. But without Lucas, the funnel was gone, and these people, though I'd spent years in their company, were strangers again.

"Whatcha writing?" Summer asks.

"Logical fallacies," I say without further explanation. She doesn't seem to mind. She's accustomed to adults talking. "Whatcha drawing?"

Next to her pony there is a green leafy plant. I ask her if that is what the pony eats. She shakes her head. "The pony eats hay. This is a marijuana plant." She says *marijuana* with perfect diction, and the leaves on the plant really look like marijuana. The pony is sort of watching over the plant.

"This is my plant," Summer says. "It's not as big as Daddy's plant even though I put all the Miracle-Gro on it."

"So this plant is in your yard?" I ask.

"It was. It's not anymore," she says. "Me and Daddy had a competition—"

"Daddy and I—"

"Huh?"

"You say *Daddy and I*, not *me and Daddy*," I say. "Trust me."

"Daddy and I had a competition," she says, pleased with herself. "Who could grow the biggest plant. His was always bigger no matter how much Miracle-Gro I put on mine. He said if mine grew bigger than his, he'd buy me a pony. A real pony. It never did, so I just got this one." She knocks the plastic horse away with the back of her hand like she is disgusted with it now.

"What happened to it?"

"What?"

"Your plant."

"One day I was out in the field playing, and up in the sky I saw a helicopter. It found us."

"What'd you do?" I think about Pamela Randolph Walsh and all those police cars in her driveway.

"I ran all the way back to the house. I didn't stop to catch my breath. I yelled, 'Daddy, they found us. Daddy, Daddy, they found our weed patch.'"

Cal must have explained to her that what they were doing was illegal and that at some point the police might come for them. Summer knows things little girls shouldn't know, and at the same time, she is perfectly innocent and childlike: Cal's little girl.

"What happened?"

"We put all the weed into trash bags as fast as we could. Then we took the trash bags out to the cans."

"Why?"

"Daddy said maybe they wouldn't look there." She looks at her paper, not me, when she talks. Using her green crayon, she colors in more marijuana leaves. The plant is huge now, bigger than the pony.

"But they did look there," I say.

"Yeah, one of the cops put Daddy in handcuffs, and then another cop took me into the living room and said I shouldn't be afraid. I didn't like the way he looked at me. He eyeballed my tangles—I hadn't combed my hair that morning. I wanted to keep my tangles. I yelled, 'I ain't afraid of no cops.'" She stops, looks up at me, and corrects herself. "I should have said, 'I'm not afraid of cops.'"

I nod. "Very good."

"Then I ran back into the kitchen where they were talking to Daddy, and he told me to get the duffel bag from the hall closet." She continues, "I knew where it was already, back behind all my toys."

"What was in the bag?"

"Twelve thousand dollars." She says this matter-of-factly, like an adult.

"Cash?"

"Yep, the bag of Benjamins." By the way she says it, I can tell that's what Cal called it. "Daddy said, 'I'll be back in two hours.' Then the cops took him."

"Was he?"

"One hour and forty-eight minutes," she says, mimicking the rotation of a clock's hands with her finger in the air. "I timed him on the oven clock."

"So they didn't arrest him?" It occurs to me as I ask a little kid this question that they did arrest him but it went away. The twelve grand was to pay off the cops and the prosecutor and the judge and maybe several other people in the county. Twelve grand, and poof, the whole thing never happened. Just like that. Small-town liberty.

"Now we're on the up and up," she says. This too is one of Cal's expressions.

My conversation with Summer reaffirms my plan to get rid of Yag. I convince myself that this business with the Wrestler is dangerous, that the way he treats women is inexcusable, and that he has brought an element into The Final Final that none of us, least of all Summer, wants or needs.

I ask her what she wants to be when she grows up and she says she's not sure, maybe a veterinarian. I tell her that's a good idea but she should keep her options open, apply to colleges someplace other than the U., go to New York or Boston, make the big bucks. She has ambition, I can see. The hard part will be pulling herself away from her father.

My eye catches Jimmy and Yag at the bar, chatting with Amelia. Sliding off the chair, I whisper to Summer, "I need to use the loo." She asks what that is, and I tell her it's British for toilet, to which she giggles.

Then I slip the wallet into Yag's jacket, which hangs on a stool near the pool table drying out, and make a beeline for the bathroom. I empty my bladder, wash my hands, and take a long, hard look at myself in the mirror. There's nothing to do now but wait.

RIGHT UP UNTIL LUCAS and I started trying to get pregnant, I'd spent all my sexually active years trying not to get pregnant, which I defined as success. The minute I went off the pill, that experience of success shifted to an experience of failure. Weird, right? One day, not getting pregnant is success and then, wham bam, it's failure, just like that. And my sense of failure was nagging and persistent because it hit me every month like clockwork.

It was during one of these monthly mental reckonings that Lucas and I went to a party at Samantha's house. The occasion was her daughter's first birthday.

Lucas and I were among only a few childless couples at the party. Samantha had a full bar for the adults but that didn't make the party fun. At one point I found myself separated from Lucas, in a circle of moms. After each of them swapped stories of the endearing mischievous acts committed by their precious children—throwing up on the Persian rug, eating an entire box of macarons carried home from Ladurée in Paris, refusing to put on clothes—I smiled knowingly and said, "Sounds like my Addie!"

Sienna, the neurotic, bake-sale tyrant with the hungry-spirit kid, replied, "Oh, you must be relieved to have a babysitter today."

And I said, "We just leave her home alone. It's no big deal."

After letting the joke linger for less than a minute, Samantha informed her, "Addie's a dog." I couldn't tell if Sienna was offended by the joke or by the comparison between a dog and her four-year-old. Either way, she didn't talk to me for the rest of the party.

I asked Samantha if I could borrow a charger because my phone needed juice. When she pulled it out of the odds-and-ends drawer in her kitchen, I glimpsed a roll of "I voted" stickers. She caught me looking and said, "Oh, these? I keep them on hand in case I don't have time to vote. It's no big deal. Everybody does it. Here, take ten." Momentarily, I considered declining but it occurred to me that I could stick them to my chest on random Tuesdays and really cause a stir with the politically informed set. I shoved them into my wallet and walked away to plug in my phone. That's when I noticed: all the outlets near the floor were covered with childproof guards. Samantha's prodigious use of outlet guards would come to haunt me later, when I had a child of my own. I would look at my unguarded outlets as if they had eyes watching me, each outlet with two sockets: four eyes for every outlet multiplied by, say, three outlets in every room, not to mention the six-outlet power strip behind the TV. A twelve-eyed power strip can register a lot of judgment all at once. I never did anything about it, though, because I thought, rationally, *Electrocution by outlet is statistically very unlikely*.

Samantha's house is a Pottery Barn house. All the walls are some shade of taupe, and the tan chairs are topped with perfectly placed, color-accented throw blankets. A level-five finished house.

There are five levels of drywall finishes. Most people think of walls as smooth and perfect, or old and cracked, but in the end, they think a wall is a wall. This implies that drywall guys are always working to level five, which means they've applied three layers of joint compound to the tape and screws, they've sanded, and then they've applied a skim coat. In reality, level five is not the default; it's the exception. For one thing, there's plenty of wall that gets covered up—by tile, by wainscot paneling, by cabinets, et cetera. Does the wall need to be mirror smooth if it's covered floor to ceiling? And most people don't have level-five finishes in their basements and garages. No one notices or cares. Lucas probably notices, I suppose. He probably walks around judging everyone's walls.

Occasionally, we'd go out to eat or walk into a store and he'd look around with pride and say, "I did these walls," and I'd say, "Wow, smooth." But we had plenty of surface area in our own house that wasn't level five, and Lucas was perfectly fine with that.

Lucas and I assigned levels, one through five, to a variety of situations. The categorizations were unscientific but usually pretty accurate. Our yard, with all those weeds, was level-one manicured, in reference to which Lucas once said, "We all experience self-loathing to some degree." Level two was Spanish rice made by throwing everything in the rice cooker at once: mushy, edible but not delicious. The rug under our coffee table was level-three clean—it looked okay because Lucas loved vacuuming but if you put your nose right up to it, you could smell dog. Antolini's served level-four pasta, which was always delicious but the plating was imperfect, and the noodles weren't always al dente. My tits, according to Lucas, were level five, which meant he adored me. Sometimes when we got drunk, we'd have meta conversations about our conversations reaching level six, but level six didn't really exist—there's nothing smoother than smooth— even if we were several whiskeys deep.

There was something off in the image of Lucas drinking a beer in Samantha's level-five house—a dead space, lacking cosmetic flaws—his posture stiff, altered to match his surroundings, and beyond posture, his facial expression, uneasy and tight, a stress vein appearing just above his temple. He didn't belong in a place like this: a beautiful flawed man inhabiting a taupe consumer world.

On our way to the car, I informed Lucas that if we were lucky enough to have a child, I would not turn into Samantha or Sienna. I would not be *that kind of mother*. I would be more like a French mother—I'd raise my kid like the little adult I already wanted him to be, my *enfant sauvage*, born from my womb with ingenuity and a taste for aged cheese.

———————

ANOTHER TEXT FROM SAMANTHA flashes across my phone: *Where are you? I'm at your apartment.*

I reply: *Why are you at my apartment?*

Picking you up!

I'm not home.

The Final Final is only eight blocks from my place but Samantha won't think to look for me here. She'd never suspect I spend all my free time at a townie bar (I'm good at hiding my transgressions), and anyway, as far as she knows, this is Lucas's bar, always was.

Outside, the sky remains open. Through the darkened front window, I watch the rain come down in torrents. Thunder cracks. I'm not leaving the bar anytime soon. Fancy Pete calls the storm a "doozy." We are all happy to be in this familiar place, comfortable and dry, drunk or well on our way to it, but we know we'll have to leave after last call. God willing, the storm will be long over by then.

I google Elisa Monfils. Her website says she's the *Henry Ford of human productivity*. I'm not sure what that means but I'm embarrassed for her. A free app is available for download. It's called "Unstuck." The description makes it sound like a fertility app but instead of tracking your cycle, basal body temperature, and cervical fluid, it tracks your *stuck-ness*: procrastination, negative thinking, and emotional consumption. Sounds like a new way to procrastinate. No thank you.

If the U. invited her to speak, we've sunk to a new low in scholarship. She is based in Boston, which is ground zero for the corporate psychobabble that passes for sociology these days. It doesn't surprise me that she knows Grace.

Grace has a husband and two kids: a life outside of work filled with soccer games and family dinners, and doing whatever parents these days do to get their kids into Ivy League schools. She is one of those people who get by on four hours of sleep. A live-in nanny cooks and cleans. Grace's strategy is to outsource all tasks that aren't "touchstone moments." Whether she does them, or pays to have them done, correlates to the impact on the development of her kids. Personal grooming, oversight of chores, some chauffeuring—touchstone; laundry, bathroom scrubbing, cooking—not touchstone. She eats with her family but doesn't cook for her family. Grace is the kind of perfect I find exhausting, and though I wonder if growing up in her shadow will fuck up her kids in incalculable ways, I tip my hat to her. I really do.

THIS IS THE MOMENT when I've had enough to know I will be hungover tomorrow but not so much that I don't care. I've always been able to hold my liquor. I don't slur words. Anger has never been a problem. Apathy, maybe. In fact, my personality generally gets better after several drinks. In business school, we all took the Myers-Briggs, and I found out I'm a "contained extrovert." After a few drinks, I'm just an extrovert.

But getting drunk isn't all fields of poppies. The flip side of a good binge is a hard hangover. And kidneys be damned, ibuprofen has become my oh-God-make-it-stop drug of choice in my thirties. Gone are the days when all it took was a greasy breakfast and a hard run.

In the company of friends, revelry usually overshadows any accounting for tomorrow. But right now, I'm paying attention. And my anticipation of a hangover is almost physical. My body and mind feel good, comfortable and loose, a little absent, perhaps, but there is this barely noticeable anticipation of sickness, a physical premonition, as if my mind is telling my body, *Here's an itty-bitty taste of tomorrow.* It is the physiological equivalent of receiving a text that reads, *Let's talk about this later.*

I need to switch to water for a minute, so I catch Amelia's eye.

She is a one-person dish-washing assembly line. There are three sinks behind the bar. Actually, they're behind and under the bar so I can't really see them, but I see her hands moving in and out. The Final Final also has a star sink, where Amelia can press a glass, rim down, into a rinser, which shoots up water to clean it one final time before she pours a beer. She doesn't always use the rinser, though, depending on a combination of factors—whether she's pressed for time and how well she assumes the customer will tip.

Amelia dunks the glasses in hot soapy water in the first sink, then shuffles to her left and rinses them in hot water in the second, half-soapy from the glasses that passed before, and finally she dunks a third time in a sink of cold, mostly clear water before wiping them down with a towel. It's a germophobe's nightmare. Drunks assume the alcohol will kill anything left behind, which may be true, but it doesn't kill whatever's left inside us—all those *if onlys*.

———

LUCAS TOLD ME ONCE that he was like water flowing downstream, over, under, and through all the various impediments that hold other people up. He was proud of this fact, and it was part of what made him so likeable, so easygoing and fun. I, like everyone else, loved this about him, until I grew to resent it.

"What're you doing over there?" Lucas called to me from in front of the TV.

"What does it look like I'm doing?" I was in the kitchen unloading the dishwasher so I could refill it with the new stack of dishes that had accumulated. Every third object I pulled out was still dirty, crusted with old food. I held up a fork with yellow egg webbed in its prongs.

"Jimmy's at the bar. He wants us to meet him," Lucas said.

"Are you constitutionally incapable of rinsing the dishes before loading them?"

"Just leave it. I'll do it later."

"That's just it—you'll do it later. And then I'll have to redo it later." I held up a steel pan dotted with what looked to be blackened tomato paste. "At least let Addie lick it clean before you load it."

"I don't think she liked that one. I burned it," he said.

"What exactly goes through your head when you place a crusty pan in the dishwasher? Is there a voice telling you that this time it will be different? The god of the dishwasher will kick it up a notch? This time, the pan will come out shiny and clean?"

"I don't like washing the dishes before washing them. That's redundant," he said.

"No, Lucas, what I'm doing right now is redundant." I held out a mug with a ring of black coffee on the bottom.

"I'll do a better job next time. Just leave it. Let's go to the bar."

"I have zero confidence you'll do anything different next time."

"Why?"

"We've had this conversation before."

"My aversion to redundancy created cognitive dissonance, which forced me to forget we've ever talked about this before," he said. "I want to do a good job on the dishes, but I can't."

"Your aversion to redundancy?"

"To doing the dishes before the dishwasher does them."

"The dishwasher doesn't do the dishes. I do them."

"Maybe we need a better dishwasher," he said, laughing already at the joke I knew he was about to make. "One that doesn't talk back."

"We've talked about this at least six times. That's not cognitive dissonance. It's motivated forgetting."

"It's really sinking in this time," he said. He came up from behind and put his arms around my waist. He tickled me and I squirmed. Addie ran over to us and bounced up and down.

After wiping the coffee out of the bottom of the mug with a sponge, I placed it back in the dishwasher. "I don't feel like going to the bar tonight."

"I promise I'll clean up tomorrow," he said. "Come on. It's Friday night."

"Why don't you meet Jimmy, and I'll stay here with Addie?"

"He wants to see you too."

"No, he doesn't."

"I want to see you."

"I want the kitchen to be clean."

He watched me scrub the sink for a minute. "Just one drink," he insisted. "Then I'll walk you home."

"I'm wearing yoga pants."

"Then you will be the best-dressed person at the bar," Lucas said.

I had on yoga pants because earlier in the evening we'd had sex, and afterward I'd thrown on clothes that were comfortable for lounging. Back then, we were very regimented about having sex on and around the time I ovulated. The sex was still good but it was also purposeful. Each time it came with the slightest dual twinge of hope and failure. Hope that this time it would work; and failure, because chances were it wouldn't.

In my right hand, I held our plastic slotted spoon. There were grains of rice stuck in the slots and caked on the back, remnants of the pineapple fried rice we'd made for dinner. I poked Lucas in the gut with it and jumped backward, holding him off with the spoon, an extension of my arm. He batted it with his hand. Then he grabbed a spatula and we began to fence. Addie got in on it, dancing on her two hind legs for as long as she could, holding her mouth open just enough to turn the vibration of her vocal chords into a playful growl. I pointed the spoon at her. She put her nose to it, feeling me out, determining if I meant to give it to her.

"Sit," I said. She sat. Like Lucas, she listened when motivated. I gave her the spoon.

"You're buying the new one when she chews that one up," Lucas said.

"Someone has to get the rice off, and we both know it's not gonna be you," I said.

"Two drinks," he said.

"I'll go for one," I said.

"One whiskey, one beer," he said.

"Ordered simultaneously," I said. We had a deal.

If my math was right, this was the night Lionel was conceived. We made Lionel and then went to the bar where I had what would be my last whiskey for the next nine months.

———————

THAT NIGHT AT THE bar we talked about death. Upon arrival, we seized the front tables with the unearned swagger of investment bankers on the squash court. We spread our legs. We stretched our arms. We made ourselves big.

All of us were there—Cal and Summer, Fancy Pete, Short Pete, Yag, Jimmy, Lucas and me, a motley crew of eight. Summer was in the second grade at the time, and her class had just finished reading *White Fang*. Her child mind was preoccupied by death—specifically, how awesome it was that a dog could kill a man in under three minutes with only his teeth. Summer barred her big, gapped bunny teeth and snarled. The men cheered her on.

She sucked Coca-Cola through a straw. Then she peered up at the crew, lifting only her eyes. Releasing the straw from her lips, she asked, "If you could, would you want to know when you were gonna die?"

I looked around the circle, from guy to guy. One by one, they took long, hard pulls from their drinks. Then Jimmy said, "Are we talking imminent death, or death in old age?"

"That's the point, stupid," Cal said. "You only find out if you agree to the terms."

"What terms?"

"What is *imminent death*?" Summer asked.

"Let's say you find out your daddy's gonna die tomorrow," Yagla said. "That's imminent." He caught my look of disapproval. "What? It was her morbid question. Jesus, Em, lighten up."

"Imminent just means soon," I said to Summer. "In the near future."

"Okay, yeah," Summer said. "Would you want to know if you were gonna die *im-mi-nent-ly*?"

We were in the groove, which is, as far as I can tell, the whole point of drinking. It is a looseness of the body and a dialing back of the conscious mind, not a dulling so much as a minimizing. Both the number of thoughts and the duration of rumination are cut, hour by hour, according to a long-tail curve: the x-axis being drinks and the y-axis being thoughts. The point at which the curve bends from the head to the long tail, the fat part of the curve—that is the groove.

Everything that anybody said was hysterical, laugh-out-loud, feel-it-in-the-gut funny. Lucas ordered a round of house shots and a pitcher of Amber, and Amelia served us before making drinks for all the strangers at the bar who'd been waiting longer.

We didn't bother to clink our glasses together, but as Cal lifted his from the table, he said, "To imminent death." Some of us repeated the toast, and all of us shot 'em down, including Summer, for whom Amelia had made a virgin shot.

Lucas stretched his arms wide, opening up his full wingspan, and wiggled his body. It wasn't a dance, because there was no rhythm to it. It was an outward expression of inward joy. These were the moments Lucas lived for, the good times, *the groove*: friends, conversation, revelry. There was nothing special going on; the night was like a thousand that came before; and, at the same time, it was better.

Lucas stopped wiggling and said, "I'd want to know because then I'd be happy just to be."

"You mean you'd live it up," Yag said.

Lucas hadn't thought about what he'd actually do with his final days—he knew more about what he wouldn't do: namely, drywall a building. "Well, I wouldn't want to spend my final hours hungover," he said.

"So no drugs?" Yag inquired, aghast.

"I might do drugs but I wouldn't burn time trying to find drugs."

"If your death was imminent, it'd be pretty easy to get drugs," I said. "You could just call up Cal and tell him you were about to die. He'd hook you up."

Cal nodded.

"I wouldn't need to go out in a blaze of glory," Lucas said. He looked at me, and either he forgot a bunch of his buddies were listening or he was too drunk to care because he said, "Really, I'd just want to spend the time with you and Addie." We did not yet know about Lionel, and if his soul existed somewhere in the ether, it was beyond Lucas's purview. His wing closed around me. He pushed his forehead into mine and kissed me.

Cal said, "Gross—get a room." He looked off across the bar with this huge, sappy smile on his face.

Jimmy looked lonely.

Martin Yagla rolled his eyes, wanting not what we had, wishing, probably, some hot young thing would walk through the door.

Short Pete was content to be in the company of friends.

Fancy Pete had a girlfriend at home and a project going in his woodshop.

Summer spoke directly to Lucas. "Yeah," she said. "I'd want to know too. I'd ask Daddy to take me on an adventure."

"Where would you go?" Lucas asked.

"You guys could come too," she said. "We'd get out of here. We'd take a journey up the Mackenzie like White Fang."

"Sounds like a great idea," I said. "Lucas is basically Canadian anyway."

He nodded. He was in.

Cal ordered another round of shots. This time, he didn't have to say anything, because we all telepathically understood we were drinking to Youth. Summer had reminded us there was a world beyond this place, a world for all of us that held the possibility of adventure.

TAKING A SHOT OF Fireball is like eating a corn dog at a county fair. Do it occasionally and it's ironic, a quick jaunt to an unfamiliar world: class tourism. Do it often, and lose your self-respect: *Abandon all hope, ye who enter here.*

Yag and Cal are having a shot. Fireball shots are three dollars every day at The Final Final. The unspoken custom here is to bust out the Fireball to help a fellow barfly cycle through the five stages of grief: denial, anger, commiseration, perseveration, and drunken stupor. Dumped by your girlfriend? Fireball. Dog died? Fireball. Can't pay off your gambling debt? Fireball.

As far as I can tell, Yag is in the second stage of grief (anger) and Cal is trying to cool him off. "I'll kill him before he goes near my mom."

"These things have a way of working themselves out."

"They cheated," Yag says. "Just can't figure out how. You shoulda seen the hands. It wasn't mathematically possible."

"Did I ever tell you about when I went twenty-eight months without running water?" Cal asks.

True story. Not twenty-eight hours, or twenty-eight days—twenty-eight months. Cal's spirit animal is a honey badger.

Poised to enter the third stage (commiseration), Yag orders a second round of Fireball shots on Cal's tab.

Cal begins his story. "I planned to leave town for a month during slow season, and decided to turn off the water. The ranch is old as shit, so the water could only be turned off at the stop box near the street. The box wasn't even on my property. The shutoff was up the street in front of the neighbor's house. Public Works told me only thirteen houses in the whole county had stop boxes located that far away—but, no problem; they'd send someone out to shut off the water.

"The service guy used a key at ground level to close the valve, which was buried six feet underground. Shoulda been routine, but the box was old, and when the guy turned the key, he broke the valve. The water was turned off, but there was no way to turn it back on."

"Moron," Yag says.

"The guy reported back to Public Works, and Public Works said I was responsible for replacing the stop box, and to bring it up to code, it would need to be moved a hundred and seventy feet, to the front of my house. That required excavating the street. They gave me an estimate. The combined cost of excavation and a new stop box came to nearly eight grand. Can you believe it? Eight Gs. I had a guy who said he would do the excavation for five, but he couldn't go any lower because he'd have to rent equipment."

Classic conversational narcissism: Martin owes the Wrestler ten grand, and Cal's way of empathizing is to tell a story about owing a similar amount of money with the same amount of indigence. In the outside world, people might not put up with this kind of thing, but bars have their own rules. If you're the one buying the shots, you have license to talk.

"That's fucked up," Yag says. "The service guy broke the valve. You break it, you buy it."

This all happened before Summer was born, and before Cal's general contractor business took off. Eight grand was not a drop in the bucket by any means, but he could have swung it. He had the money in his freezer or mattress or buried in the backyard somewhere. Or, it's possible he didn't have the money at all but pride prohibited him from admitting as much. Whatever the case, it wasn't about the money for Cal; it was a matter of principle.

"Fuckin' A right," Cal says. "I refused to pay but the town didn't back down. Some asshole at Public Works actually told me I could sue them if

I wanted to make my point in court. I told them, 'I don't sue people for shit like this; only you people do that!'"

"So the water remained off?" Yag shakes his head at the world he knows to be unfair.

"I started showering at the community rec center after work. I got to know all the homeless people there. When I had to take a shit at home, I used a bucket. I took my clothes to the laundromat on the other side of town.

"Things started to snowball from there. Because I was pissed at the town, I noticed there was something wrong with my gas bill. I didn't like the way they were reading the meter. They were just estimating the data, basing it off my five closest neighbors. On the bill, it was called *neighborhood estimation*. I knew I wasn't using nearly as much gas as my neighbors because, for one thing, I had no hot water, and also I wasn't running the furnace at the time. So I refused to pay that bill, and the gas was shut off too."

At the time, people around town started talking. Cal didn't have water or heat. He was living like a savage.

Yag says, "I would've marched down to Public Works and burned the fucking building down."

"If I'd done that," Cal says, "I'd be in prison right now. Or dead. That's my point. You gotta hold the course. Wait 'til things right themselves."

"The town eventually came around, then?" Yag asks with a twang of disbelief.

"Not exactly," Cal says. "Evie was about to graduate from college at the U. I asked her to marry me and move in. She refused to shit in a bucket. She called Public Works. The guy who answered the phone took pity on her. He told her if I came down to the office after five p.m., after everyone else had left for the day, he'd give me a used stop box. I could dig up the old broken one myself and replace it.

"I called Lucas and we did the back-alley deal with the guy from Public Works. Then we drove to the house to dig a hole six feet deep. We dug straight down, shaving dirt from the sides. Lucas brought out his Shop-Vac and we used it to suck up dirt, emptying it thirty times over.

"It was obvious when the water came back on because Evie ran out of the house screaming to turn it off again. Some of the pipes had burst. I said no way—now that the water was on, nobody was gonna turn it off. I pulled Lucas out of the hole by his ankles, and we went inside and capped the pipes. Later, I ran all new piping by myself."

"If you did all the work, didn't the town win?" Yag asks.

Amelia serves them a third shot of Fireball. Cal raises his glass to Yag and says, "To getting so drunk it doesn't matter." Drunken stupor: the fifth and final stage of grief. Cal doesn't take the shot, though. He turns his head toward Summer and hands it off to Martin, who takes both, rapid-fire.

"At the end of the month, I got a call from the Water Department. A woman said, 'Sir, we have a problem. We've identified a twenty-eight-month gap in our billing cycle.' She couldn't figure out why. She'd never seen anything like it before. I calmly explained that the water had been off for twenty-eight months, and now it was back on. She informed me that even if I hadn't used any water, I was still responsible for the sewer fee, which was thirteen dollars a month. I told her to send me a bill. I'd pay it. I'd never been delinquent on a bill."

Cal believes his name is on a list somewhere, but I highly doubt it. If the government had the wherewithal to surveil every crazy white guy in town, they'd put eyes on The Final Final, and as far as I can tell, no one gives a rip about what we do here.

"Sure, you could say I lost," Cal says, "having gone so long without water and all. But here's the kicker: within the year, the town installed a new stop box across the street. No one notified me, but I watched it happen while I drank in my lawn chair."

"Fuck, man. I don't have your stamina," Yag says. "Those assholes cheated, and they're gonna get away with it. I should break in and light the poker table on fire. Send a message."

Cal puts his hand on Yag's shoulder, a wise father calming a hotheaded son. "Wait it out. Pay off your debt. The water eventually comes back on."

I can't help but smile into my drink. The passage of time, all twenty-eight months of it, didn't solve Cal's problem, as he insists. Evie solved his problem. She picked up the phone and forced him to get out of his own way. If Yag doesn't do something crazy first, his mom will solve his problem. I'd put money on it, if gambling didn't seem like such a bad idea right now.

A WHILE BACK, I noticed a pattern in my students' presentations. They'd finish a section, like a SWOT analysis, or an exploration of Porter's Five Forces, or a rundown of KPIs, and then they'd say, "Now John's going to talk about the financials," or, "Here's Alice with our recommendations." Students assume these are transitions simply because they hand off the proverbial baton.

One day, a group came to me and asked where they should put the financials in the deck. The simple question of *where*, not what or how, made me realize that MBAs think of transitions in the wrong way. They think, *How do I move from one point to the next?* when really they should be thinking about how one point builds into the next. If content is optimally structured, the transitions don't feel like handing off a baton. They feel like shifting a manual transmission at about 3,000 rpm. In other words, transitions should feel natural—like the right time to shift—and if successful, the engine gets a boost.

The engine, or in my students' case, the content, dictates the shift. But unlike an engine, which is mechanical, content is organic. It is a living extension of the speaker, and transitions aren't optimized at fixed points (the financials do not always come toward the end). I encourage my students to command transitions to work to their advantage, which is easier said than done. After beginnings and endings, transitions are the most important aspect of any presentation, whether it's a stock pitch, or product launch, or an old story much told at the bar.

FOR OUR FIRST WEDDING anniversary, Lucas and I took our bicycles to France with the goal of escaping tourist traps and exploring the countryside. On our third day, in the hills to the west of a town west of Lyon, we came across a tiny village. In its heyday, two hundred years prior, the village was home to approximately five hundred people.

Today, it has one business: a juice bar run by a jolly old lady who makes crepes on request, and her husband, who keeps bees and sells jars of honey. They have a big, old, lazy dog that hangs by the man's side all day long. The juice bar is located right in what was once an active town square.

Lucas and I parked our bikes and watched the old woman press the oranges for our mixed juice. Then we walked to the middle of the square, where we found the statue of a man holding his hands behind his back, as one might do when taking a leisurely stroll.

There are so many statues in France that it's impossible to care about any of them, but this one caught my eye for two reasons. First, the subject smiled, a rarity for European statues. And second, the inscription on the stone base read *Le Maire*—simply, *The Mayor*. There was no name on the statue—I found the name, Gerard Dupris, later, back in a library in Lyon.

And he wasn't actually the mayor. In the nineteenth century, this district was unincorporated and had no governing body.

On Dupris's fourteenth birthday, his mother, who had fallen gravely and mysteriously ill, died suddenly. Later that year, his elder sister and primary caretaker died in a tragic accident, according to legend, falling into a ravine. By sixteen, Dupris fell in love with a beautiful girl from the village. They married quickly and conceived a child. His young wife, who bore a son, died during childbirth. Dupris never loved another woman. Dupris's son was, quite literally, raised by the village. He helped the bread baker deliver morning loaves across town. The villagers fed his belly with homemade treats and his mind with stories. He lingered in their homes and brought joy to everyone who knew him. He grew up to be very handsome and charming.

Dupris and his son farmed the land that their family had worked for generations but they also roamed freely, traveling by horse, and developed friendships throughout the provinces. They cultivated reputations for trustworthiness and sincerity, and they began to broker deals, first among merchants and landowners, and then among the ruling class.

They were welcome in monasteries and palaces; they attended feasts as guests and distributed rations to the poor as volunteers. They spoke many local dialects. They could have chosen wives for love or wealth or status, but they broke many hearts instead. Their bond with each other, forged through death, was singular and unbreakable.

Dupris and his son returned regularly to their village, bringing gifts of knowledge and medicine and invention that created great prosperity. The village had an annual festival in the town square when father and son returned for the winter months. It erupted spontaneously when they rode into town and ended as many as seven days later, when the wine jugs ran dry.

After their final journey together, and on the third day of the festival,

Dupris's son, less than twenty years old, virile and muscular, stepped into the wrestling ring, a favorite pastime among the youth in the village. In the third round, he grabbed his chest and collapsed. He was immediately unresponsive and died quickly.

Gerard Dupris was not yet an old man. Having lost his only companion, he stopped traveling but did not shut himself off from the townspeople. The village prospered for the remaining years of his life, and though it was small, it became known for art and culture and for the annual festival.

He had already planted the seeds of success but only after his son's death did people begin to tell his story. Some called him *L'Ange de la Mort* because he danced with death so gracefully; those who knew him well called him *Oncle*; most called him *Le Maire*. Known for his sunny demeanor and toothy smile, Gerard Dupris was the de facto leader of his petite village.

Among the five hundred or so inhabitants of the village, there was one sculptor. In 1837, one year after Dupris's death, the villagers commissioned a statue of the man they called The Mayor.

This story fascinated me, not because it was weird—though in the period of the French aristocracy, it was quite unusual for a peasant to achieve such notoriety—but because very little of it was written down anywhere. Dupris was not someone kids read about in history books. He was not even a particularly interesting historical figure. He didn't start a war, or end a war; he didn't invent anything; he wasn't a craftsman or a philosopher, and according to legend, he wasn't much of a lover.

The statue itself was cataloged in Lyon, which was where I found Dupris's name, but for the rest of the details I had to hire a translator to talk to the remaining villagers—less than twenty now—most of whom were very old. They had learned of Dupris from their parents, who learned of him from their parents, who were possibly kids or maybe not even born yet when the statue was erected. It was an oral history and so it was my-thologized in ways that were entirely believable to me.

The third and final section of *The Breakout Effect* was about Gerard Dupris. His story was about death and perseverance. At the time I wrote it, both were strangers to me.

I admired Dupris, and in many ways, he became the hero of my book. Certainly, among my three subjects—Pamela, my father, and Dupris—he was the one who found happiness, or, if not happiness, a kind of spiritual wholeness that I couldn't define. Lucas later called it the Tao. Whatever it was, it was inaccessible to me. Dupris was many things, but he wasn't a mother. If he had been, he'd have blamed himself for letting his son set foot in a wrestling ring, or for not making sure his wife had proper medi-cal care, or for not being present when his elder sister fell into the ravine.

But Dupris was a man, like Chuang Tzu, free to drum on an inverted pot and sing.

———

GIL AND HIS SILENT sidekick—I mean, second wife—are back. They did a lap around the bar and found themselves right back where they started, next to me.

"You know what it was? You know how I knew Lucas was gonna buy that place?" The volume of his voice jars me. He doesn't give me the opportunity to tell him I don't want to know. "I could see him envisioning all them things he was gonna do." He says *them things* in an intentional folksy tone because he figures some people find it endearing.

"Did Lucas ever fix up the porch?"

"Yep," I say, looking only at my whiskey. I fight like a fool to appear ticked off, when what I really feel is my insides turning to salt water. *That fucking porch. If only we'd just let it rot. If only. If only.*

Amelia recognizes something—I'm not sure what. She holds my glare for a few seconds and purses her lips. She knows. Aldrich Gilfillan does not know. I assumed everyone in this town knew everything about everybody, but I realize now that either Gil is completely tone-deaf, or he simply doesn't know. He thinks I still live with Lucas. He thinks we're still married. No one told him what happened to us.

This sudden realization of my own anonymity feels fantastic. Part of pain is managing other people's reaction to pain—the things they ask and the things they avoid. When people ask questions, they usually focus on some narcissistic need to show they care. They conflate empathy with the desire to display empathy, and they want answers that will make them feel good for having asked the questions. Strangers want to be thanked for their concern; friends want to be told how much their support means. They do not want to hear uncomfortable truths. When a soldier comes home from war, he doesn't sit around at dinner parties talking about how his platoon mate took a piece of shrapnel and bled out in his arms, requesting only that he tell his wife and child how much he loves them. He might show off a scar from a physical wound that has healed over but he doesn't mention his fractured mind that will never heal.

I've only said about three words to Gil but he's still hovering, not taking the empty seat next to me at the bar but not moving on either.

"Welp," I say. "Nice talkin' to ya."

He hands me a card. "Let me know when you and Lucas are in the market for a bigger house."

I lift my whiskey off the bar and push it toward the second Mrs. Gilfillan, who has not spoken a single word. She's holding a Budweiser bottle by her side. She lifts it to my glass and lightly clinks it against the rim. I think we are both, telepathically, toasting her miraculous endurance of Gil.

Before Gil walks away he says, "When you see Lucas, tell him hello."

I LIKE A MAN who can fix things, who knows his way around a shop, who works with his hands. That's what we all say. That's the romantic version. But any woman who has ever lived with this kind of man knows the do-it-yourself life is one lived in a constant state of *almost-done*. She comes home to find a hole in the wall that he's cut out with a saw so he could access some electrical wiring. He finishes the wiring but doesn't bother to seal up the hole—even though he installs drywall *for a living*—because it's not pressing, because it can be done later, because there are twelve other things that require attention first. Or, all the furniture has been moved to the middle of the room so he can paint but he doesn't get it done in one weekend, so you sit on it like that for days. Or, there's a layer of dust everywhere because he sanded something, which may or may not be toxic.

Other people—the lawyers and doctors of the world—hire professionals, and it's not sexy but it gets done in forty-eight hours, and then they live their perfect, clean, nontoxic lives, and they have time to throw dinner parties or go to PTA meetings or whatever it is that they do. Sometimes I look at the pale skin of some of my colleagues at the U., baby-smooth hands that are only used to type, and I think to myself, *Who do their wives ask to open jars?* and then I imagine their gentle sex, and I find myself making a bored face—an expression Lucas could have read with one glance.

The house on Catherine Street was the night-and-day opposite of the monstrosity I grew up in: a six-bedroom, eight-bathroom, Tudor-style mansion in Wilton, Connecticut, built to look old in the late 1970s. My home with Lucas was like Baby Bear's porridge. Every inch of it was lived in: the books on the shelves were our favorite books, the kitchen was stocked with everyday equipment—cast-iron pans and spatulas—the couch was good to curl up on, as opposed to the designer sofas and chairs of my youth, which were only meant for display.

I still think about all the woodwork that Addie scratched up—wood doors and windowsills, floorboards and paneling. Lucas and I spent hours together stripping it—one of those projects we stumbled into ass-backward. Possibly, Lucas thought these things out in advance, but I always just found myself in the middle of them. If memory serves, we decided to strip all the woodwork because we wanted to stain it dark, and we wanted to stain it dark because I had chosen a peachy color for the walls, and we had purchased one gallon of paint for thirty dollars, thereby locking us in. Lucas referred to the peach as *titty pink*, which I guess meant flesh toned, though it was really more apricot. He then decided the only way titty-pink walls would look good would be if the woodwork was very dark, and then a week later and we were stripping, stripping, stripping. I didn't protest because it was exactly where I wanted to be, hanging out with Lucas.

We finished just more than half of the woodwork, basically everything in the living room and kitchen, except for the window frames—we didn't make it to the dining room—before we decided to table the project for a year. We were sick of scraping, for one thing, and I wanted to devote more time to my book. Other projects demanded Lucas's attention—some of the wood on the porch was rotting and the entire exterior of the house needed to be repainted. Did I want all the woodwork to have the same smooth, dark finish? Yeah, sure I did. But to be honest, I didn't give a rip either.

WHEN I COMPLETED *THE Breakout Effect*, I gave the draft to Lucas to read.

Pen in hand, he read it within forty-eight hours. He flipped over the last page and said, "Let's go to the bar and talk about it," which was different from "I love it," what I wanted to hear.

It must have been a Monday or Tuesday night and damn cold outside, because I remember stepping in from the frozen streets to an empty bar. Only a couple of the high-top tables were occupied by grad-student types. The regulars were all home for the night.

Lucas flopped down and stripped off his coat and gloves. He requested a whiskey, half rocks, and riffled through the manuscript, finding the second section, the one about my dad.

I could see all his notes in the margins, in three different colors of pen, and I knew this conversation wasn't going to make me feel good. Lucas wasn't the rubber-stamping type. I ordered a Cherry Coke and braced myself.

No one was playing the jukebox, so Amelia put her own music over the sound system, mellow and bluesy, the right tempo for the beginning of the week, something we could sit with for a while as we talked about the matter at hand. Amelia didn't ask what was on the paper, though I suspect she already knew it was my book. Lucas and I had been talking about it for months.

Lucas said, "Do you know what I'm going to say?"

I glanced down at the marginalia and noted the red lettering, all caps: *NOT LIKE THE OTHERS*. I told Lucas I had no idea what he had to say.

"You don't give your dad any credit," he said.

"That's the point," I said. "He doesn't deserve credit."

"Pamela and Gerard get the benefit of the doubt. Your dad doesn't. Why is that?"

At this point we were only about ten minutes into a conversation that I knew would last hours, and I was already chewing on the ice at the bottom of my soda. I asked for a refill, waited for Amelia to put it on the table in front of me, and watched the bubbles. "He was a shitty father," I said.

"Your dad's not so bad. I mean aside from cheating on your mom—"

"That's one big aside."

"Your mom is a bit of a battle-ax, not to mention a drinker."

"That came after," I said, suddenly defensive of mothers everywhere.

I'd taken a test and confirmed it: I was pregnant, finally, after many months of trying. I was still adjusting—fatigued, short on breath, head in a fog. Lionel was growing inside me. He had an X and a Y chromosome. And all his DNA.

PERHAPS LUCAS WAS RIGHT. My mother did drink. But my father definitely drove her to drink *more*. Mom suffered from postpartum depression. Or, maybe having me just triggered something that had been in her all along. However it originated, the depression came and went in bouts. There were days when she didn't get out of bed. There were good periods too. She took me out for milkshakes and French fries. We snapped our fingers and swayed to funk music in the kitchen. She taught me how to cook real Italian food. She wasn't Italian but she became an expert after she married my dad. Her herb garden featured basil, rosemary, thyme, and oregano, the Italian staples, and she employed techniques from the old country, like cooking chicken *al mattone*. She claimed Uncle Nic taught her how to cook.

I remember Uncle Nic as jolly. He snorted when he laughed. The guy was always cracking a joke, even when the situation called for restraint. In many ways, he and my mom were cut from the same cloth, which was why they got on so well. They both liked a good dirty martini. They were also both prisoners of their own minds. When I was eighteen, Uncle Nic shot himself in the head in the New York City apartment my dad rented for him. Dad refused to go to the funeral, which my mom planned. At the time, I thought this was just his way of dealing with grief.

Uncle Nic left one letter when he died. It was in an envelope with my father's name on it. I dug it out of the trash can in the kitchen.

Caro Fratello,

Busy, busy, busy.

I'm sorry for dipping out on Mattea. A stronger man would have shut the thing down a year ago, tied up loose ends. The restaurant is a source of pain for me. Not because it failed. Because I know it will continue to fail. As tough as you are, you won't shut it down—not immediately—either because it was my project or our mother's namesake or, probably, both.

Every month, you'll review the books, and you'll be reminded of your little brother, losing money from beyond the grave. Three or five or ten years down the road, you'll pull the plug on it. Whoever winds it down, sells off the equipment, won't bother to strip the sign, MATTEA, and you'll happen to walk by on your way to that hip sushi joint. You'll try to look away, but out of the corner of your eye, you'll see it, empty and abandoned, with a weathered awning and a homeless man sleeping in the doorway.

This is not how I want you to remember Mattea. I want you to remember the day I pitched you the idea in a garden of potted herbs, with the promise of simplicity—hand-rolled pasta, house-cured meats, table wine, espresso. I want you to remember where it all started, in our mother's kitchen.

If I owned the restaurant, I would give it to Emma. She'd know what to do with it. Seeing as you own it, I suppose that's entirely up to you, and knowing you, I have no doubt you'll succumb to some free-market, invisible-hand idea, related to what's best for her, incentives and all that, and you'll figure you'd be doing her a favor if you left her out of it. That might be true.

As for me? Remember me for the only things I was ever any good at: making Emma smile, re-creating Mamma's Bolognese, and, in the end, holding you to your own standards: never throw good money after bad.

Nico

Busy, busy, busy was a Vonnegut reference. Uncle Nic was an aficionado.

Some years later, my dad met me in San Francisco, where I was living, and on our way to dinner, a homeless man tripped and fell on the sidewalk just a couple of feet in front of us. The guy was so close to the entrance of the restaurant that my dad literally had to step over his body to get to the door. I was young at the time and sort of in shock so I just followed his lead. From inside the restaurant, I looked out and watched the man gather himself. Upon seeing my expression, my dad grabbed my arm and said, "A man's worth is no greater than his ambition." Biographies and military histories, along with the *Wall Street Journal* and a few select business periodicals, comprised most of my father's reading list. Marcus Aurelius fell squarely within his bailiwick.

Something about the word *ambition*, spoken through my father's lips, reminded me of the word *abomination*, and I realized the two weren't so far off—abomination was simply an exaggerated form of ambition. For the duration of the evening, I pushed the food around on my plate in shame while my dad ate heartily and talked about San Francisco real estate. He tipped generously.

When I told my mom this story, she said, "Of course that's how he feels. Why do you think he didn't come to Nico's funeral?"

Dad probably would have invested in every two-bit business idea

Uncle Nic ever had, but the one thing he would not forgive was the obvious eventuality: one day the spaghetti would stop hitting the wall. He despised what he perceived as the opposite of ambition: giving up.

Though my mom always blamed the other woman for their divorce, I'm sure it had everything to do with how he saw her depression. In his mind, it was only weakness. I never forgot what he said to me that day in San Francisco.

––––––––––

"YOU NEED TO FORGIVE him," Lucas said. "And if you can't forgive him, you need to set aside your personal feelings for the benefit of this book."

"It's a business book," I said. "Forgiveness has nothing to do with it." I really believed this was true. The book wasn't a memoir. There was no mention of his affair, or his absenteeism. I didn't even mention the homeless fellow he stepped over in San Francisco. Whatever meanness Lucas identified in the draft, I couldn't see it. I was blind.

Lucas noticed my defensiveness and we both knew this would be easier if I was drinking. He suggested we go through the other sections first, Pamela Randolph Walsh and Gerard Dupris, and he ordered himself another whiskey.

"You know Maker's is the same price as Bulleit," I said, judging his choice.

Lucas had mapped out through lines in both sections, scribbled in different colors of ink. He called Pamela's *HIGH TOLERANCE FOR PAIN*, and Gerard's *TAO*. Each subject had different and equally complex equations, which included but weren't limited to their unique stories— Pamela's bookkeeping father and Gerard's relationship with death. In both cases, their stories clearly mattered in some essential way but their personal attributes allowed them to persevere, which was really the key, because if they hadn't, then their stories would be just that, stories, and not worth the paper they were printed on.

Lucas was right, of course. The stories were the mechanism for the subjects to break through their respective resistance levels, but beyond the mechanics of breaking out, there were all those devilish details of character and grit. Pamela Randolph Walsh and Gerard Dupris and my father all possessed both in abundance.

When we finished talking about the sections devoted to Pamela and Gerard, Lucas got up and went to the bathroom. On his way back to the table he stopped at the bar and asked Amelia for a cigarette. They didn't sell cigarettes at the bar but that worked out just fine for Amelia because Lucas tipped her an extra dollar or two for every one cigarette he bummed, which was a pretty good return on investment.

Lucas caught me rolling my eyes at him as he headed for the door. He walked over, and before he grabbed his coat, he rubbed his shadow of a beard all over my face and said, "Enjoy it before it smells like cigarettes."

"Gross," I said. "Get outa here." But I couldn't act mad, because he was helping me with the book, and also because we were both now acutely aware that *Lord, give me chastity but not just yet* applied more than ever because *just yet* was approximately six months away for Lucas, though it had already imposed itself upon me.

By the time Lucas came in from the cold, I had read his notation in the section on my father. Green, all caps: *AMBITION*. My father's through line. When Lucas looked at his own penmanship, he said plainly, "You have it too. So will he," and he put his hand on my belly, and it was the first time we gave Lionel a gendered pronoun, and it was also the moment I started imagining what he would be like, what kind of man he would be. I felt like a mother, protective of the precious life inside me, *all that for which I lived.*

The best racket my dad ever ran was teaching me that I was worthy of success, financial and otherwise, that I deserved it. I never doubted that I belonged in beautiful places, hallowed institutions with manicured quads and ivory towers, palatial offices in skyscrapers that kissed the heavens, in summer homes with private beaches, and multi-acre ranches under big blue skies. That feeling never goes away. I could fail a hundred times and it would remain within me.

It's not entirely a class thing. I can say that. Though class has something to do with it. Lucas's mom ran the same racket. As far as I can tell, it's a dinner-table thing. At least, that's where our parents ran the racket— at the dinner table. That's where they told us the world was our oyster, over and over again, from the time we could listen. And we believed it.

So I remember thinking, *Yes, Lucas is right; our child will be ambitious.* We would make sure of it over pastas and roasted chickens and burgers cooked on the grill.

We stayed for a couple more hours, long enough for Lucas to switch from whiskey to beer, long enough for me to fall in love with him again, as I did every time we hung out at the bar together.

Later, I rewrote the section on my father. I didn't forgive him, as Lucas hoped I would, but I gave him the credit he deserved, and overall, the book was stronger for it. By the end of the new draft, I realized my initial hypothesis was wrong. The story doesn't matter more than the person. The story and the person are one and the same.

9PM

THERE'S A LULL AT the bar. Only a patient warrior stays at the same place from early evening to bar close.

I look around for Cal, secretly waiting for him to discover his missing wallet. He will have to take Summer home within the hour. This suits him just fine. He likes to be home early, where he can smoke a joint and kick back in his recliner, or roam around his property in the predawn light: an insomniac's constitutional.

He shows Short Pete something on his phone. I lean over, hoping to see a picture of a naked lady, but it's a home video of a big honkin' gun.

"Check this out, guy. I bought a tactical twenty-two. Laser on the front, twenty-five-round mag, adjustable stock," Cal says.

"Beauty," Short Pete says.

"I got a scope for it too. This baby is lethal up to four hundred yards. In a situation, if we need to bug out fast, this is the one I'm taking," Cal says.

There's something about the way Cal says *in a situation* that appeals to me. I imagine he has planned for the gamut of possible, however unlikely, situations, ranging from social unrest to alien invasion.

Short Pete is three-quarters of the way through the twenty-dollar bill he put on the bar when he came in. Every time Amelia serves him a gin and tonic, she takes away a few dollars and change. He's on just two legs of his low-back stool. His right knee pushes against the edge of the bar. He uses it for balance so he can tilt backward and rock forward. This is the least suave way a man can possibly position himself while sipping a gin and tonic. I try to imagine James Bond teetering on the back two legs of his bar stool. I can't; it's impossible. There's something innocent about the way he moves. He does it to occupy himself. He's not self-conscious about the way he looks, and he isn't worried about falling. He encounters the chair like a kid: part game, part instrument of sitting.

"Ever fallen off?" I ask.

"A bar stool?"

"No, Pete, the wagon." I smile.

"Honey, none of us have ever been on the wagon," Cal says.

"Jimmy was in AA for a while," Short Pete says. Jimmy is hovering behind us, taking a break from the pool table. Cal, Short Pete, and I are all bellied up to the bar.

I swivel around to include Jimmy in the conversation. Motion makes me feel the alcohol. I'm sober enough, but everything around me—the faces, the signs on the wall, the glow of the jukebox—everything appears a little bit grainy, like I'm watching the night unfold on an old TV.

"I've never fallen off a bar stool, no," Short Pete says. "Amelia would kick my ass right out of here."

"House rule," Amelia says. "Don't fall off your stool."

"I thought the house rule was don't fall asleep at the bar?" I say.

"I seen many a sleeping beauty get thrown outa this place," Cal says.

"That's Murphy's rule." Martin Yagla looks at me. "Lucas Murphy's rule, not the famous Murphy's rule."

"That's Murphy's Law, ya dumbass," Cal says.

"Murphy's Law dictates that Pete will fall off his stool," I say.

Yag grabs Short Pete from behind and gives him a tug. Short Pete gropes for the bar but it's too late. His eyes pop open wide. Yag holds him there, suspended halfway to the floor. Then he pushes the chair with Pete still on it into its upright position: four legs on the ground.

"The golden rule," Yag says. "I didn't let you fall."

"Rule of the jungle," Short Pete says. "Do that again and I'll kick your ass." Everyone looks at one another and laughs.

"Whooeee, why all the rules?" Cal says. He grabs his belt and gives his pants a little tug.

"Let's put on some Ja Rule," Yag says. He walks over to the jukebox.

"The half-your-age-plus-seven rule," Short Pete says.

"Yag doesn't know that rule," I say.

There is a jukebox etiquette at The Final Final. When someone plays a song that offends the sensibilities of the regulars, they verbally shame the person. They usually leave girls alone—they are a protected species in this bar, rare as they are. For this reason, all kinds of pop songs go unchecked—Taylor Swift and Katy Perry and Adele have all driven me to order another whiskey many times over. But all guys are fair game, college kids, old codgers, even the regulars themselves. As far as I can tell, there are three songs you absolutely cannot play: "Sweet Child o' Mine" by Guns N' Roses, "Come On Eileen" by Dexys Midnight Runners, and "Margaritaville" by Jimmy Buffett. "Beast of Burden" by the Rolling

Stones is okay, but only under certain circumstances (late enough so everyone is sufficiently drunk). You also cannot play anything by Neil Diamond. Billy Joel is acceptable, though. I once witnessed the entire bar sing along to "Captain Jack." If you play "Have You Ever Seen the Rain" by Creedence Clearwater Revival, and it happens to be raining outside, you're a fucking hero.

The jukebox is yet another test. The guys use it as a measure by which to judge people, based on whether the entire bar is subjected to something unforgivable. Once, a guy played Mariah Carey and received so much verbal abuse he left his full drink on the bar.

"So many goddamn rules," says Cal, repeating himself.

"Live free or die." I make a rock 'n' roll sign with my hand.

We decide to write up a list of bar rules, but in the end, we can agree on only one:

THE FINAL FINAL HOUSE RULES:
#1 KARMA

———

ONE WEEK BEFORE MY due date, a rash spread across my belly: a peony firework, cherry red and dazzling. It didn't hurt or itch. It seemed more like an announcement than anything. Or maybe a pronouncement. *I am here.* The doctors ran tests and found nothing. The baby was fine. They told me he could arrive at any moment.

My mother said that I had introduced myself in the exact same fashion, and that she had no way to confirm it, but she suspected my dad had done so too. "That baby is telling you he has the power," she declared. "It's in his blood."

"Genetic peacocking," I said. "Someone should give you a Nobel Prize."

"I'm just telling you what I know," she said.

"Why a rash? Why not a kick?" I asked.

"All babies kick. Kicks are boring. That baby wants everyone at attention. He wants the doctors scared; he wants Lucas scared; he wants *you* scared. He is your father's grandson. Don't forget that."

Investors are the only people in the world who profit off pessimism. Dad did it in the early eighties when there were still buildings in New York no one wanted to buy, and he did it again in 2008 in the midst of the credit crisis. The key is waiting until everyone else is looking at a big, scary rash, and they freeze, and then bam! You make your move.

That was the day my water broke.

———

AFTER LIONEL WAS BORN, as many as three times a week, a homemade meal, plus enough to have some left over, appeared in the kitchen. A pot roast, a batch of lentil soup, a casserole. It varied. I accepted this charity because I was physically exhausted from breastfeeding and sleep deprivation and planning my upcoming book tour. Plus, I felt less guilty about Joan cooking than I did about Lucas cooking, either because I assumed she didn't have anything better to do, or because of some unconscious sexist bias I'd rather not admit.

The details were always a little fuzzy on how the food appeared on the stove top. Once, I asked Lucas if his mom had a key. My tone was probably accusatory or maybe I rolled my eyes, because he insisted Joan did not. I made it very clear that I did not want my mother-in-law to have unbridled access to my house. Maybe Lucas met her at the house when she came by, or maybe she left it on the porch and he brought it in. Most likely, though, she had a key.

Lucas's father married his mother when she was young and because she was hot. They were barely twenty. The old codger was a workaholic who built his drywall business from nothing. When he wasn't on a job, he challenged himself with projects like building a boat. He was the restless type, so he either had to be drywalling or building boats, which meant he didn't have much time for Lucas or his mother.

When Lucas was a young boy, his mother started seeing a therapist. Her primary takeaway was that her family's domestic life was not her sole responsibility. She abruptly stopped cooking and cleaning. She also explicitly told eleven-year-old Lucas that his happiness was not her problem. Then she went to an ashram in India for the better part of a year.

These days, spending time at an Indian ashram is no big thing. The plane ticket is pricey but no one bats an eye. It's like buying the six-dollar eggs because the yolks are orange. Back in the eighties, when Joan did it, it was like leaving the Shire to travel to the gates of Mordor. People would have been impressed if they weren't so distracted by the magnitude of her maternal failure.

The casseroles might have been her way of making up for her own absence, but they felt more like an indictment of the choices I was about to make: day care, business travel, supplementing with formula.

EVERYBODY, NO MATTER WHO they are or where they come from—everyone over thirty—drinks for the same reasons. They have problems they cannot solve and subjects they'd rather forget. They drink because relationships are hard. They drink so self-loathing doesn't get the better of them, even if that self-loathing comes from drinking too much. They drink because to be alive is to be in pain.

New York bankers, with their designer suits and Italian shoes, and townies, with their flannel shirts and workman's boots, both consume two things in excess: whiskey and cocaine. Why? Because they haven't figured out how to let the light in.

"What's in the bag?" I ask. Cal is carrying a cheap, black nylon backpack. From the way he holds it, I can tell he's not carrying anything heavy.

He starts unzipping the bag. "I have a croissant, headphones, and a bottle of water."

"You have a croissant?" I ask.

Cal pulls a grease-soaked brown paper bag out of the backpack. He gives it a little squeeze. "Croissants are fucking delicious."

"I bet you can't even spell *croissant*," Short Pete says.

"Of course I can spell *croissant*. I eat one almost every day. C-r-o-s—"

I give him a little poke in the gut. "Maybe you should lay off the croissants." I change the subject. "I'm trying to decide what Addie and I should do in the event of the apocalypse. We'd probably make our way out to your place."

Cal has a big piece of property outside of town. He calls it *the ranch* but it's really just a one-story ranch-style house.

"Combine resources?" Cal nods vigorously. "Money's no good in an apocalypse scenario."

"How's business these days, anyway?" I ask.

"I'm doing three times what I did two years ago. I just got this kitchen remodel. Eighty Gs." Cal gestures like he's throwing a lasso, catching some invisible beast called Money. Then he's right back on the apocalypse scenario. "Everyone will need to pitch in—building, hunting, cooking. Lucas'll do the shelter." He looks at me when he says this. "Sorry, honey, we knew Lucas first. He's in."

"Postapocalyptic shelters don't need drywall," I say. Postapocalyptic shelters have level-one finishes.

"Lucas can do odd jobs too," Cal says. "He doesn't finish projects, but he sure can start them." He winks at me, laughing.

WHENEVER CAL OR ANYONE else asked Lucas whether he'd finished a project, he'd always say the same thing: "Everything left to do is just cosmetic." I'd heard that sentence so many times it became a running joke. Lucas would find me home writing in the middle of the day, wearing yoga pants and no makeup, my hair pulled up on top of my head sloppily, and I'd say, "Everything left to do is just cosmetic." Or Lion would have boogers coming out of his nose and spaghetti sauce all over his face, and I'd say, "Everything left to do is just cosmetic." Or Addie would get into the trash, tear through it, spread it everywhere, and we'd come home to a veritable garbage dump in our living room and say in unison, "Everything left to do is just cosmetic." If you start saying this enough—I mean really take it on as a mantra—you start to realize it's actually true. Food, shelter, clothing, sleep, education, healthcare—even these most basic needs are, to varying degrees, both essential and nonessential, maybe 80 percent necessary and 20 percent cosmetic for middle-class folks, and 20/80 for upper-class folks, or 10/90, more realistically.

The truth beyond economics is that people have different definitions of beauty, and when I was with Lucas, every hole and exposed joist and visible tuft of insulation was beautiful, like a freckle on a bare chest or a gap between two front teeth.

When Lucas took out the wall between the kitchen and the living room, he had to move an air duct. He completed the ductwork but left a hole in the floor (because it was just cosmetic). Through it, you could see right down to the basement. Lionel's birth should have inspired us to seal it up. The looks on our friends' faces—on Samantha's face—the you're-a-bad-mom looks, might have served as warnings. It wasn't like Lionel could fall into the hole, though. It was about four inches by four inches, big enough, maybe, for an adult to twist an ankle, but it didn't pose a real threat.

I can say also, in our defense, it wasn't a laziness thing. I can say that. Other things were, like the way we maintained our lawn, or as Cal affectionately called it, our *weed pit*.

The hole was different. Addie was always dropping her ball down there. I'd go get it for her and she'd stay on the first floor, peering down at me through the hole. I felt a weird affection for the hole, the kind of affection a person might feel for something so ugly it's cute.

Eventually, Addie taught Lion to put things down into it. After nosing her ball down one night, she stood over it with her ears perked up, and Lion clapped like she'd performed a profoundly difficult trick, one that she'd come up with on her own without any promise of treats. The treat, I suppose, was the joy of watching Lucas or me get up from the couch. After that, I started finding Lionel's toys down in the basement. Sometimes these toy drops would be secrets between him and Addie. On other occasions, he'd hover over the hole, turning his face to the right so he could spy down into it with his left eye.

Lionel was not allowed into the basement. There were too many dangerous objects down there. When we installed the baby gate, I marveled at my child's curiosity. Addie was afraid of the basement steps—she could see through them because they didn't have risers. The basement was the one place she wouldn't follow us. She was content to stay where she was. Lionel's mind worked differently. The place we didn't allow him to go was the place he immediately wanted to be.

For Lionel, the hole in the floor was a glimpse into another world, a world of laundry and spiders and tools, and I can only imagine the Candy

Land he dreamed up for it. There wasn't a woman in the county who could put her hands on her hips and shake her head, and make me want to seal off that hole. I never asked Lucas to fix it.

———————

CAL CONTINUES TO HASH out the apocalypse situation. I shouldn't have brought it up.

"Bottom line," Cal says. "Lucas cannot make the decisions. We'd never get anything done. Have you ever seen that guy order a sandwich? Once, I waited for ten minutes while he decided whether he wanted a slice of tomato on it." This is not true. Lucas doesn't like tomatoes on anything. This was a point of contention because I love tomatoes. Tomatoes and mushrooms. I put them on everything. "Actually, ordering the sandwich isn't the main problem," Cal continues. "Eating the sandwich—now, that's excruciating." He pantomimes taking a bite of a sandwich, masticating the air in his mouth very slowly. "Takes, like, an hour." This is true. Lucas eats slowly. Cal, on the other hand, can put away a foot-long in under five minutes.

"What can I do?" I ask.

He shrugs. "Ain't no stock market in the apocalypse, hun. Don't you worry your pretty face. You can still join us."

I'm on Cal's good side because I encouraged him to invest twenty thousand dollars in the market and his investment is doing well. Guys like Cal don't trust the market. He puts money in the bank so he can run his business, but as I mentioned, he's one of those bury-the-cash-and-jewelry-where-only-I-can-find-it nutjobs. Though I imagine Summer knows all his secrets. The idea of owning stock is anathema to a guy like Cal.

It took me several hours and three straight nights at the bar but eventually I wore him down and got him to set up a brokerage account. He called "his guy" at the local bank and had him transfer the money into it. Then I gave him a hot tip.

But Cal is right: in the apocalypse, my stock tips won't be worth a damn thing.

"I could write everything down. Record what's happened for future generations. That's a really important job," I say.

"You can just look pretty," Cal says.

"Looking pretty is not a basic need. It's like drywall," I protest.

"Sex is a basic need." Cal has this big, dumb grin on his face.

"I'm not having sex with you. Even if you're the last man on the planet."

"Not even for the benefit of the species? Okay, fine; you can cook. Lucas can cook too. He's a feminist." Cal draws out *fem-min-nist* slow and smooth. He adds, "I have enough bottled water to last us six months."

"Food, water, and shelter," I say. "And friendship."

Cal raises his bottle to me. He pours whatever's left down his throat. "Let's go, Beautybelle," he says to Summer. I picture them driving home in Cal's truck—Summer with her legs up on the dash, Cal telling her how she will rule the world someday. It doesn't matter to Cal what she does with her life. She'll always be his Beautybelle.

Summer lifts her head. "Can we stay a little longer?"

"It's almost ten," Cal says.

"Nobody here minds." She looks at me.

I nod.

"Amelia," Cal says, "tell her what's what."

"No children after ten," Amelia says, flashing a smile.

"Unless you're a man-child. Then you can stay 'til close," I say.

Summer laughs and allows Cal to slip a clear plastic poncho over her head, before putting on his rain jacket. Then he reaches into his jacket pocket to pull out his wallet so he can pay his tab. The wallet's not there. He searches in the other pocket, and then, even though he knows it's not there, in the breast pocket.

"Who took my wallet? Someone took my wallet!" He looks at Summer. "Did you see anyone suspicious over here?"

She shakes her head no.

"Shit," Cal says.

"I'm sorry, Daddy. I wasn't watching," Summer says. She feels responsible.

Cal kisses her on the head. "No, no, Belle. It's not your fault. I didn't mean that."

I call across the bar, "I saw Yag creep over there about an hour ago."

Collectively, every head turns to Yag, who is at the pool table, about to take a shot. He looks up, flabbergasted. "What the fuck, Emma? I didn't go near that table."

"Sure you did," I said. "When you and Jimmy came in from your smoke. Jimmy went to the bathroom and you hovered over there by Cal's jacket."

The look on Yag's face indicates his desire to attack me but he doesn't have time because he is blocked by Cal and Jimmy.

Jimmy says, "Come on, man. We know you need the cash."

Cal says, "My wallet has twelve hundred dollars in it. I need that money back."

Yag throws up both hands. "Search me. I don't have your fucking wallet. Emma doesn't know what the fuck she's talking about."

Cal pats him down, finds nothing.

Jimmy walks over to Yag's rain slicker, which is draped on a stool next to the pool table. By the way Jimmy holds it up, everyone can tell it's heavier than it should be. He pulls the wallet out of one of the pockets.

"That's not mine," Yag says. "It's my jacket but I have no idea how that got there."

I look down into my drink.

Yag points across the bar at me. "She did it. She put it there."

"Why would I do that?" I say.

"Because you're fucking crazy. You've always been a crazy bitch."

"Leave her out of this," Jimmy says. He hands the wallet to Cal.

Cal counts the money. It's all there. He walks over to Amelia and pays his tab.

They briefly discuss what to do about Yag. There's no way they'd call the cops, and no one's going to lay a hand on him. Cal is holding Summer's hand. He shakes his head at Yag, showing him he's disappointed. He says, "This is our bar. I don't want to come here having to worry someone's gonna steal from me."

Yag protests again, "I didn't do it. You gotta believe me."

"How about you take a couple weeks," Jimmy says. "Pay off your debt. Get your head on straight."

"Typical, Jimmy. Some things never change. You and Lucas can shut me out whenever you want, but you can't ban me from the bar. You don't own the place."

"I can," Amelia says. "Take a month. Then we'll reassess."

"A fucking month? Jimmy said a couple weeks."

"We all know you're not going to pay off ten grand in a couple weeks," Jimmy says. "A month is reasonable."

"You did this. This is all you, Emma," Yag says. "This is no different from when you told me I wasn't welcome in my best friend's house."

"If you need work," Cal says, "I can throw some your way."

"Ban Emma from the bar," Yag screams. "She's the one who took the wallet. No one wants her here anyway." He closes his eyes and runs his hands over his bald head. He's calculating something—I can't tell what. He snatches his jacket from Jimmy, looks at me, and says, "Emma, step into my office." Then he heads straight for the ladies' room and lets the door shut behind him.

Jimmy and Cal both make a move toward the bathroom, but I stop them. "He wants to talk to me because he thinks I did something to him. I'll handle it," I insist, telling myself I'm doing it out of kindness when really, deep down, I'm worried Yag might actually convince someone I took the wallet.

I did what had to be done. And anyway, it's not permanent. It's just one month and then, as Amelia said, *we'll reassess*. How civilized. If only everything worked that way. If only the justice system worked that way, or deportation, or illness. *Let's just give it a month, and then come to terms.*

"Holler if he gives you any trouble," Cal says. "We'll be right here."

───────────

"WHY ARE WE IN the ladies' room?" These are the first words that spew out of my month upon seeing Martin Yagla sitting atop the closed lid of the toilet. The swinging, louvered saloon doors, which cordon off the toilet from the sink, hang open. From my position, having just entered through the heavy door that separates us from the rest of the patrons, I feel a certain intimacy, perhaps a shared insanity.

"The men's room is dirty," he says. "You and I both know I didn't go anywhere near Cal's jacket. Why'd you finger me? Why'd you set me up?"

Even if Yag is not conscious of his intent, I'm sure he chose the ladies' room because, deep down, he knows Cal and Jimmy will leave us alone in here. I don't feel threatened, though, which has something to do with his demeanor. His body language suggests he just wants to talk.

"Did you see what just happened?" he asks. "Jimmy's trying to excommunicate me. My best fucking friend wants me gone."

I'm surprised that Yag considers Jimmy his best friend, but I don't say anything.

"Ever since Lucas dipped out—"

"What do you mean since Lucas dipped out?" I interrupt.

"We don't see him anymore, not since—" Then it hits him. "They hang out without me, don't they?"

"I wouldn't know," I say. "I mean, they've been friends for so long they have their own way of communicating."

"They think I've never lost anyone," he says. "Like they have."

The fake pine smell of the bathroom hits me again.

"That's not how it works, Martin. I know you want to make sense of it, but loss doesn't push people together. It tears them apart. If Lucas and Jimmy are still close, it's because they found a way around the loss. They tapped into something that existed long before we ever knew them. Bottle rockets in the backyard or summer nights in the cemetery." I'm not sure if this is true, or if I'm saying it for Martin's benefit or my own. He's not really listening.

"You know I took an extra year to finish med school?" he says.

"I know that, yes."

"Everyone just assumed I went off the deep end, like I went off my meds or something."

"So why did you?" I ask.

"I was in love," he says. "Just once. I loved her as much as Lucas loves you."

"With who?"

"Maeve," he says. "Jimmy's sister."

I do a little mental math. Yag's time in med school coincided with when Jimmy returned home. Maeve's cancer had already spread.

"When Jimmy arrived, he made us stop seeing each other. I wasn't allowed in the house."

"Why?" I ask, even though I know why.

"Same reason you later banned me from your house, I guess." He shrugs. "Jimmy said she was too fragile for me."

"She was dying," I say for no reason.

"Exactly," he says. "And I loved her. I loved her and I wanted a little more time with her, and she wanted more time with me. One night I snuck her out. Jimmy was at the bar. Their parents went to bed at nine. Maeve asked to see a ten o'clock movie, just to feel normal for a night. It was a good idea until we ran into Lucas, who understood Jimmy's wishes and sided with him. He ratted us out, of course. Jimmy was at the theater within ten minutes. He dragged her out in her wheelchair as she protested. I would've fought him but Lucas held me back." He chuckles. "I thought Lucas was my bro. To tell you the truth, we weren't close. We weren't anything. Just two guys who hung out at the same bar."

There are other women at the bar—the group of college girls that came in for shots. One of them could barge in at any time. I bolt the lock on the outer door, an action I usually forgo because the toilet stall is private. Yag is telling me something he needs to tell me, for whatever reason, and I don't want to be interrupted.

"I'd told my parents I couldn't go anywhere that summer. They'd planned a trip to Montreal, but I didn't want to be away for two weeks, so I insisted on staying behind. Jimmy and Lucas made sure I never saw Maeve again, though."

"You loved her," I acknowledge. "She must have known."

"She died that summer." Yag starts crying. I've never seen him like this. I always thought he was just another Peter Pan asshole.

"Imagine if Lucas was dying," he says. "And someone thought you were so worthless that you weren't allowed to say goodbye."

I can imagine exactly that, I think. Except *someone* would be me. I'd keep myself away.

I squat down to look at Martin at eye level. Shifting my weight from the balls of my feet to my heels, I realize I can't hold the position for very long. My knees ache. I drop my butt to the floor and sit cross-legged at his feet. My body reminds me how badly I need to pee. I will hold it for as long as I can. "So why'd you keep hanging out with Lucas and Jimmy?"

"We took a break," he says. "Maybe six months after Maeve died, I started seeing them around the bar again. I dunno. I guess I was lonely."

Looking at Yag now, I can see how Maeve would have been attracted to him. He has smooth, milky skin, almost feminine, and before he lost it, he had a mop of curly blond hair. He's short for a man but not too small, not scrawny. He's lean and muscular, and in his twenties, he wouldn't have carried the softness on his gut. To top it all off, he has these beautiful, serene green eyes—eyes that, until now, I don't think I've ever looked into. I want to tell him Lucas and Jimmy were wrong to keep them apart. I want to say *I'm sorry* because that's how I feel, but sorry doesn't mean anything. I wish Yag had told me this story before I'd planted Cal's wallet in his jacket. If only I'd known his story, or considered he had a story at all, beyond what he'd shared with the guys at the bar, I'd have cut him some slack. *If only. If only.*

My feelings toward Martin are softer now. I even decide to give him a pass for the succession of young girls, one after another, each one more attempt to bury the memory of Maeve.

I point at the bathroom door. "Those people are your friends. Lucas too."

"Jimmy sold me out in a hot second when you planted the wallet.

You know what? I'm glad you did it. Now I know where we stand. It's got nothing to do with his sister."

"It's been a long night. Jimmy's drunk. No one's thinking straight, yourself included."

He wipes the tears from his face. "Beer tears. That's what my mom calls them," he says. "Screw Jimmy. He and Lucas can have their sad-sack friendship."

"Lucas always cared about you," I say. "I'm not sure if he can be there for you now, but that's got nothing to do with you."

"How am I gonna come up with ten grand anyway?"

"Borrow it from your parents. Go to work for Cal. Pay it back over time." I stand up and shake my legs out. "Give me the stall for a minute, or I'm going to piss my pants."

He stands up and walks over to the mirror.

I close the swinging stall doors, yank down my jeans, and talk as my bladder empties. "Any minute, some drunk college girl is going to start banging on this door, needing to pee," I say. "Here's what we're gonna do. We're gonna walk out into the bar. I'm going to tell everyone that I planted the wallet, that it was just a gag. I'll buy everyone a round as a show of goodwill, and the apologies will come just as quick as the blame. Then you'll play another game of pool with Jimmy. Take the edge off. And we'll all go home and tomorrow will be another day."

I flush and step out of the stall to wash my hands. He nods, seemingly pleased with the plan. As I begin to unlock the door, he puts his hand over mine. "Everything you do turns to gold," he says. "Your book. The fund. Maeve was the only one who made me feel like somebody."

"I am a mother—" I begin. He throws me a look of recognition, and I don't have to finish the thought. He accepts my use of the present tense, or doesn't question it. I was a mother. I am a mother. I will always be a mother. Even Martin Yagla understands that. We unlock the door together and exit into the bar.

There's a girl waiting outside on her phone, legs crossed, holding in her pee. She looks annoyed. "What?" Yag says to her. "Never fucked in the bathroom?" We both laugh at the look on her face, mouth contorted upward in disgust.

I point at Amelia and tell her the next round, for all the regulars, is on me. Then I come clean about the wallet.

I READ SOMEWHERE ONCE that drinking is healthy for relationships. Statistically speaking, couples who drink together are more likely to maintain lifelong bonds. Never mind that the study was probably funded by the alcohol industry. This finding was congruous with what I believed to be true about relationships, in spite of the fact that my parents had split and Lucas and I had also split. I'm not talking about a glass of wine with dinner. I'm talking about a sustained habit of drinking together for several hours at a time. The kind of drinking that forges pathways of communication that would not otherwise exist; the kind that replaces therapy altogether. Lovers and friends can cover quite a bit of ground in eight hours of uninterrupted time. Aside from college dorms, that kind of time only exists in bars.

Sometimes I think that's where Lucas and I went wrong—we stopped going to the bar together. Maybe if we'd kept up the habit, we could have worked through things. Maybe we'd still be together. Don't get me wrong: the bar can't make the pain go away. Drinking can, for some hours, but it always comes back. The bar is simply a place where a person can live with the pain, because it isn't home, with the trappings of loneliness, or work, with the slow torture of avoidance. It is just a place where one human in the world chooses to be among other humans.

We didn't stop going to the bar when we had Lionel. We met here twice a week, when my class let out at four o'clock. Lucas's mom watched our son on those days, and she seemed happy to spend a few extra hours with him.

On weekends, we'd have friends over for barbeques in our backyard, or, every now and again, we'd take our son with us to the bar. Some combination of the chatter and the clanking glasses put him to sleep as a baby, and everyone seemed to appreciate his wide-eyed wonder as he started to grow. The regulars all called him Lion, and they let him sit in their laps and grab on to their legs, dangling from bar stools. Amelia gave him maraschino cherries, on the house, which I pulled apart into little pieces so they could slide down his tiny throat. For our little Lion, the bar was a tiny world, better than a playground.

We stopped going to the bar when I started traveling to promote my book.

––––––––––––

AFTER THE FIRST FEW months of touring, exhaustion set in. I'd been doing it so long that the excitement had waned but not long enough to fully acclimate. I can't remember what city I was in at the time. Tolstoy said, *Happy families are all alike*, but what he really should have said was, *Hilton Garden Inns are all alike*. That was the reality of my life: hotel art, patterned carpets, forced air.

FaceTime had a special ring, not even a ring, really—more like a digital beep, quick and repetitive. The sound of joy—it always preceded a glimpse into Lucas and Lionel's world: our home on Catherine Street.

I sat cross-legged in bed, holding my iPad up high, level with my face so my chin looked good. Lucas appeared, only half on-screen. He moved from the kitchen to the living room. I caught a glimpse of his left hand, holding a cup of tea.

"Since when do you drink tea?" I asked.

"Oh, this," he said, angling the camera toward his mug. "It's a hot toddy."

"I want one," I said.

"Check this out!" Lionel's little back appeared on the screen. He sat on the floor, facing the wall. The plastic baby tool set that Lucas's parents had given him was next to him on the hardwood. From it, he'd taken what looked like a drywall trowel, a flat rectangle with a handle protruding from the middle of the backside. Lucas had apparently also given him some joint compound, which was all over his hands and arms. "He's my little apprentice," Lucas said.

Lionel stuck a glob of compound on the wall with his left hand and then attempted to rub it in with the trowel. Lucas panned back to his own face, again only half on-screen. He put his drink down on the coffee table. "Hang on, he needs help," he said.

He sat down behind Lionel with his legs bent around him. Lionel handed him the trowel and, for the first time, saw my face on the screen. His eyes lit up. He raised his arms to the air. He squealed.

Lucas ran the tool across the small section of wall near the floor in a fluid motion, smoothing out the mud. "Like this," he said. Lionel's attention shifted from my face to the wall. He grabbed the tool from his father's hand.

Lucas repeated, "It's fun. It's fun. Isn't this fun?" as if he were trying to talk himself into it. He reached back toward the coffee table for his drink, and on-screen I could see the face I loved so much, half covered by the mug.

"Maybe he'll take up the trade someday," I said.

"Oh, the kid will know how to drywall," Lucas said. "But he won't go into the business."

"No?"

"He's independent, like his mom." Lucas pushed his body back so he could lean against the edge of the couch. Lionel maintained focus on the wall.

"He does seem to like it," I said.

"How'd the talk go today?" Lucas asked. "Did you give someone hope?"

"Doing my part," I said.

"Restoring faith in capitalism by charging thirty bucks for a hard-cover?"

"Teaching people they are special," I said. "I'm like Rachael Ray for wannabe bankers and consultants."

"Capitalism at work!" he said. "You should launch a product line focused on longevity."

"Goop already exists."

"Immortality, then?"

"'Caius is a man, men are mortal, therefore Caius is mortal,'" I said. "Lemme see Lionel again."

Lucas turned the camera back to Lionel. He had a clump of compound in his hand and it was smeared on his face, across his cheeks, on his lips, and into his mouth. He flashed a devilish smile. "Shit," Lucas said. "Put that down, child."

"That stuff's probably toxic!" I yelled.

"It's not toxic," he said. "I mean, maybe just a little."

"How much did he eat?"

"I dunno. I was talking to you."

"You're supposed to be watching him. Who gives their baby toxic joint compound to play with?" Lucas put down the phone. I could only see the ceiling fan. "What are you doing now?"

"I'm wiping him off."

Lionel started crying.

"You need to call poison control," I said.

"You call poison control," he said. "I'm busy. You're just sitting in a hotel room."

"I'm a thousand miles away, and I'm not the one who let him play with a toxic substance."

"I told you I don't think it's toxic, at least not until you eat a lot of it."

"You just said you have no idea how much he ate."

"I know it wasn't a lot. He probably just put a little in his mouth and swished it around. He's fine."

I opened my laptop and googled *baby ate drywall compound*. I clicked on hospital-data.com, which had a page about accidents related to children ages zero to five ingesting caulking or spackling compounds. The site estimated 1,029 accidents over a ten-year period, which didn't seem like a lot. I scanned several instances. They all said, "Examined and released without treatment."

I googled *how to make edible playdough* and read the recipe aloud for Lucas.

"Em," he said. "I don't need you to google for me."

"Well, you clearly need help," I said.

"So come home and help me."

THERE'S A VOICEMAIL ON my phone from Grace, time-stamped fifteen minutes ago. I figure I should check it. She's usually more of a texter.

Emma, I need you to take an Uber to Samantha's house. Please. We've incurred considerable expense, both in time and money, to arrange for Elisa to meet with you. This is important. If you won't do it for yourself, do it for me and Samantha.

She tells me to take an Uber because she suspects I'm already drunk.

A *New York Times* profile on Elisa Monfils reveals that she's something of a therapist for Wall Street junkies and Silicon Valley nerds and D.C. attorneys. She talks them off the ledges of their high rises.

Oh my God—I get it now. Grace planned an intervention. I text her immediately: *What the hell, Grace? Are you worried I'll appear on MSNBC with a bottle of whiskey and a doobie, and all our investors will back out?*

It's not about the fund, Emma. It's a birthday gift. Elisa works with the best of the best. Steve Jobs was her client. She doesn't mention Elon Musk or his doobie.

Today is my thirty-fifth birthday. I'm not advertising this fact at the bar, because people over twenty-one who still celebrate their birthdays are either narcissistic or simpleminded or both.

STEVE JOBS WAS OFF HIS ROCKER!!! I write.

Steve Jobs sat atop an empire, she retorts.

Well, he's dead so if he's sitting atop anything, it's a money bag in the fourth circle of hell. I shake my head and add an eye-roll emoji even though emojis are beneath me.

Everyone uses consultants from time to time, Emma.

Call it what it is, Grace. It's not a consultation. It's an intervention.

She doesn't deny it. She texts, *Pick up the phone, Emma.* It vibrates in front of me on the bar.

Even if she believed my lie about driving up from the city, she would assume I made it home by now. I slip out back. Standing under the overhang next to a can full of cigarette butts, I take her call.

"Where are you?" Grace asks.

"I stopped at the bar for a drink." I picture her pinching the cartilage between her nostrils. "I have no interest in your little intervention."

"You're stuck, Emma, in a terrible and understandable loop. We think Elisa can help you out of it."

"You and Samantha have no idea—"

"I know," she says. "I can't even imagine—"

"That's just it," I say. "You don't have to imagine. What happened to me would never happen to someone like you. Your life is perfect."

"We've known each other too long for you to believe that, Emma."

This is true, of course. Less than a year after her son was born, Grace was diagnosed with breast cancer. I was with her when she tried on bras and contemplated whether anyone would notice that her fake breast sat higher than her real one. Her daughter, the oldest, repeated kindergarten after falling behind and was later diagnosed with multiple learning disorders by a throng of specialists. Her mother died last year in Taiwan, where she'd moved when she divorced Grace's father late in life after many unhappy years in Ohio. These are just a few examples from the last five years, the ones I know about. So yes, even Grace is like drywall, all those layers of mud plus a skim coat. But her eyes are so clear and bright, always looking toward the future. Sometimes I forget she has a past.

———

I'M TIRED. I MISS our old bed, the one I left behind when I moved out. The guy at the mattress store told us we should buy the biggest bed that fit in our bedroom, so Lucas and I picked a king. It occupied most of the room, with just barely enough floor space for a dresser against the opposite wall and narrow passageways on either side. When we told Lucas's dad about the purchase, he said, "That's so bourgeois."

It was a great decision. That bed was a home within a home. It was where Lionel said his first word.

He cried out from his crib around six a.m. I remember it was a

Saturday, because on weekdays, Lucas was always up by six, getting ready to head out to a jobsite.

Addie jumped up and sat, ears perked, at the foot of the bed. She was the most awake of all of us, anxious to rush downstairs and wait for Lucas to fill her bowl. Together, they plodded down to the kitchen. A bit later, they scurried back upstairs.

Lucas carried Lion into our room so I could feed him. I propped myself up in bed with pillows, gave him the bottle, and watched while he filled his tiny belly. We'd switched to formula pretty quickly, much to Samantha's chagrin. She'd sent a series of articles espousing the benefits of breastfeeding. I deleted her emails before clicking on the links. Lion was a hearty little thing, strong and growing. We could tell how smart he was by the way he explored the world. If Samantha wanted to judge us for giving him formula, that was her prerogative. I didn't give a rip.

When Lionel finished, he fell asleep on my chest. I scooted down, a little closer to Lucas, and let myself drift away. Addie knew well enough to give us a little more time, but our half rising had riled her. She wanted to be a good dog, her deep desire was to please, but she couldn't help herself. She jumped off the bed, ran downstairs, her nails clicking on the wood, and back up again. She returned with her ball, which looked like a tennis ball but it squeaked when she closed her jaw around it. As soon as I heard the squeak, I fake-scolded her. "Addie, shhh! No playing on the bed!"

This was an invitation to play, of course. Lionel was awake again now, sleepy but gleeful. He turned from me and toward Addie, opening his arms. She dropped her ball on our clean French linens and licked his face. He smiled with his perfect cherub mouth, showing his tongue and little teeth that had just come in.

"No playing on the bed!" I repeated.

Lucas grabbed Addie by the neck and began to wrestle with her. He put his hand in her mouth, gripping her fangs, shaking her head back and forth.

I picked up the gross, slobbery ball from our duvet and threw it on the floor. Addie mistook my gesture for a game of fetch. She jumped down off the bed, picked up the ball, and jumped back up. She dropped it from her mouth and it rolled toward Lionel. He said, "Ball!" and clapped his hands together.

Lucas picked up the ball and shook it in front of Lion's face. "Yeah, it's a ball. It's a ball!"

Lion repeated, "Ball."

Lucas repeated, "Ball."

Lion repeated, "Ball."

Lucas said, "That's right! It's a ball." He threw it off the bed. Addie fetched it. She stood over us, holding the ball in her mouth, waiting. Addie was never a good listener. Perhaps we gave her mixed signals.

"No playing on the bed," I said. Lucas and Lionel laughed. Addie wagged her tail.

After I moved out, the post office forwarded mail from Catherine Street for a full year, and every time I saw my old address with that yellow forward sticker, I thought about this morning, together on the bed with my family. Each time, it was hard to catch my breath again.

10PM

TIME IS SPEEDING UP now. A full hour nearly escapes my notice. There's an old-school wall clock in the corner of the bar. Its face is a beer advertisement, noteworthy for its orange-beaked toucan and the words *Always time for a GUINNESS*. Bar time is warped. It starts out real slow, the minute hand creeping along, and then, wham! Quarters slip away. The minute hand becomes irrelevant; the hour hand accelerates toward last call.

My body is tethered to the bar. The lights have begun to blur over, like a photograph with a single object in the foreground and everything else rendered in the abstract, colors and shapes. The bar is more an extension of self than a place. The room and the objects—the chairs, the wood, the glass in my hand—are me, and I am them. I could not walk the line, but I can still sit on my stool and order another drink.

Summer's wish to stay longer has been granted. She hasn't taken off her poncho but she's back at the front table with another Cherry Coke. Cal is drinking a fresh Bud Light with the same gangly kid he was talking shop with earlier. I take a closer look. He's baby-faced, barely old enough to drink. He's wearing cargo shorts and a white undershirt, and he has a tattoo on his right side, which extends from the middle of his forearm, across his elbow, to the bottom third of his bicep, just below the line of his T-shirt sleeve.

"Snow season is just around the corner, if you can hold out a few months," Cal says. It seems odd to be planning for snow in this late-summer heat, as hurricanes ravage the southern coast and wildfires tear through California. Every time the door swings open and a regular steps outside for a smoke, I am reminded of the deluge of rain that fills our gorges and turns our sleepy creeks into gushing streams. I think about Lucas's rain barrel and the soaker hose he hooked up around the backyard perimeter, where I said I would plant flowers but never did.

Cal and the kid agree on details in the corner. The kid adjusts his black flat-billed cap. The logo on it is old-school Adidas, the trefoil. It's not a new hat made to look old—it is vintage, circa '91 or '92 maybe, before the kid was even born, and well-worn.

Cal owns a plow that hooks onto his pickup truck. Various businesses around town contract him to clear their parking lots. This is not particularly lucrative. When business slows in the winter months and school lets out for break, he and Summer would just as soon take his fifth wheel down to Florida and hang out in RV parks with retirees. Nevertheless, he always seems to stick around so he can manage those relationships and make sure his truck is available for plowing.

On a regular basis, Cal tells me how much he grossed in the preceding year. He has upgraded his fifth wheel three times. His current model is more than forty feet long with more than sixty gallons of fresh water capacity. It has a queen bed and a fifty-inch flat screen, which is, incidentally, bigger than my TV at home. I know all of this because Cal talks about it, each feature and gadget, a point of pride. He talks about the bad stuff too—when he's had a down month, or issues he's had with credit card debt. When I was growing up in Wilton, people never talked about money, or rather, they never spoke about it directly. They talked about the market sometimes, about having a good year, or about tax reform or interest rates, but never dollars and cents.

The kid says, "Yes, sir. I can be available first thing in the morning."

Cal shakes his hand.

The reason Cal hooks the snowplow on to his truck every winter isn't to make a few extra bucks. It's because some skinny kid with an arm covered in tats needs the work, and Cal is in a position to provide it.

Eventually, he'll pass his business on to someone. He'll probably meet him here, at The Final Final. He'll take him under his wing. He'll sell him everything, all the equipment and his client list, for a fraction of what it's worth. Summer will be long gone by then. She'll have a big job in a big city.

Cal takes the open seat next to me. The gesture suggests he's forgiven me for the wallet drama, though he doesn't say anything about it. I don't want his pity if that's what he's offering. He checks his phone. I can't tell if he's happy or disappointed that there's no text asking him to come home.

His ex-wife, Evie, is an ultraliberal animal lover. Mostly I encounter her through Sarah McLachlan–style posts on social media. I rarely see her around town, although I know she still lives here and remains part of Cal and Summer's life. When she stopped chasing bands around the country, she stayed put long enough to get a master's degree in plant sciences from the U. Cal barely graduated from high school. Evie told me once that she asked him to make her a cup of tea and he called in from the kitchen, "Ya want shamoolie?" After realizing he was reading the chamomile box, she said, "Yes, please, make me some shamoolie." He was present when she told me that story. He laughed about it. Nothing embarrasses Cal, not since he started pulling in more money than he can spend.

Every morning, Cal wakes up at five a.m., three hours before Summer stirs. In the kitchen, he turns on Fox News and makes a pot of coffee. He says this is his favorite time of the day, a time when he can be alone with his thoughts. By thoughts, I assume he means ideals: Second Amendment rights, and First Amendment rights, and pulling himself up by his boot-straps, and low taxes, and minimal regulations, except when his neighbor violates the zoning laws by building too close to the property line (then regulate the shit out of that!). Cal wants to think things without being told he's wrong or stupid. And I totally get that. Everyone wants that.

When I look up, the kid in the Adidas hat is gone. The girls are gone too, huddled under umbrellas arm in arm, heels slipping on wet pavement as they make their way to the heart of town.

Only the regulars remain: Cal and Summer, Fancy Pete, Short Pete, Yag, and Jimmy. I'm still here. Alone but not alone.

MY ATTENTION SHIFTS. YAG puts his cue down, yells out to Amelia for a round of shots. "Hey, Jimmy, when's the last time you saw Lucas?" he asks.

Jimmy shrugs. "Two, three days ago, maybe? He had a tree down in the backyard. I helped him clear it out."

"Could've called me," Yag says.

"It was a two-man job," Jimmy says, focusing on his shot. He's not picking up on Yag's agitation, even though it's evident in the volume of his voice and the way he paces around the pool table. Jimmy thinks they're just shooting the shit.

I think about how Jimmy used to leave the bar with Lucas and me, follow us all the way home, and call a cab from there. If I had a bike, he'd walk it for me. Lucas never asked why he didn't just call a cab from the bar. We always assumed he wanted to keep the party going. I know now that he just didn't want to be alone.

"We used to be like Kirk, Spock, and McCoy. I'm McCoy, of course. You're Spock," Yag says. "Or like the Beastie Boys."

Jimmy doesn't ask Yag to expound on how their personalities correlate to Mike D, MCA, and Ad-Rock. He stares at the balls on the pool table, unwilling to engage, as if to say, *The old days are behind us; too much has happened*.

"Dude, ya know who was hot in high school?" Yag is yelling now. Amelia perks up, as if she knows what he's going to say before the words escape his lips. She holds off on making the shots. "Your fucking sister."

Jimmy doesn't say anything at first. He continues to shoot the balls on the table, even after he misses. "Don't talk about my sister."

Everyone knows the saying *The straw that broke the camel's back*, which implies there is a significant amount of other straw that the camel carries and is aware of. The cliché is overly generous in regard to what she bears knowingly. The truth is that she carries around all this straw but it is weightless and invisible, and if it does have weight, which it might, she denies its existence. So when the final straw lands, the camel must instantaneously bear the burden of that straw and every single other straw that had gone unattended for so long. Essentially, the saying is misleading because the last straw is not incremental. It isn't just one more straw. It is the straw that reveals and magnifies all the straws. It is the moment when attention is drawn to everything that's been carried—every wrong, every hurt, every loss. And the camel breaks.

This is bad—worse than the Wrestler, and worse than the wallet. If only the sparrow could find its way in now, at this late hour. It would be a welcome distraction.

"She looked so good in those sundresses," Yag says.

Jimmy props the cue against the table and approaches Yag. "Don't talk about my sister."

"I'm just saying she was hot. It's a compliment. You can take a compliment, right?"

"Shut up." They are face-to-face.

Amelia is watching like a hawk from behind the bar. She yells out, "It's time to go home, boys. Time to get out."

Yag ignores her, grabs his crotch. "Dude, especially after she lost all that weight." He starts laughing. It's an ugly screech.

Jimmy puts his left arm around Yag's neck and pushes his face in front of his right fist. Before Jimmy punches, Yag says, "She must have lost sixty pounds."

The sparrow: a premonition. Disaster is imminent.

Jimmy starts in. He is enormous and strong but he's pulling his punches a little bit. He's a teddy bear, not a fighter.

Cal tells them to settle down. He says, "Jimmy, forget about it. You're gonna wake up tomorrow and take a shit and it'll be a whole new day. You'll just wish the shit was before the shower."

Short Pete laughs at this. They're not seeing what I'm seeing. Jimmy wants to kill Yag. And Yag is a wily little fucker.

Yag wiggles out of the headlock. He's holding a Budweiser bottle in his right hand. He rotates his shoulder, throwing his arm out in a haymaker motion. He strikes Jimmy across the face with the bottle, following through with every bit of upper-body strength he can muster. The bottle shatters on Jimmy's face. Blood rolls down into his eye before Amelia can say, "Get out now, Yag, or I'm calling the cops."

Cal is standing next to Summer with his hands on her shoulders. If she weren't his foremost concern, he'd be on top of Yag right now. Short Pete is standing, mouth agape, but he stays out of it. Fancy Pete is nowhere in sight, in the bathroom, maybe.

A thick vein protrudes from the middle of Yag's forehead. He lets out a low, guttural noise, which sounds more animal than human: a badger whining.

"Why do I have to leave and Jimmy gets to stay? He started it."

"You're not worth the air in this place," Cal says.

"But he started it!" Yag jabs his pointer finger toward Jimmy's chest and rotates his forearm like a screwdriver. He's desperate for someone to take his side, which is not the same as forgiveness. Deep down, he knows we all chose Jimmy a long time ago.

I conceptualize Forgiveness: how it feels, soreness trailing a hard workout—microfractures in the muscle cells; how it looks, a serene face, wrinkled but not without luster—crow's feet, evidence of a million bygone smiles; how it wears, like an old, cozy sweater—the reason winter is a welcome intrusion. If Memory and Nostalgia are sisters, Forgiveness is their godmother. She is old; she is wise; she carries neither the judgment nor the worry of motherhood. She operates stealthily, by example. She is easily ignored—a wallflower at a party passed over for a flashier woman, or rowdier repartee.

Amelia picks up the phone.

In a single, fluid motion, like a dance, Yag twists his body away from the pool table and toward the bar. He pulls a hunting knife out of his pocket and opens it. He waves it toward Amelia. "Put the phone down."

She complies. *Never comply with demands. Always fight back.* That's what the experts say. I took a self-defense class once.

Yag grabs me, nearly pulling me off my stool. His arm is wrapped around me like a hug, his left hand holding me down by the breastbone while his right pushes the knife toward my cheek.

"You," he says, "are a total fucking bitch. Five minutes ago, you acted like you actually cared. Now you have nothing to say? You pile on with all these assholes. You want me gone. Just like when you told Lucas he couldn't be friends with me. You know how long I've known Lucas? Twenty goddamn years. Since we were sixteen. And then you came along and told me I wasn't welcome in *his* house. Well, fuuuck you. It was his house before you and it's his house after you."

Music plays on the jukebox. I recognize the song but not the singer, some young pop princess. Her voice drives me crazy. I look at Amelia, wondering if she'll cut the sound. She doesn't. The queue of songs is long. We haven't gotten to mine yet.

Cal says, "Put the knife down, Martin. Come on. You don't want to be doing this now." He gestures toward Summer, who is frozen. "My little girl is here, Yag. We're all friends here." Everyone knows Cal is packing a gun. His right hand is under his maroon blazer. The gun is still in the holster as far as I can tell.

Yag pushes the knife closer to my eye. Everything slows down.

MY BODY IS HERE, in The Final Final, a limp target, but my mind is in the Adirondack Mountains. Lucas and I are on a white-water rafting trip, a last hurrah of sorts. I am three months pregnant with Lionel. I don't tell anyone official I'm pregnant, because pregnant women are not supposed to do anything fun.

The river has a good mix of class-three and class-four rapids. Easy enough for novices but challenging enough for a moderate thrill. We are given life jackets and placed into one of two rafts leaving at the same time.

Each raft has a guide. Lucas and I share a raft with two other couples and a guide who introduces himself as Monty. His full name is Mario Montenegro. Monty is bearded and buff, an obvious outdoorsman. He knows the river—every rock and every current—like he has a map imprinted on his subconscious.

A guide called Kilo leads the other raft. He doesn't explain the origin of the nickname, but we joke it is related to selling drugs. He speaks slowly with an affectation that isn't quite a stutter.

Monty tells us the river is at her finest—the rapids fierce and fast. It will be a good day. He yells, "Out," and we jump into the cold water to acclimate, learning how to pull one another back in. Grab the vest with two hands. Find leverage. Push down, pull up and in.

Monty is a practical jokester. When the river is calm, the rafts duel. Monty pops out the bridge that holds in two fake front teeth and smiles. "This is what happens when you take an oar in the mouth. Keep 'em suckers in the water at all times!" He pulls a water balloon out of his bag and aims for the guide on the other raft. He misses and hits a scrawny, nerdy-looking guy on the side of his head, right in the ear. Everyone cheers.

The guides pull out water guns. They pump water into them from the river and start a war. Everyone stands up in the rafts. Lucas and I grin at each other. We are in love. I pick up a balloon and chuck it at the other raft. It clips Kilo and bursts on the floor of the raft.

The two rafts drift closer to each other and the battle escalates. Kilo jumps onto our raft, grabs Monty, and throws him off. "You fuckin' idiot—" Monty yells, but not soon enough. Kilo grabs my shoulders and throws me off too just before Monty finishes, "—rapids!" My body is in the water heading for a class four. My life jacket keeps me buoyant. My hands hold on to my pregnant belly.

Why did I come on this trip? What was I thinking?

Kilo is now in the wrong raft, leaving his own raft guideless. The rafts surge forward, approaching the rapids. I am pulled forward as well, but the rafts are already some distance away. There is no chance I will be pulled in. I watch Monty swim toward the shore. He climbs up the wooded edge and runs to a rock perched over the rapids.

How could I put my baby at risk?

Lucas is still in our raft, which is wedged in some rocks—stuck. Kilo calls out orders, attempting to lead the raft through the rapids. Lucas scans the water, looking for me. I can see him but he can't see me.

I feel hands on my life jacket, pulling me up and in. I find myself in a boat of strangers, two girls in bikinis, one lean tan guy, no life jackets except the one I'm wearing.

We navigate the rapids and drift awhile before stopping in a cove below. I am shaking, expressing gratitude. I tell my new friends I'm pregnant. I tell them I made a mistake. Reckless. Selfish. Dumb. The guy who pulled me in says he's going back upriver to make sure everyone else is all right. We watch him run up on shore. He swims the rapids again, freestyle.

I look back to the shore and see Lucas and Kilo running toward us.

"Hey!" I yell. "I'm here!"

When Lucas sees me, his stance relaxes. He drops the oar from his hand.

Kilo puts his arm around his shoulder. "Hey, man, I'm glad she's okay. Everyone is okay." Lucas twists away.

Monty, now back in our original boat, guides both rafts toward the cove. The tan guy who saved me is in the other raft. He takes the hand of one of the bikini babes and climbs toward me, into his boat. He and Monty help me back into my raft.

As my new friends float away, I turn back to Lucas and Kilo, standing onshore. Lucas is holding the oar again, now threatening to take a swing. Kilo's hands are up, protecting his face. I've never seen Lucas threaten a man before. I've never even heard him raise his voice. He always walks away, jaw clenched. Now, he looks like he could kill Kilo.

"Lucas, stop!"

We exist in this state: capable of violence, suppressing our urges, which are instinctual and maybe justified. While we fight quietly with our minds and hearts, quibbling with words and drinking away pain, rage continues to burn.

MY HEAD IS BACK where it belongs. Martin Yagla is talking to me. "You think you're better than us. Always in the city or on a plane to some place that's not here. You want to know the funny part? Whenever you left town, Lucas invited me over. We played poker and drank beer and smoked cigarettes on the porch. That's right, *Mrs. Murphy*, we smoked tons of cigarettes on your porch. What's it to you, anyway? You weren't there. Lucas did what he wanted. Sometimes he made us wait to smoke until the kid was asleep. Point is, *I was there*—"

A new song comes on the jukebox, an Eminem song. I don't know if Yag added it to the queue earlier or if he just likes it, but whatever it is, he lets go; he releases me. He is transfixed. He pushes backward off me and dances along the narrow corridor of the bar. He pretends his hunting knife is a microphone. He may actually think the blade is a mic. His mind might be telling him he is onstage.

A sharp, high-pitched scream escapes Summer's mouth.

Cal points his handgun at Martin. He must have pulled it when Yag released me. Without turning his head, Cal's eyes dart toward Summer. He says, "Belle, you know what to do."

She crouches under a table, half hiding, half trusting Cal, her eyes glued to him. Short Pete kneels down next to her, his arm around her shoulder.

The gun is aimed at the center of Martin Yagla's chest. Because of my proximity and the fact that Cal is on the other side of him—the three of us in a scalene triangle formation—I can see down the barrel of the gun.

Most people do their best to avoid looking down the barrel of a loaded gun, so I should be clear. In actual fact, I can't see down it. I see it. I see a black hole that a bullet is designed to emerge from. There's no looking down into the hole. It's just black. But it's right there, pointed at Yag's chest. And it's scary as hell.

The barrel of the gun, the blackness, alters time. I see the future. I see a world inhabited by all of us, but Martin isn't breathing. Martin's dead. I see a hole in his chest and blood all over the floor. The cops come. An ambulance arrives. The body is taken away in a bag on a stretcher. Amelia takes a mop to the vinyl and soaks up all that blood, squeezing it out in a bucket. Everyone claims that none of us are to blame, that circumstances were out of our control. But no one believes that entirely, and each of us, in separate and isolated mental chambers, bears responsibility. We are each individually aware of this reality—we are responsible—but unwilling or incapable of acknowledging it to one another for fear that a reckoning would be the end of us. So we don't. For a while, it works. We return to the bar. We shoot the shit until we can't anymore, and then, one by one, we stop coming. Soon, we are strangers.

I guess that's what people mean when they talk about looking down the barrel of a gun. There's a lot to see there.

Yag either doesn't notice the gun or doesn't care, because he keeps rapping into his blade.

The music stops. Silence falls over the bar. Yag looks at the gun, then at me, then at Jimmy: one, two, three. His knife hand falls to his side.

"I was there that day too," he says. "Yeah, you know, *that day*." He trans-fers the blade to his left hand and lifts his right up and motions downward.

Lucas didn't tell me this. *Yag was with them.* Martin Yagla: banned from setting foot in our house. He smiled at my baby with his grotesque, falsely white teeth. He touched my baby with his soft, little hands, the same hands that grope girls from the U., children of a different kind. He spoke to my baby with his vulgar tongue, the same tongue that insults decency. My instinct is to attack, to gouge out his eyes with my finger-nails, to sink my teeth into his flesh, to thrust my knee into his balls, again and again and again. I want to leave him on the floor, bleeding and impotent. I'm not a human being anymore; I'm an animal.

I lunge forward. I don't get more than six inches away from my stool. Jimmy holds me back, arms wrapped around my waist.

"Bet Lucas never told ya that, huh? I was *there*." At first I think he's bragging but then I realize he's sobbing. He bears responsibility.

He lifts the blade to his own throat.

The gun goes off. A single shot. Louder than anything I've ever heard. And then: dead silence. No one so much as gasps.

Blood soaks through Yag's T-shirt, his left deltoid a deep, bright red. He grips it with his right hand, dumbstruck, and the blood oozes out of the cracks between his fingers, rolling down his arm.

"You fucking shot me!"

The spell is broken. We need to figure out what to do; Yag's next move is impossible to predict.

Yag looks at Jimmy, then at me. Whatever pain he's experiencing forces an ugly grimace, so that's what everyone sees: pain. I look harder because I want to know what's under all that pain—not what his body feels but what his mind feels. It's pain too, of course, all mucked up with synapses on neurons sending signals through the spinal cord to the brain, but it's also more than that. It's deeper. It is profound loneliness, the kind that only exists when a person is out of options, when there is nowhere to run and no one to turn to, and all you have is yourself, your own mind, which is the greatest punisher of all. I see this because Martin Yagla and I aren't so different, because it's the way I've felt for a long time.

"That asshole shot me," Yag says, as if he wants us to act on this information, restrain Cal, take the gun away. No one moves. No one answers his call.

Cal holsters his gun and says, "Give me some towels, Amelia. It's a through and through. Nicked his shoulder." More like it tore through the middle of his shoulder, but no one corrects Cal's interpretation.

Martin turns to run out the back door. He yells, "This bar sucks!"

His rain slicker is all that remains of him. Outside, the rain is still heavy, a translucent gray sheet of indistinguishable drops. I imagine Yag sprinting home, drenched in blood and water, clothes stuck to his body, eyes squinting to see through the gray. If he runs fast and the police don't pick him up first, he will be in his parents' basement in twenty minutes. He might not lose too much blood. His mind will process the night like a dream, and he will deny that any of this ever happened at all.

11PM

ABOUT FIFTEEN MINUTES HAVE passed since Yag bolted, and no one has done anything, unless you count Amelia popping the tops off a round of Bud Lights that Cal ordered to calm our nerves. The only people in the bar are Cal and Summer, Jimmy, Short Pete, Fancy Pete, Amelia, and me. It's possible a neighbor heard the gunshot but there are no sirens in the distance, which means no one reported it. A single shot could have been a truck backfiring or a firecracker, which kids are apt to set off at all hours of the night around here.

"We need to call the cops," I say.

"No cops," Cal says.

"Martin was shot. He should go to the hospital," I say, looking at

Jimmy for support. He says nothing. Short Pete and Fancy Pete sit next to each other facing the bar, as if this is just another night.

"The bullet grazed his shoulder," Cal says. He's over at the far wall, behind the pool table, dislodging the bullet from the Sheetrock with the paring knife Amelia uses to cut limes. He slips it into his pocket. "It's nothing more than a flesh wound."

"There was a lot of blood," I say.

"Nothing an ACE bandage can't handle. Dr. Yag can patch himself up just fine."

"He held a knife to my throat."

"Sack up," Cal demands. "You're fine."

"Cal, your daughter just watched you shoot somebody." I throw up my arms.

"Summer hates cops." He looks over at her and she raises a small fist in solidarity.

"Jimmy, got an opinion?" I ask.

Jimmy shrugs.

"You guys are acting like children," I say.

There was a knife at my throat. Someone got shot. A ten-year-old child saw the whole thing. And these guys are just going to drink beer and pretend it never happened.

Amelia eyes the phone handset, which is off its base. She's ambivalent. Cal notices this too. "No cops," he repeats.

We're all drunk, with the possible exception of Amelia, and drinking more because we need the booze to cut the edge of adrenaline.

"Everyone knows you don't invite cops into a domestic dispute," Cal says. "That's how people get hurt. We're a family. We'll handle this like a family."

Short Pete and Fancy Pete nod in agreement.

"And what if Yag hurts himself? Or someone else? What if he goes home and slices his parents' throats before taking his own life?"

"Don't be dramatic, Emma," Cal says. "He's probably sleeping it off as we speak."

"Amelia, give me the phone," I say. I could just go over and pick it up, or use my cell, but I want Amelia's tacit support. I need someone to back me up, and I assume, for no other reason than she is a woman, she will be rational.

She shakes her head. "You're outnumbered, Emma. Sorry." It occurs to me that Amelia doesn't want the cops to come, because the story will be all over the news—*Shooting at The Final Final*—and the place will become even more of a backwater townie shithole than it already is.

"Emma," Cal says, his tone firm but full of feigned compassion, like a negotiator talking me off the ledge. "Martin always found you judgmental, but we—the rest of us—don't think that's true. You want what's best for us. You worry about us. You care about us. Even Yag. But the police will only make this worse. For all of us."

"You don't have a permit for the gun, do you?" I ask.

"I have a license to carry," Cal insists.

"Just not a license to shoot a guy." Jimmy chuckles. I should slap him. This is serious.

So many things can go wrong in a matter of just minutes. Of all people, I understand this. As far as I know, Martin Yagla doesn't own a gun but what the hell do I know? This is Upstate New York, and he is a disaffected white guy who will never achieve his full potential. I also don't know why the guys are so adamant about not calling the cops. All the *family this* and *family that* and *we don't trust the cops in our domain* is a sack of garbage. I'm pretty sure everyone is just afraid the bar will get shut down, and they'll have no place to drink.

I SIT ON THE closed lid of the toilet and collect my thoughts. The time on my phone reads 11:34. For all I know, Yag's already dead. I do the adult thing and call 911. I say there was a shot fired in The Final Final, and a man with a knife has fled. The operator asks if the shooter is still in the bar, and I say yes, but he's one of the good guys. It was self-defense. My heart sinks because Cal's right—he's going to take some heat for this.

My decision to make the call from the bathroom isn't cowardly as much as it's a personal precaution. If I'd tried to make it in front of the guys, they would have physically stopped me, and I've had enough of that for the night.

The 911 operator tells me to stay on the line, but I say quickly that everything is fine now, we're all safe, and hang up.

Everyone is huddled together, now on a second round of Bud Light. There is an open bottle, presumably for me, lonely on the bar top. I pick it up and announce the cops are on their way.

I expect the guys to give me shit, to say Yag was right after all—I am an *uptight bitch*—but no one does. Shit-giving comes from a place of love, not anger: a lighthearted pastime. They hang their heads in acceptance, as if they already knew it was coming but just wanted one more drink together.

THE IDEA FOR THE hedge fund came to me on a plane. I was headed home from a talk I gave at Michigan's Ross School of Business. One of the students asked a question about the predictive value of stories, whether I thought there was an arbitrage opportunity. A good question. The short answer was *yes*. The longer answer was that figuring out the opportunity would be very, very tricky.

It's not like I'd never thought about this before. Heck, I named *The*

Breakout Effect after a financial concept. And, as I mentioned earlier, a major news event can lead to a breakout. But you can't trade people like securities, and even if it is theoretically possible to predict when a human being will break out, the likelihood that this event would translate to the movement of a security is remote.

Still, the kid's question got me thinking: *How do you humanize a company or a product?* You find a story about the people running the company, the people cleaning house at the company, a whistle-blower, a savant who emerges out of the woodwork, a woman whose dad was a bookie. These people are the protagonists of publicly traded companies.

Protagonist is a term most business people haven't used since high school English class, but only when an investor understands what it means to be a protagonist in the corporate world can he or she begin to predict when a story might be sufficiently humanizing to move a stock. In effect, investors should stop thinking about people in the Freudian sense, as id, ego, and superego—as human capital—and start seeing them in the Shakespearean sense, as actors on the corporate stage.

A researcher would first need to find those special, needle-in-the-haystack stories. This would be the easy part. A story doesn't move a stock by merely existing. It isn't told in a vacuum. It blossoms in a political and cultural climate. It undergoes a process of galvanization—word of mouth, social media, mainstream media. There are hundreds and sometimes thousands of complicating factors.

But the kid from Michigan was onto something—stories could be predictive. They exist before, sometimes long before, they have an impact on a person, company, or stock. With the right models, a reasonable amount of intuition, and some media savvy, a couple of old pals from Harvard could make a significant amount of money.

Lucas and I did not discuss the fund much initially, though he was aware I'd been making calls and had a partner in Boston—Grace Hu, my old friend from Harvard. When I wasn't on the road, I was glued to my computer.

Eventually, I asked Lucas if he was okay with investing some of our own money in the fund, to which he said, "You earned it; do whatever you want," and went back to playing with Lionel. Then I mentioned we could extend the offer to his parents, and he looked at me like I was an alien with no understanding whatsoever about what they sacrificed to accumulate their nest egg. Anyway, I extended the offer to them as a kindness. My own father invested an enormous sum of money.

3:17 A.M. GLOWED GREEN on the clock when Lionel cried out. I thought, *If only I could sync his circadian rhythm with the alarm*, which was set for 5:30. I had to be in the city before noon.

Lucas reached over and touched my back gently. It was the subtlest push in the history of the world: *You take this one*.

These latest middle-of-the-night outbursts were not motivated by hunger, as they'd once been. We assumed they were spurred by dreams, scary dreams, though I could not fathom the nightmares of a one-year-old. Tickle monsters? Sad bunnies? A global Cheerios shortage?

Lucas continued to snore (how was that possible?), which created a kind of chorus with Lionel's shrieks. Addie sat, alert, on the end of our bed, ready to bolt into Lionel's room with me. Her ability to dip in and out of sleep all day and all night was a gift.

I rolled out of bed onto my feet but my body wasn't ready to stand so I ended up in a wobbly downward dog.

Lionel stood up in his crib, grabbing the wooden slats like prison bars. He was red faced, with teary, squinted eyes, and his mouth was open in the shape of a hamburger so maximum sound could escape. An effective technique. No one ignored this kid.

He always hated the crib like it was a punishment. Who could blame him? For the first six months of his life he got to sleep in our king—Lucas, Addie, and me, all the company he ever wanted, like a party. When I left town, Lucas caved, a result of his own loneliness, and invited Lion back. And then there was the guest bed right next to the crib, which Addie jumped on in the middle of the night because she liked Lion's smell and no one stopped her from pulling back the quilt and getting into the soft duvet. Lion wanted to be there with her, his protector, a warm furry thing offering face licks and limitless snuggling.

But the crib was safer, and I insisted on it most of the time, save an occasional nap when we figured the battle over where to sleep would lose the war, sleeping at all. *If only. If only.*

Picking him up from the crib, I felt how heavy he'd become, how he'd miraculously grown into a big boy, hearty and strong. There was a time, just a month or two prior, when he just wanted to be held, but now he squirmed violently, arms flailing. He didn't nuzzle into my chest as I hoped he would; he pushed off.

I cycled through emotions so fast I couldn't keep track of them: annoyance, longing, rejection. In hindsight, I see this was love—complex, intense, and painful—but at the time, it felt like something else. The longer I held Lionel, the louder he wailed.

I remember thinking, *It's okay; he'll love me later.*

Lion threw a right hook to my ear. The pain was real. For some reason, Addie wanted in on this horseplay. She stood on hind legs, pushing her nose into the action.

Lucas called out, "Bring him in here." The image of Lucas reclined in bed struck me with fury. We'd had fights about Lionel sleeping in our bed. As a newborn, co-sleeping made it easier to breastfeed in the middle of the night, and Lionel was a cuddly little thing, secure and happy. Later, I advocated sleep training, and consistency, though I had no control over what Lucas did when I was on the road. Whatever we were doing wasn't working.

I ignored Lucas, and the crying grew louder, if that was even possible. By then I was sitting down on the bed, holding Lionel's legs with my left hand and attempting to rein in his arms with my right. Addie sat on the floor but kept her nose out of it.

"He'll calm down in here," Lucas muttered, groggy. What I heard was, *He'll be happy when he's in bed with his dad.*

"Baby, what do you need?" I whispered. "It's okay. It's okay—"

Between sharp, high-pitched squeals, Lion said, "Zoo. Zoo. Zoo. Zoo. Zoo." It seemed like a coded answer to my question. I had no idea what it meant.

I spoke to the dog, the only one less likely than me to know what was going on. "Did he have a dream about the zoo? Did an animal escape?" I hated zoos. We'd never taken him to the zoo. "Did Lucas read him a book about a zoo? Was it Joan? Did Joan take him to the zoo? That's an hour drive. I did not authorize a trip to the zoo! Maybe Lion thinks he's in a zoo? Is his crib a cage? Does he feel trapped?"

Addie crossed her paws and looked at me like I were an insane person.

An errant tear morphed into full-on weeping as soon as I processed why I was so upset. I felt, at the same time, both devastated that I was about to leave my child, and relieved that as soon as I hit the road, I would have four hours to myself. I could not reconcile the pain of being away with my desire to be away.

Lucas appeared in the doorway. His presence made me realize that I held my son not like a mother but like a nurse on a psych ward, focused solely on restraint. I turned his body around so he faced me and squeezed him into my chest. His head bobbed back. "Zoo. Zoo. Zoo," he repeated.

Lucas walked around us to the other side of the crib. A stuffed monkey, a gift from Joan, was on the floor in the corner. "He wants Chuang Tzu," he said, gently pushing the stuffed animal into Lionel's face, giving him a rapid series of monkey kisses. Lionel grabbed the monkey and smiled.

"*Chuang Tzu*?" I said.

"That's the monkey's name," Lucas said. He tightened his lips and took a deep breath.

"No, it's not—" I started.

"He's a Taoist monkey."

"His name is *Monkey*," I said.

"He *is* a monkey. His name is Chuang Tzu." When Lucas said Chuang Tzu, it flowed quickly. It sounded like Ju-an-zoo.

"Why would a baby have a Taoist monkey?" Lionel sat in my lap, happily playing with Chuang Tzu. Snap of the fingers: his mood shifted. Addie jumped up on the bed so she could sniff the monkey. Their happiness fueled my feeling of being left out. None of this had anything to do with me.

"The reason his name is Monkey," I said, "is so Lionel can learn what a monkey is."

"He's not a monkey," Lucas said. "He's an organic, cotton plush toy that my mom overpaid for at the craft fair."

"You just said he *is* a monkey!" I said.

"Well, he can learn about monkeys while learning about religion."

"*Religion*?" I wasn't sure if Taoism was a religion or not. The whole idea of it seemed anti-religious. I'd taken a Zen Buddhism course in college, which, granted, was not Taoism—but in the middle of the night the distinction was lost on me—and at the time it did not play like a serious subject. In fact, it seemed an insane stroke of luck that the professor, with his signature tuft of gray chest hair poking out from his short-sleeve rayon button-down, and his slow-talking mellow vibe, had woken up from a drug-fueled haze and found himself with tenure.

"It's not a big deal," Lucas said. "I just gave him the name a few weeks ago. Lion likes it. It doesn't mean anything."

"Maybe next time, you should let me in on your inside jokes."

"It just happened. Lionel was playing with the monkey on the floor, and I looked over at the bookshelf, and we started calling him Chuang Tzu."

"Well, to be fair, Lionel calls him Zoo."

"Right, sure. We can call him Zoo."

"Shall we spell it T-z-u?" Lucas picked up on the sharp tinge of sarcasm in my voice.

"Monkey's fine," he said. "It's just—"

"It's just what?"

"It's cool that we get to teach him things. That's all. We get to explain the universe, the world, all the animals and plants and bugs," Lucas said.

"And the Tao," I added.

"And the Tao," he repeated.

"He might be a little young for that, Lucas."

"You can teach him about business and investing." I'm sure Lucas meant this sincerely but it came off like a dig: *I'm going to teach our kid the mysteries of the universe, and you can teach him about money.*

Lucas reclined next to us on the bed, and I put my head on his shoulder. Lionel's breathing grew heavy. He clutched Chuang Tzu as he drifted off to sleep. We were all there in that moment: Lucas, Lionel, Addie, and me. We fell asleep together like that: four bodies on top of the duvet. Then, from the other room, I heard my alarm go off.

Lucas took him from my arms, placed his head on the pillow, and tucked his little body under the covers. Addie curled up at his feet. Before I could say, *We should put him in his crib*, Lucas said, "I'll stay here with him. You go shower." I didn't protest. They all looked so peaceful—a man, his son, and the dog—their bodies close, their breathing synchronized.

———

ON MY WAY OUT of town, I had to drop Lion off at my mother-in-law's house because Lucas had to get to a jobsite. I wanted to leave Lion on the doorstep in his stroller, ring the bell, and run, but I'm not a psychopath.

Joan invited me in, offered a cup of coffee, and wouldn't take no for an answer. While I gulped it down, she fussed over Lion. "Where are those red pants I gave him?"

"They are already too small, Joan. We told you not to spend money on clothes. He's growing too fast."

"Hi, dollie. You're a big boy, aren't you? Such a big boy."

I looked at my watch. "I have to run, Joan."

"Where to this time?" she asked.

"Just a quick trip to New York. I'll be back tomorrow," I said.

Joan lifted Lionel, holding him up by his torso, legs dangling. He rotated his head, looking from her to me and back again. He smiled. He giggled. She said only, "How can you leave this little angel?"

I thought about asking her how she left her *two* little angels for eight months, when she ditched the family to sojourn to an ashram in India, well before *Eat Pray Love* made that kind of behavior socially acceptable.

Instead, I did something I'd never done in front of Joan before. I broke into tears.

She looked at me, woman to woman, mother to mother, and said, "I admire you. You know that, right? Lucas does too. He probably doesn't say it, but he does."

On my way out the door, an outlet guard caught my eye. Like Samantha, Joan plugged all the outlets in her house, but they were the kind of plugs that any child with a modicum of intelligence could simply pull out, and what I never understood was, if Lion was inclined to shove a fork or a paper clip or a wet finger into an outlet, why would Joan assume he lacked the wherewithal to first pull out whatever lamp cord or plug blocked his way? But these were just intellectual ideas, rationalizations, really, and in the end, I still felt like a bad mother.

———————

WHEN GRACE AND I traveled to New York City for business, I stayed in Brooklyn, mostly because I felt guilty that the town house—my father's wedding gift—remained largely vacant save the caretaker's weekly visit. Grace preferred to stay in Manhattan.

Waiting for Grace in the lobby of her hotel, I crunched the numbers. In the US, there were approximately twenty-five hundred children treated in the prior year due to wall outlet shock accidents. That statistic came from a site on the internet called statisticbrain.com, which seemed reputable enough for this back-of-the-envelope analysis. Something like twenty million children ages zero to four were alive in the US at the time. That meant 0.01 percent of kids stuck metal objects or wet fingers into sockets. If I counted five- through ten-year-olds, also candidates for misplaced aggression directed at electrical outlets, the number of incidents was more de minimis. When I thought about how many kids were traumatized by anxious, overprotective parents that year, probably in a double-digit percentile, 0.01 percent started looking pretty good. And sure, adjusting up for households that were completely locked down in terms of child safety, maybe there would be, like, ten or twenty more incidents every year, but that didn't even move the needle, statistically speaking.

Back then, this type of analysis brought no comfort, though I did it anyway. Motherhood does not account for statistical likelihoods. Low-probability events—lightning, child abduction, poisoned candy—share the same tonal qualities as ordinary hazards: wall outlets, toxic substances, a hole in the floor. I think maybe this is nature's twisted prophecy: you can worry all you want, but you'll never predict the thing that will destroy you.

———

THE ANSWER TO JOAN'S question (*How can you leave this little angel?*) was that we were in Manhattan to celebrate. We had just publicly announced the fund, and Grace organized a dinner to mark the occasion.

Grace and I were among a small cohort of women who managed portfolios at hedge funds. The number of women at the very top of major funds? We could count them on two hands. Literally. Grace invited all eight to celebrate with us.

Lionel was one year old at the time, and I was blindly feeling my way through motherhood. Naturally, I treated these women like objects of sociological inquiry. Two of them were divorced without children; three were married to men who understood that their careers were not nearly as consequential as their wives' careers; two were lesbians—one was married to a woman who stayed at home with their child, the other, happily childless; Grace and another impeccably dressed supermodel-type were married to successful attorneys, and relied heavily on nannies; and then there was me—the hot mess, tired all the time, missing my baby, husband, and dog all the time, wanting a drink most of the time.

Grace chose an East Village restaurant called Side Pony because the owner and head chef, Francesca Jones, was a new friend and her object of curiosity du jour. Grace was interested in food and restaurants, but she was more interested in the violent potential of kitchens—knives, flames, egos. At Harvard she'd dated a nontraditional student—an older guy, late twenties, who worked as a chef in Amsterdam before matriculating. He'd make her fancy meals on the electric burners of the dorm kitchenette, which was romantic until it wasn't. When she returned to the dorm after a midnight study session with a guy from her econ class, the boyfriend led her to the kitchenette for toast and poached eggs, insisting the water had already come to a boil. She never told me exactly what transpired in that little kitchen, but the scars on her hand and forearm were plainly visible. The boyfriend was thrown out of the dorm but not the college. He claimed it was an accident.

Francesca bore a twin scar. Hers was much worse, extending from her neck to her elbow, with more raised scar tissue. According to her memoir, which Grace had given me for my birthday, another line cook, frenetic, had accidentally dropped a pan of hot oil on her. Incompetence was, of course, a sin of a very different nature. Nonetheless, Grace and Francesca were now officially bound to each other.

We all arrived at eight o'clock. The hostess seated us at a kidney bean–shaped table in the rear corner of the restaurant, elevated two steps from floor level, as if it had been a stage at one time. Over the table, nailed to an exposed beam, there was a small placard that read *LA FAMILIA*. The space had a shabby chic look, homey, if home was impeccably decorated. I felt good there, at the center of the table, ravenous. I raised my glass to Grace before acknowledging everyone else.

The server arrived with an amuse-bouche paired with bubbly wine, and shortly after, Francesca dropped by to greet us. Grace embraced her, and a couple of the women gushed about her memoir, calling it powerful and irreverent.

Before I knew it, Francesca's white coat had come off, and she stood before us in a gray, ribbed tank top, revealing her scars. Someone said, "In your memoir, you chose not to identify the line cook who did that to you."

"Are you asking if it was a man? I'm not sure it matters," Francesca said. "But I will say that I've never worked with a woman so careless around hot oil. I've seen women trip and fall, and drop hot plates, and cut off the tips of their fingers, but I've never seen a woman injure another person on the line. We only hurt ourselves."

We ate until we were full, course upon course, all designed by Francesca for us. The amount of power around that table, measured in net worth or political influence or sexual prowess or raw intelligence or spiritual gravitas, whatever, rendered all other symbols of power—the presidency, the bull, a Tesla in space, a big swinging dick—nothing more than limp reminders of the past: anecdotes and jokes.

By midnight, most of the other patrons had cleared out. The women were polishing off the last of the wine and a few of us had ordered digestifs. Two men remained at the bar, banker types (commercial, not investment, by the looks of it), occasionally glancing over at our table. Our waitress delivered ten colorful glasses of rum punch, the potent house special, made with three kinds of rum, liqueur, and fruit puree. "From the gentlemen at the bar," she said, slightly blushing. By the look on her face, the way her bow-shaped mouth went sideways into a smirk, it was clear she understood the men's mistake. She was smart not to stop them, though, because the tip on a $150 round was probably worth her while— plus, she must have known we'd have some fun with it.

Amrita Khullar, who managed a $24 billion fund, leaned toward the waitress and, in her gorgeous British accent, said, "Please thank the boys for their lovely gesture." As she said this, she took a punch glass from the waitress's hand.

Grace flashed me a look, and I could see that thing in her eyes: ambition. I hadn't realized until that moment just how big Grace wanted to go. Our current fund was just a pilot. How had I not seen it? Grace didn't want to run a small fund—she wanted to manage billions.

Grace said, "Yes, and then put the drinks and the rest of their bill on our tab."

The other women clinked their rum punches together, toasting themselves. The waitress said, "Are you sure?" but what she really meant was, *Why?*

Grace shrugged. "Oh yes; we're sure."

Clapping ensued, and more drinks. When the men walked out a short while later, with heads slightly bowed, we all got a nice obligatory wave, which we returned wholeheartedly. After Francesca closed the kitchen, she joined us for the remainder of the night, which extended into the wee hours.

The attitude around the table could be summed up in one and a half words: fuck 'em. No one said it outright, though. It was all very civilized. And I remember thinking, *Power is dangerous but less dangerous in the hands of women.*

That night at Side Pony was the happiest time of my life. I know I'm supposed to say the birth of my son was the best moment, and—don't get me wrong—it was among the best. But that night in Manhattan was the culmination of everything—Lucas, Lionel, and Addie, my partnership with Grace, and above all, the work that made all of it sweet, special, worth the sacrifice. I felt like I could fly.

Still in our proof-of-concept phase, Grace and I had made only a series of small trades with our own money. At any time before we called on our capital commitments, we could have simply shut the whole thing down. But I am my father's daughter. I am that girl who woke up early to rearrange the pens in his briefcase while he took calls. I am that girl who wanted to know what a *manure* was so I could be one someday. And I think, even though Lucas gave me a taste of it, I am a woman who is not supposed to be happy.

SIRENS APPROACH.

The cops look at our IDs, write down our contact information, and take brief statements: *Who started it? What happened next? Which direction did he go?*

They take Cal's gun but don't bag it like TV cops do. I roll my eyes at their sloppy police work, knowing, at the same time, there's nothing to investigate—no fingerprint analysis or testing for gunshot residue necessary. It's Cal's gun; he fired it; everyone knows it.

One of the cops tells Cal he's going to take him down to the station. Cal asks if he's under arrest. The cop says no, but Sheriff Redman wants to talk to him there. Pointing at Summer, the cop says, "Your daughter can come too." Cal agrees to go. Red is in Cal's coffee klatch. They meet at eight a.m. every Friday at Jimmy's place.

The rest of us are told we can stop by the station tomorrow to give official statements. One officer asks Jimmy if he wants an ambulance.

We'd all forgotten about Jimmy's face in the hubbub. A jagged line, deep red, extends from the middle of his forehead to the edge of his eyebrow, just shy of his temple. Smeared to keep from dripping into his eyes, there is dried blood on the side of his head and in his hair. He says, "No doctors." I expect the cops to insist, but they don't. They are in a hurry to leave, anxious for action. On their way out the door, they say they will look for Martin Yagla.

Just like that, they're gone.

Amelia hands me a clean towel. I tell Jimmy his wound might open up again, he might need stitches, offer to take a cab to the hospital with him, but Jimmy doesn't have health insurance and doesn't trust the system. "I started the fight," he whispers.

"Yag instigated. Everyone in this place will back you up," I say.

"You'll never see him in here again. Don't you worry about that," Amelia says.

There's something worse than the blood crusted on Jimmy's brow. He's crying. I've seen more grown men cry in the last two years than I have in a lifetime. Who's next?

WHEN I WAS A child, my dad had this old movie camera with film reels. He never watched the film or tried to digitize it. Later, I realized the camera just gave him something to do so he didn't have to talk to people at family gatherings. After he split, I took a few of the reels from my mom's house and set up a projector so I could watch them. The footage is silent, so it's just a lot of smiling and waving and baby fat. Everyone seems so happy. Old film reels are the physical manifestation of nostalgia. Digital video does not have the same effect, perhaps because you can hear all the words.

My last happy memory on Catherine Street is an old reel I play over and over again in my head. The only sound is the click-click-clicking of the reel, but as it spins, I remember the idea of sound in notes and chords and laugher and guttural almost-barks. My brain layers audio over the reel, which creates an eerie sort of distance, like the whole thing exists in memory, but it happened in another dimension, where the woman is me and isn't me—she's the woman I used to be. I see her and stare.

Jimmy is over with this new girl he's seeing. He looks at her like he's falling in love. Her last name is Woodford, which inspires Lucas to pull out the stepladder and stretch to reach the bottle of Woodford Reserve that is hidden away for a special occasion.

The girl holds the bottle next to her face, posing with it, moving it from one cheek to the other, a huge smile stretched from ear to ear. We open the bottle and Lucas pours two neat for Jimmy and him, and two on the rocks for the girl and me.

The girl asks Lucas to put on *Graceland*, and—this is the sound layer—Paul Simon's voice fills the room.

Lionel is dancing. I'm holding him on my hip and his arms are out-stretched, moving to the music. We're all singing, even Lucas, who never sings. The reel spins. I see our mouths moving. I see our heads tilted back.

I look down at the floor and the hole is there, but I don't give it a second thought. I'm not worried Lionel will catch a foot or the Woodford girl will twist an ankle. In a flying dream, do you worry you'll crash? You can fly, remember? That's the whole point.

Addie's with us too. This is her optimal situation: everyone together in our kitchen, dancing around, touching and not touching. She slips between us, stands on her hind legs, and puts her front paws on my thigh.

Lion wants to be down on the floor with her, so I bend over and put him on his feet. His legs aren't quite ready to hold his weight. He drops to his butt. Addie's tongue juts out. She licks him on the face.

Lucas grabs me, swings me around, dips me backward, pulls me in, kisses me on the lips. It's the kind of public affection that would normally embarrass him but we're all drunk, and Jimmy's eyes are glued on the Woodford girl.

Lion puts his little hands on Addie's back and pulls himself to his feet.

We all look down at them: Lion's feet move to the music. He sticks his diapered butt out. His fingers grip Addie's fur. His cherry-red lips turn upward. Addie, stirred by the dancing just moments ago, is now calm. She stands still. If she moves, he'll fall again.

There's a glitch in the reel. We are suspended in time: Lucas with his arms around my waist; Lionel holding on to Addie beneath us; Jimmy with his eyes on a new love. Memory is an infinite loop.

Jimmy squats down, his enormous frame folding in on itself. He reaches for Lionel, puts him on his shoulders. Lionel wraps his legs around Jimmy's neck and dances all the way to the ceiling.

I see my kitchen full of dancing bodies. I taste a hint of whiskey on Lucas's lips. I hear my child giggle. I feel Addie's wet nose against my leg. But the reel is grainy, the colors tinted in sepia, and the music stops, and then I remember: this is what I had and lost.

———

I GET JIMMY UP on two feet, his arm around my shoulder. The smell of kitchen grease on his clothes is still strong. I can almost feel it rubbing onto me as I hold my arm around his waist. "Amelia, you got a first aid kit in this place?" She tells me to take Jimmy down to the basement. The kit is mounted to a wall down there.

I've been in the basement before with Lucas. On nights when his buddy Jacob used to bartend, he'd let Lucas go down there to grab bottles for him and use the staff-only toilet. Lucas took me down with him once and we had sex standing up, against the cold, rough cellar wall. That was a long time ago now but the smell carries me back.

The first time Lucas and I made love was at the house on Catherine Street. I climbed on top of him. He looked at me, first at my breasts, my stomach, my hips beneath his hands, and then into my eyes. He said, "I haven't had this in so long." I knew he wasn't talking about having sex, or even about good sex. He was talking about love, or maybe having sex with someone he loved, which is good but different than good sex—it is sex that exists atop a series of reference points, all time and experience operating like construction lines.

After he finished he said, "I've never had this." I hadn't either. I'd loved other guys, sure, but not like this, not like Lucas. It was different, and because it was different, the sex was different.

I've had sex with exactly one person since the divorce, a stranger. It was raw and drunk and a little bit sad. It was a reminder of what was once mine, and I welcomed that pain.

Something about the dankness of the basement brings me back to wilder days—times when I was willing to bear the strangest discomforts to have Lucas inside me. Now, suddenly, on this night when the sparrow breached the threshold, when I saw a younger version of myself in the mirror, I want him again. It is a sudden, discernable moment, not a gradual change.

I close my eyes. Wrapping my arms around myself, I feel his firm arms, his rough hands, his long gaze. My body aches with the distinct desire to be penetrated, and it is an ache only Lucas could satisfy. Jimmy, even if he weren't such a loyal friend, couldn't relieve the feeling, nor could a stranger. I wonder if some other woman has eased this ache for Lucas, and I guess that she has, but only temporarily.

Ellis, the waitress from Antolini's, dances into my head. Perhaps she fulfills Lucas's longings as I no longer can. She is sexy—all that blond hair flows down, covering her breasts as she sits on top of him. He pushes her hair aside, over her shoulder, so he can see her. He admires the tightness of her stomach and the curve of her hips, and the way she moves: fluid, a dancer in the bedroom as she is a dancer in life. This doesn't make me jealous. It turns me on.

Aside from the constant inflow and outflow of kegs and boxes of booze, nothing in the basement has changed in years. On the far side, there is an old washbasin sink, which is operational, and the toilet, which now has a brick on the lid and a handwritten note: *DO NOT USE.*

I run warm water over the towel Amelia gave me and wring it out. Jimmy stacks two boxes of booze, one on top of the other. He half sits so his face is at my shoulder level. I put the warm towel across his forehead, eyes, and cheeks. The blood soaks through it. I rinse and repeat.

With the exception of Jimmy holding me back from Yag, this is the closest I've ever been to him physically. We've never so much as hugged. Everything I feel for Jimmy—respect, friendship, love, even—exists in reference to Lucas. Without Lucas, Jimmy is unknowable to me.

I'm wearing a tank top and ripped jeans. Though I'm relatively small chested, cleavage shows at the top and at the side. My hair is pulled back in a tight ponytail.

If Jimmy is aware of a possibility of intimacy, he doesn't show it. His gaze extends beyond me.

"It's true. Yagla was there," he says. "We both were."

"Beers in the backyard—Lucas told me you were there. He just left out the part about Yag."

"Martin was running his mouth like always. He gave Lucas a hard time for not wanting to party."

"You mean do cocaine?"

"Or whatever. He asked Lucas if he ever wished he wasn't tied down. Then he went on and on with his usual bullshit." Jimmy pushes back his shoulders and mimics Yag running his hand over his head, as he always does before he makes some inane point: "*We never have fun anymore, man. All for what? Baby talk? Diapers? You're not even getting laid. What's the point of having a wife if her hot ass is in another state? So she can call you and ask you what we're doing? Force you to lie to her because you're hanging out with me? Seriously, man, I don't get it. What's in it for you?"*

"What'd Lucas say?" I ask.

"He said, 'I'm in it for *them.*'"

"Think he ever second-guessed himself?"

"You and Lion were the only two things he didn't question," Jimmy says.

AT SUNSET, I LIKED to take Lionel outside to sit on the porch swing. As a newborn, the rocking soothed him, and as he grew, the change of scenery distracted him. We'd look out at the trees. I'd say, "This is the world," and he'd stare, eyes wide open. One evening, I noticed a bolt, which fastened the swing onto the joist, was coming loose. Lucas reached up to the ceiling and pulled soft wood out with his bare hand.

Over the course of several weeks, Lucas and Jimmy rebuilt the roof over the porch, climbing out onto it through the window of Lionel's room, hammer and nail in hand. They worked every weekend in the hot sun with their shirts off. I don't think Lucas paid Jimmy, except in beer. I can only assume Jimmy did it for the same reason I obliged a nonstop series of DIY projects—he liked spending time with his friend.

After the last of the soffit board was nailed in, Lucas reattached the porch swing. I arrived home after nine that night, because I'd been away on business. Lionel was already asleep in his crib. The outside light was on, and Lucas sat on the top step, a glass of whiskey in his hand and Addie by his side: my welcome party. He told me to peek under the swing.

Lion had dipped his little hand in paint and left a print. Lucas handed me the paint tray where he'd saved some of the deep blue, the same color Lion used. He said, "Let's add ours too. Then I'll cover them with sealant."

Those three handprints will be on the underside of that swing as long as the swing remains. Lucas made sure of it.

Neither of us said anything for a while. We let the happiness sink in.

Then Lucas said, "The only thing left to do is paint the trim on the roof."

"I'll help paint," I promised.

"Okay," he said. "We need to finish it before the temperature starts to drop."

It was a promise I did not keep. Regret is a leaky faucet, drip, drip, dripping. I don't know how to make it stop. In the old days, Lucas would've fixed it. *If only I had helped paint as I said I would. If only. If only.* At the time, saying I'd do something and not following through with it didn't seem like such a big deal. But the thing about keeping a promise is you don't need a crystal ball. You just do the thing you said you'd do, and karma takes care of the rest.

RAINWATER SEEPS THROUGH THE old stone foundation, creeping toward the drain at the lowest point, turning dirt to mud. Jimmy and I are on the dry side, closest to the stairs.

"After we finished the primer coat on the trim, we went out back for beers," Jimmy says.

"I know. Lucas told me," I reply. I think, *Please stop*. Then I think, *Keep going. We must keep going.*

"Lucas was so happy after he put Lionel down," he says. "Lionel called him *Dadda*. He said, 'Dadda, *pen, pen!*' He said it three or four times."

"He had started to form sentences," I say.

Jimmy nods. "It was the first time he called Lucas *Dad*. Lucas thought he wanted the door left *open* so Addie could run in and out."

"But you don't think that's what he meant?"

"Yag and I were in the backyard. Lucas came out and told us that Lionel kept saying *pen*. We were drinking beers and cracking jokes about Lucas raising a writer. We didn't put it together."

Jimmy's wound cracks open again because of the way he's contorting his face. I hand him the towel and he wipes blood and tears and snot.

"You think Lion was talking about the open window." I know two things immediately. One: Lucas also believes this. And two: it is ridiculous.

I consider the bright-red peony that appeared on my belly right before I went into labor: Lionel's ambition manifest. It wasn't Lion who tried to warn me. It was my own body. The rash was mine, not his.

Lion was an adventurous child, not a careful child. He wanted to go everywhere he wasn't supposed to go. He wanted to touch everything he wasn't supposed to touch. He wanted to taste everything he wasn't supposed to taste.

He was a sneaky child. When he could, he hid his explorations from us, only letting Addie in on his secrets. I found objects I thought were out of his reach under the sofa and down in the cushions. In his diaper, I found a tiny gold pendant from one of my necklaces, which I didn't even know he'd gotten hold of, let alone swallowed and passed.

And he was bold. He waited until I was busy sorting three different puzzles dumped in a pile with a couple of dog KONGs, or Lucas went down to the basement to grab the laundry, and then, right under our noses, he swiped a cracker or a piece of cheese from the coffee table, putting one in his mouth and giving the other to Addie. I only caught him once, but I always noticed when all the cheese was gone.

It was not in Lion's nature to tip us off.

THE NIGHT BEFORE I left for Cambridge, Lucas and I argued.

From the couch, he watched me pull my noise-canceling headphones out of the drawer and place them in my suitcase. Lionel was in the middle of a long crying spell. We were still trying to break the bad habit of letting him fall asleep in our bed before Lucas carried him to the crib. He was thirteen months—old enough to fall asleep on his own. We needed our own time, adult time—drinking time and TV time and conversation time. So we put Lion down on his own and let him cry himself to sleep.

My mother had given me a couple pieces of Rimowa luggage. German quality. Quite pricey. Addie hated it. She stood in the middle of the floor next to it and leered. I could always tell when she felt sad because she'd just stand there, frozen, which was different from when she felt physically ill, which would drive her under the coffee table. When she felt good, which was most of the time, she'd either carry her ball around, goading us to play, or curl up on the couch like a love bug. The suitcase depressed her. She knew what it meant. Her tribe would be forced apart for some period of time that was mysterious to her, only discernable, perhaps, by some vague sense of circadian rhythm or sublimated memory of prior encounters with the suitcase, an approximate recalling of daily runs, or lack thereof, or an accounting for meals—two days, four meals. In the human sense (hands on a clock) time was a mystery to the dog, but in a metaphysical sense (fundamental reality) she understood perfectly: the amount of time I'd be gone was too long.

As Lucas watched me, I read his thoughts. "The headphones don't work on crying."

He smiled. "Maybe I need them to drown you out."

I pointed to my suitcase. "Well, you'll have some peace for two days."

Addie sulked; she moved away from my suitcase and rested her head on the floor between her paws.

Lucas pulled me toward him. He remained seated on the couch, and I stood over him. "How many more stops on this tour?" he asked.

"It's not a tour anymore," I said. "The book has been out for a year."

"So, indefinite?"

"The money is good," I said.

My agent had been scheduling me for a talk a week, more or less, since the book tour ended. I'd spoken at Facebook and Google and Stanford and Wharton—places like that. Honestly, the speaking engagements weren't about the money, which was nothing compared to the fees Grace and I stood to earn from the fund (2 percent of total assets, 20 percent of profits).

I liked being in front of audiences. Lucas didn't know it, because he'd never seen me give a talk, but I was good at it. I was dry and funny and self-deprecating, and best of all, I made people feel like they were worthy and capable of change. It was the holy grail of self-help.

Lucas abhorred fighting, having always preferred to eat his rage, so we almost never did. But something made him ask me not to go on this trip.

He looked tired because he'd done more than his share, taking care of Lionel and working on the house. Either because of this or in spite of it, I had all the power.

"Addie misses you when you leave," he said.

Addie sniffed around the coffee table, attracted by a Reese's Peanut Butter Cup wrapper, remnants of Lion's bedtime treat. Her manner was slow and cautious. She tested us, baiting us to say no. Then she lifted it delicately and ducked under the table to lick whatever essence of peanut butter was left behind.

"Not Lionel?" I pulled away from Lucas and busied myself with picking up Lionel's blocks and putting them back in the box.

"Not as much."

"Because you let him sleep in the bed with you. And then I come home and he cries and cries when his mean mom puts him in that crib. Why do you always make me the bad guy?"

Lucas didn't respond for a minute. He fidgeted with a rubber band. "Remember how you were so proud of yourself for not marrying your dad?"

"Yeah, I married for looks instead." I laughed. Lucas either missed the joke or didn't find it funny.

He continued, "You're always talking about how fucked up he is and how he doesn't even know his own daughter and how he gave that horrid speech at our wedding about something you said when you were ten because that was the last time he had a conversation with you."

"That's all true."

Lionel wailed upstairs. Lucas looked at his watch. It'd been about fifteen minutes since we'd put him to bed. On the road, I exhausted my mind thinking about how much I missed Lucas, Lionel, and Addie, but I actively avoided thinking about Lucas's role at home—feeding Addie and Lion in the wee hours of the morning, taking them out for a walk, dropping Lion off at his mom's on the way to a jobsite, picking Lion up on his way home: feeding, changing diapers, soothing, petting, bathing, crying, crying, crying.

"All I'm saying is maybe he's not such a bad guy. Maybe his priorities are just a little screwed up because he's rich."

"It's not about being rich, Lucas. This isn't a class thing. He was a shitty father."

"You promised you'd help paint the trim." He got up from the couch, walked into the kitchen, and poured himself a bowl of cereal. There was a time when he would have stepped outside for a cigarette instead, but he had kicked the habit after Lionel was born. Then he stood and ate at the counter instead of carrying the bowl back into the living room.

"I talked to Cal about it," I said. "He's coming by to help tomorrow and Friday."

"You talked to Cal about it?"

"Yeah, I told you I'd help and I can't, so this is how I'm helping. It's all paid for. It's done."

"I'll call Cal in the morning and tell him I'll do it myself."

"I already paid for it, Lucas."

"He'll give us our money back." He spoke with a mouth full of cereal.

"Cal does this for a living."

"I'll do a better job myself. Jimmy will help if I need it."

"Okay, how about you do it with Cal? That way you can make sure he does it right."

"I want to make sure *you* do it right."

"I'm sorry, Lucas."

"Sorry about what?"

"Look, I paid Cal a thousand dollars. He needs the money. Harvard's paying me more than that, after taxes. Do the math."

"Nice after-tax analysis," he said. "What about everything else?"

"Taxes are relevant."

"Listen to yourself, Emma. What about doing something together? How do you value shooting the shit?" He fell silent for a minute. Then he added, "If you really want to do the math, make sure you factor in all that money your dad has dropped on Harvard over the years."

Having never attended college himself, my father was an atypical university benefactor. At the age of eighteen, when I set foot on Harvard's campus for the first time as an incoming freshman, I was taken aback by his name recognition there. He didn't have his name on a building, or anything as gauche as that. But, upon introducing myself to an upperclassman at a bar, he said, "Oh, like the fund." My dad had endowed an equity portfolio, which was managed by select Harvard MBAs under the supervision of an advisor. Harvard named the fund after him. I'm sure my father's reasons for never mentioning this to me had to do with protecting my ego.

When I graduated, he told me, "No one can ever take this away from you," and he was right in some ways: the benefits of the Harvard pedigree, a BA and, later, an MBA would follow me in the form of assumed intelligence at every turn—nothing would change that—but he was wrong too: *he* took it away from me, or at least he took away my perception of it as my own, the naive assumption that I prevailed in a meritocracy.

My dad continued to donate to Harvard long after I graduated. A couple of times a year, he flew up to Boston on his company jet and met with Harvard MBAs who wanted careers in private equity. This was not a recruiting exercise on behalf of his firm. He did it for himself.

"Don't diminish my accomplishment," I said, and then, because I wanted to win, "It's not like I work for him."

The funny thing is I thought I didn't care about money. Lucas and I had chosen to live a simple life, in an affordable town. What I found when I made money wasn't so much that I cared about it, felt the need to spend or hoard it, but that it simply changed my relationship to one thing: time. Deep down, I began to believe my time was more valuable than other people's time, more valuable than Lucas's time. And that changed everything. Because being a wife and a mother, being a human being, has everything to do with time.

"Why are you doing this?" Lucas asked.

"Doing what?"

"The constant travel. Bailing on everything. Missing our son grow up."

"I'm not missing Lion grow up."

"He changes every day. You're missing it."

I thought for a minute about what he was saying, wondered how he knew to say the thing that would hurt. "I'm doing this because *I want to be somebody*. Because I don't want to be Ivan Ilyich." Immediately, upon uttering these words, I realized that what I was doing, the travel, the focus on money in and money out, was what Ivan Ilyich would have done, and what Lucas was doing, building a life, was what happy people did.

Lucas placed his bowl on the floor for Addie to lick clean. Then he picked it up and put it in the sink without bothering to rinse off her drool. Together, they moseyed back into the living room and flopped down on the couch. Lucas bent his knees so Addie could sprawl out at his feet.

Lionel had finally stopped crying. I imagined his tiny face, the way his lips parted ever so slightly as he slept, how his hands curled around his monkey's tail. In the old days, I would have been lying with Lucas on the other side of the L-shaped couch, our heads meeting in the corner, pressed against each other. I would have stayed in that position for as long as I could, even when his snoring drowned out the TV.

"It's ironic," he said.

"What?"

"You were so proud of yourself for not marrying your dad. Turns out I married him."

"Well then, I guess it's time for my affair."

Addie stirred and got up. She stepped over Lucas on the couch and stopped in front of me. She licked my hand, looking for pets. "Thanks for the lick, Boogers." I spoke directly to her. "You know I'd never do that, right?"

Discharge collected around her eyes, probably due to allergies. By contrast, Lion's snot and other bodily fluids had always been more responsibility than amusement.

What I wouldn't give now to wipe his face again! What deal I wouldn't make so that I could hold him still as he squirmed. How happy I'd be to let his nose get all crusty if that's the way he preferred it.

The truth was I always yearned for an adult child. Even before Lionel was born, I knew I was playing the long game. Some women love babies and nursing and holding tiny, little bodies against their skin. And some women love their children's affection, the endless stream of questions, the wide-eyed wonder. And some women love soccer games and piano lessons, I suppose. It's not that I didn't like these things, or that I wasn't looking forward to them. It was that the thing I really wanted, the reason I had a baby in the first place, was to have a relationship with my adult child. I wanted to talk to him. I wanted to see his father in him, and perhaps some of myself. I wanted him to be a good person, kind and respectful. I wanted him to be whip smart, smart like Lucas, smarter than me. And funny.

When Lionel played with blocks, I imagined he would become an architect. He'd endure the training and work in the field for a time. He'd look the part with a checkered shirt and a skinny tie. His office would be in New York City, or maybe Philadelphia, and he'd design big glass boxes, modern buildings, until that got a little bit stale, or the office politics began to wear on him, or some leadership guru at the company retreat preached, "Always be excellent." Then he'd quit and start up his own company, designing and selling furniture, maybe.

"Oh, come on. Take a joke! I'm not planning to have an affair to be more like my father," I said. "I can't believe you don't think I'm funny. Audiences find me hilarious."

Most of my jokes were lost on Lucas. Some guys only find other guys funny. They laugh all day long at sophomoric jokes about farts and sweaty balls, and then a woman throws out a really snappy one-liner and they just don't hear it.

Addie looked up at me. I wiped the booger from her left eye.

"I think you have a good sense of humor," he said.

"You just like it when I laugh at your jokes," I said.

"Hmm, yeah, that's true." He finally cracked a smile.

This was the last real conversation we ever had.

I RETURNED HOME WHEN Lucas called to tell me what happened. He met me as I walked out of the terminal. He didn't say anything—there were no words—he just wrapped his arms around me. It was the first time I felt cold to his touch, reptilian. It's not that I expected to feel passion, but I didn't expect to feel the way I did. It wasn't hatred and it wasn't indifference; it wasn't love but it wasn't the absence of love either; it wasn't life and it wasn't death. It was cold. It was brutal. I can say that.

I felt Lucas looking at me, searching my face for something he needed, but I couldn't look back. I'd lost everything already, but if I looked, I'd lose more.

12AM

MY MOTHER METICULOUSLY PLANNED the funeral, as she'd done for Uncle Nic. She hadn't visited since Lionel was born, when she came up to help out as I recovered from labor.

Vaguely aware of her decisions, I was present when our families met with the priest. He was there to counsel us, grieve with us, and pray with us. But I was there only in body, not in mind or spirit, and there's nothing a priest can do with an empty vessel.

We congregated around a small table in the parish office, the same table where Lucas and I sat with Sister Mary Agnes only a few months prior, discussing Lionel's baptism, as he bounced on my lap.

The baptismal font is next to the casket. Eyelids lift where they fall. From dust to dust, as they say.

My mom had chosen two readings and a gospel for the funeral. As these details were discussed, I thought about Luke chapter 10, the parable of the Good Samaritan, which was the gospel I had chosen for my wedding, because though Lucas was not religious, he was a neighbor to everybody, and I believed he embodied the parable by the way he lived.

Now, I could think only of that parable's cruel prescience. Lucas and I—we were the man robbed of everything, stripped naked, and left for dead. For us, there was no Good Samaritan. No one, in this world or the next, could bandage a wound so deep and so invisible.

If Father Ed was concerned that I paid no mind to the readings my mom had chosen, he didn't let on. He was an old priest, familiar with grief.

Lion was eulogized by Father Ed in his homily and by my father-in-law, because after me, Lucas, and Joan, he'd spent the most time with him, and Lion had loved the old man's funny faces. Almost all of his words were lost on me, except for the last thing he said before leaving the lectern: "Lionel was the best of his parents, like two cans of paint mixed to create the perfect spring yellow." The best of us was gone.

After the funeral, my mother hosted a luncheon at our house. She always admired the Jewish custom of sitting shiva, mourners visiting the family home, and though she never said so, I believe she wanted to turn our house into something other than what it had become.

In spite of myself, I saw my mom in a way I hadn't seen her for a long time. If my dad understood fatherhood as a safety net, the accumulation of wealth as a contingency, my mom understood motherhood as attention to detail. She channeled her grief, planning Lionel's funeral as she'd planned my childhood birthday parties, year after year.

When I turned seven, she hosted a backward party. She put up a bunch of homemade signs that she painted backward. All the kids were told to come with their clothes on backward. We played games backward, and we ate cake before pizza, and all the kids walked around backward all afternoon. I don't know where she got the idea but I'll never forget that party. It was more fun than the fancy soirées paid for by the parents of my friends.

Over time, alcohol has stripped her of some of her pizzazz, but she kept it all together for the funeral. She had to. No one else could have done it.

I TAKE THE TOWEL from Jimmy and rinse it in warm water. He lets me lay it across his face. He puts his arms around my waist. "I'm sorry. I'm so sorry."

Lucas never told me about Lionel's last words. I never knew he called him *Dadda*, never knew he said *pen*. The reason he never told me this is clear: he thought it would cause me more pain.

"Jimmy, Lionel did not have the capacity to *warn* you. He was a baby."

"We shouldn't have left the window open. How is it even possible that we left it open?" Jimmy slumps over on the boxes and puts his face in his hands. What happened that day turned up the voltage on his sister's death, loss an unrelenting torturer. Her cancer was out of his control; Lion's fall was not.

There's something about grief that makes us dumb. Grief is the ability to reason and the absence of reason. Grief is faulty wiring. Lucas believes his thirteen-month-old son tried to warn him about the window. Jimmy believes this too. And because they ignored this warning, or didn't understand it, they bear greater responsibility.

Lucas and Jimmy never considered this possibility: Lion had not warned them of anything. Our fate was a tyranny of small decisions: a couple's decision to fix up the porch, a mother's decision to get on a plane, a father's decision to paint the trim in the company of friends, a dog's decision to jump up on the bed, a father's decision to put the baby down on the bed so he could be next to the dog, a trio of men's decision to leave the window open, a baby's decision to climb out onto the roof, and a million others not mentioned—where to live and how to live. Some were rational choices individually, good, even, but together: unfathomable.

Before now, I've never considered this possibility either. I blamed Lucas for his carelessness; I blamed myself for my absence.

I wipe mascara from my eyes. "I wish Lucas had told me Lionel called him *Dadda*," I say, tears streaking down my cheeks. I take Jimmy's hands from his face and gently lift his chin to look into his eyes for a beat, just long enough to send pain back and forth as if we share a single nervous system. I bring his head to my chest, and we remain still. His thinning hair smells of cigarettes, which reminds me of Lucas in the old days, before he gave them up.

I DIDN'T LEAVE LUCAS right away. There were months of uninhabitable fog. Lucas woke up every morning and went to work. He did the grocery shopping, and the housework, and paid the bills; he did all the things people do to get by. I was along for the ride. When I wasn't working—on Skype with Grace, digging for stories, refining our models, stretching myself to make sense of the data—I mostly hung around the house with Addie. Sometimes I took her for walks.

Before I moved out, I went home to Connecticut for a few days, leaving Addie with Lucas. I had three successive nightmares, about her choking on a chicken carcass when she was left home alone, about a coyote snatching her from our yard (coyotes do not prowl in or near town but they do in my dreams), and about an enormous tumor emerging from her head and killing her as I held her in my lap. For the remainder of the trip, I called Lucas every three hours just to make sure she was still alive. Each time, he said, "Addie's fine. She misses you, though." For those dreams, I felt guilty—for being haunted by the dog instead of my son. Grief is a wayward monster.

Addie always sulked in the evenings when only one of us came home. To her, the presence of one of her people meant the other wasn't far behind, which was usually true. She'd pace around and then stop and sit by the door expectantly. She didn't curl up and get comfortable until both of us were there and the order of her universe was restored. Lucas and I often swapped pictures of Addie waiting by the door when one or the other of us had to work late or was detained by some other commitment. The image of her waiting bestowed a profoundly satisfying sense of belonging—home was the place I was supposed to be, and because Lucas sent the pictures, I conflated Addie's desire for my return with his, which was a doubling down on joy.

When I returned home from Connecticut, I curled up on the couch with Addie and called my agent. "No more travel," I said. He thought that was a bad idea, and I could tell by his tone that he'd assumed, now child-less, I'd agree to more travel. I calmly explained that I could not leave my dog overnight. He tried to act like he didn't think I was crazy but toward the end of the conversation he suggested I see a therapist.

"Just take the dog with you, then," my agent said. But Addie hated planes and I wasn't willing to drive more than five hours at a time, so he agreed to my break. I wanted to focus more on the fund anyway. Without Lionel, I could see nothing beyond simple profit motive. There was nothing else to live for.

Turns out, Lucas was right. He did marry my father.

IN EARLY DECEMBER, LUCAS insisted that I attend the annual Murphy's Drywall Christmas party. I said I wasn't in the mood. He pulled a dress out of my closet, threw it on the bed, and claimed it would only take an hour. His exact words were, "C'mon. Be my person for an hour. One hour. I can't do this without you." I could tell he was at his wits' end so I put on the dress he'd pulled out, even though it wasn't right for the occasion and it hung loose because I'd lost so much weight.

I told myself I could do it. Then Addie pushed her hard head into my chest and I almost stayed home. Lucas tucked my hair behind my ear and pulled me up by the hand. He knew the promise of a drink would get me through the door.

There were about thirty people at the party, employees and clients, and some close family friends. Angela was there, and I realized immediately that she'd wormed back into Lucas's life.

He didn't leave my side all night. When I went to the bathroom, he escorted me and stood outside the door. The toilet off the kitchen was occupied, so he walked me up a short set of stairs to the full bath located next to the rec room on the split-level. His parents' house was a sprawling maze of extensions. Set on a large lot at the edge of town, walkable from our house, the original floor plan was an eleven hundred–square-foot, one-bathroom, stone craftsman-style house with a central wood-burning hearth. Over the years, as Murphy's Drywall grew, so did the house. Three separate additions tripled its size. No matter how big the house got, we always hung around the central hearth and the kitchen.

When we returned from the bathroom, Angela's eyes were glued to Lucas. She talked to Joan but she was really talking to him, flaunting his mother's acceptance. She attempted to show me up because I wasn't talking to anybody, least of all Lucas's mother. She looked happy, tipsy off rum punch, her voice louder than usual, more exuberant. She'd lost weight; she wore a clingy black dress. Her makeup was heavy. It made her look pale and thin lipped, and like she was trying too hard.

Lucas ignored her. At first I thought this was normal. I'd killed their friendship a long time ago. Then I realized they were actively ignoring each other, acknowledgment evident in Lucas's lack of general politeness. At one point, she stood inches away from us, ordering Bulleit from Lucas's cousin, the bartender for the night. Her eyes met Lucas's over the rim of her glass. He didn't so much as say hello, or crack a half smile; he only looked at her for a fraction of a second.

What can a man communicate in a fraction of a second? Lucas, with his large, weepy eyes, horizontally wide—rather than vertically large, as people usually mean when they say *wide-eyed*—truly wide, thoughtful and emotive, could speak volumes in a code that I knew how to decipher. With a glance, he told her that I was fragile, that I was physically present at his behest but not emotionally present, because he had no right or ability to command my mental state. He told her that it would be wise not to speak to us, and tonight there was only *us*—there was no *him*—because he wasn't about to leave my side. Later, tomorrow, maybe, there would be *him*.

In the morning, Lucas would wake up, feed Addie, and head to work at some jobsite. Then he'd stop by the old man's shop, which doubled as a back office. Angela would be there tallying expenses, planning for tax season. She'd ask him if he wanted to grab lunch, and she'd act demure and accommodating, telling him if he was pressed for time, they could just grab something quick, but she really wanted a burger from Fitzpatrick's, which was twenty minutes away and the service was slow. Lucas would agree.

A bigger person would have said hello to Angela, but I never said I was a big person. I can be quite small. I can be the bitch that Martin Yagla thinks I am. Actually, I almost did say hello when Angela was alone on the couch, digging through her purse. She pulled out objects, one by one, and placed them on the cushion next to her awkwardly slouched body: a small cosmetic case, one of those plastic, tubular tampon holders, a wallet, a handful of crumpled receipts, a pack of American Spirits. She located her phone and shoved everything back in quickly, sliding the objects into her cheap cloth messenger bag.

Watching Angela interact with the world was like listening to NPR talk about sports: painfully uncomfortable.

Angela didn't smoke. I knew this, not because I'd never seen her smoke a single cigarette at any Murphy's Drywall event, or anywhere around town, outside a bar or coffee shop, in her car, in the park—though I hadn't—but because she wasn't the type of person who smokes cigarettes. She was too much of a cat person, too into cooking and watching *The Great British Baking Show* on PBS. She wasn't a bar person. She was a homebody. Homebodies drank tea. Homebodies made soup from scratch. Angela had a pack of cigarettes in her purse for the same reason she ordered Bulleit: Lucas liked those things.

She didn't need to offer Lucas a cigarette to win him over, though. She'd already offered him something I couldn't, not anymore: friendship. Anyone with two eyes could see how much he needed it.

After the party, Lucas and I walked home in silence. Lucas wanted to stop at the corner store to buy his own pack of cigarettes. He'd taken up the habit again. I'd given up on shaming him. I said fine but I would keep walking. He could catch up. He hesitated. I'm sure this made him uncomfortable. It was late and I'd been drinking in excess. But chivalry was less important to him in that moment than cigarettes. Anyway, I was wearing heels and he must have known I wouldn't get far.

I often thought that Lucas wasn't so different from my Harvard friends. More brilliant than most of them, he could carry a conversation. He was introverted but enjoyed socializing with all kinds of people after a couple of whiskeys. He had no interest in finance, in leveraged buyouts and liquidity events and P&Ls, but all that stuff is boring to most people anyway. I teased him for his socialist leanings but he held his own when we debated the issues. One thing that separated Lucas from my friends in cities, the thing that really revealed his working-class roots, was the way he smoked cigarettes. He didn't smoke cigarettes like my artist boyfriend— the guy on Ninety-Ninth and Lex who slept on an air mattress. That guy rolled his own. Usually, he rolled spliffs. And he did it because he was an *artist*. There's a big difference between people who smoke cigarettes because they want to be cool, artists and musicians, and people who smoke cigarettes because they grew up sneaking them from their mama's packs. Lucas fell squarely in the latter camp. And he didn't roll his own. He bought Natural American Spirits, typically mellow yellow.

Lucas caught up with me a few blocks later. There was a time when we always walked home arm in arm, but I kept my hands in my coat pockets and my eyes on the sidewalk. When we got home, he tossed his phone and wallet down on the counter and went out to the backyard to smoke.

The amount of time that passed seemed longer than the burn rate of a single cigarette. When he came back in, I said, "You got a text from Angela." In the old days, I would have teased him about it, had a little fun with him, maybe gotten angry, but now I didn't have the energy.

I'd turned on the TV but hadn't bothered to find a show to watch. A regional adaptation of *Family Feud* played on the local access channel. Years prior, I'd encouraged Lucas to get together a team from The Final Final and apply to be on a local game show. In addition to *Family Feud*, there was a quiz show where teams answered questions about current events, with one night a week set aside for sports trivia, and there was a charades show, where a person on the team acted out a book, movie, or song. Lucas read everything; Jimmy remembered everything; and Martin Yagla had both mathematics and medicine stored somewhere in that crazy mind—I figured any one of these three game shows was a slam dunk.

He pulled up the text in front of me on the couch, pushed his phone in my face, and insisted I see it. It read, *I'm glad we're friends again.*

I could see how badly he wanted me to care, how he wanted me to act like I did before, say all the catty things: *She's pathetic; she lost her virginity to you.* I didn't; I couldn't. Turns out cattiness demands the ability to tap into some primal desire to defend and protect. Cattiness requires life force, imagination, and will, all of which were in short supply.

I wanted to feel imposed upon, green with jealousy, another woman's desires having infringed upon my own, her emotional and physical longings like tentacles, squeezing and choking out the oxygen—fight harder, lose more—but with the awareness that the battle was an easy victory, I had no desire to fight, and beyond battlelust, there was no other deeper desire, no love, or even awareness of love's possibility. The reflexes of my body and mind were dull and humorless, as if all my remaining energy was being used up, slowly depleted, by one thing and one thing only: survival, a counting of days, perhaps comparable to an alcoholic keeping track of sobriety, or what Catholics call purgatory, a place where time is suspended and desire is thwarted and there is nothing but waiting and waiting and waiting, and implicit in the waiting, a sense that eternal happiness exists someplace else but not here.

"I think we should split up," I said.

"You mean get a divorce?"

Lucas didn't care much for institutions. He didn't like anyone telling him what to do. Labels and titles inspired no confidence in him. He'd asked me to marry him and gone through with it because he knew I wanted it, but I'm sure he saw our bond as something more infinite. He was loyal like Addie, which is to say he possessed a pure kind of loyalty, blind and perfect and defined only by love.

Once we left Addie outside in the backyard for several hours because a simple errand turned into drinks with friends at a rooftop bar. Around six o'clock we rolled up to the house on bikes, and there she was, perched on the front porch, waiting for us. She'd found a hole in the back fence and squeezed through it. She could've explored the neighborhood, begged the kids next door for treats, smelled other dogs, but her impulse was to watch over the house and wait for her people. If we hadn't come home, she would have waited there all night, maybe even for days.

Lucas was the same way. He didn't care much about the institution of marriage, but he sure as hell cared about divorce.

He stared at the TV. I couldn't tell if he was thinking about what I just said or watching *Family Feud*.

By the way the families on the show were dressed, it was obvious that they were working-class, probably with deep roots in this town. One of the families was fat—all three generations, grandmother to grandchild— and the other skinny. Both bounced up and down and clapped to the music.

"I just need to not live here."

"Because of Angela?" For a second, he must have thought I was joking.

"Because I don't care about Angela. Because she could have texted you *The sex last night was great* and I still wouldn't care about Angela."

Lucas reclined on the couch, at the base of the L, perpendicular to the TV, his usual spot. It was cool in the house and he hadn't taken off his puffy jacket or his shoes after he came in from the backyard, so he looked both comfortable and uncomfortable at the same time, both ready for sleep and capable of flight. The way he tucked his chin into the collar of his jacket was both a metaphorical and a literal signal that he was going into his shell.

Lucas's threshold for arguing was very shallow. For a routine fight, he had about thirty minutes in him. Once we were beyond his threshold, he'd table the conversation and leave the room, picking it up again as many as three days later. He always did pick it up again, though, I think because he had to know that I was okay. Deep down, he was insecure. He carried, in his own words, some degree of self-loathing, but the heavier burden was his fear of losing the one thing that mattered to him: his family.

"I'm not having sex with Angela," he said.

"I know you're not, but I wouldn't care if you did. Knock yourselves out."

Lucas shook his head and looked away again, first at Addie, then back at the TV. It was his way of dismissing me, his way of saying, *If I look away long enough, she'll get over it*. He said, "Game shows are depressing. There's something creepy about them. Big Brother–ish. A method of control."

"We had religion; now we have local-access *Family Feud*."

"—*ist das Opium des Volkes*," he said.

Lucas had introduced me to his parents for the first time at The Final Final, about three months into our relationship. He and his dad wanted to watch some game that wasn't on regular TV, so we all met at the bar. His mom came along too, but she didn't like being in the bar much. At some point she expressed her desire to leave. The old man insisted on one more drink, and I heard him whisper, "This is family." I doubt he remembers that day, the day we first met, let alone his excuse to stick around the bar a little bit longer. It felt so good, though, for a stranger to call me family.

"I don't feel what I'm supposed to feel," I said. Before these words came out of my mouth, I hadn't thought about them at all. They were spontaneous, not premeditated, which was characteristic of breakup conversations, in my experience. But these were the only words that mattered. These were the truest words, which best approximated the reality we were living in. The irony, of course, was that these words were also meaningless because there was really no way I was *supposed to feel*, so the fact that I didn't feel it, well, then, so what? I didn't, for example, say, *I don't feel the way I used to feel*, which meant something specific because I remembered exactly how I used to feel. But there was something about the negation of an intangible that seemed almost truer than my physical and psychological reality; it was truer than true.

"You're depressed," he said. "We can make an appointment with—"

"I don't love you anymore," I said, and we both knew no doctor could fix that.

A few days later, I moved out of the house on Catherine Street. It was Lucas's house. It always was. Never mind all the sweat equity, all the memories, the three months of living without a wall.

———————

WHEN I HIRED A lawyer, Lucas said, "Why do we need a lawyer? You can have whatever you want." I insisted so he said, "I'll just use the same guy. He can do both sides, right?" I told him that would be a conflict of interest. I said it flatly, like a pragmatist.

"Have your guy do the work and I'll sign it," he said.

Sharing Addie with Lucas wasn't an option. It was too difficult for us to communicate, even through text message, even if the matter was entirely logistical. Seeing each other was like the worst migraine I'd ever had, the kind where my brain pushed against my skull until it was ready to explode, except instead of physical, it was emotional.

As we walked into the lawyer's office, I looked Lucas in the eye. "I'm not doing this to punish you," I said. "I need Addie. Without her I'd stop breathing."

The lawyer said something about there being other matters to discuss. I said, "Lucas can have the house and whatever's in the joint account."

"We can split the joint account," he said.

"Use the money on the house, Lucas. Hire a painter." The exterior of the house badly needed repainting. He'd finished only the porch and a primer coat on the trim. He stopped working on the house altogether after that.

Lucas was entitled to more than the house and the joint account. There were the royalties from the book, which I wrote while we were married and Lucas supported me, the book that he suggested I write, for one thing, and our portfolio of stocks and bonds. He'd get half of that too. It was all there in the paperwork. Lucas was aware of our financial situation, though not actively involved in the maintenance of the accounts.

He had no desire to claim ownership in the hedge fund, which Grace and I managed as general partners. At one point, my lawyer stopped and asked him if he was sure he did not want to hire his own representation.

Addie was the only thing for which I cared to fight. I had prepared a file with ample documentation: receipts for dog food, a statement from a neighbor attesting that I ran her daily, a note from our veterinarian acknowledging that I took her in twice in the last year, for a checkup and shots.

Of course, Lucas's name was on the application for the dog license. He rescued her from a local animal hospital, where a family had left her after she'd been hit by a car because they couldn't pay the bill. Lucas had a friend who worked there (of course he did—he had friends everywhere in this town), and she called him and told him she had a dog for him, and he agreed to take her. No one knew her name, so he called her Adelaide, a nod to her homeland. He watched while they mended her up and put a purple cast on her broken leg. He made sure she was up-to-date on all her shots. He paid the tab. Then he took her home and raised her as a puppy. Facts are facts.

When I pushed my folder across the table to Lucas, he said, "She's my dog," and then he corrected himself. "She's *ours*—"

He bit his lower lip. My preparedness was gratuitous. A collection of receipts and statements from outsiders were meaningless to Lucas. He had been there, after all. He was an insider. I'd known this all along. I knew it when I riffled through my receipt drawer and when I asked the neighbor to put everything in writing and when I drove to the vet's office. But it was Lucas's expression, the way he bit his lip, that made me realize why I did it.

I did it to prove my fastidiousness. I did it to show I was the one who obsessed over details: whether the bottles were disinfected, if we had enough diapers in the bag, whether the stove had been turned off, checking everything two and three times over. I did it to show how much I worried all the time: about whether my breasts produced enough milk and, if they did, whether my diet provided the right nutrients, and when we switched to formula, about antibodies, and about preventing him from sleeping on his stomach, and grapes and maraschino cherries, and the possibility of climbing up on the toilet and cracking his head on the tub.

I did it to show, as a mother, I was mentally ensconced by paranoia and guilt and longing, and, as a father, Lucas was not. And though Addie had belonged to him first, and he had known her longer, and maybe she loved him more, I was the one who should care for her.

I did it, ultimately, to blur the edges of my own guilt.

The look on my lawyer's face screamed, *Give the man his dog*, but I was paying him so he couldn't say that.

"I spend most of the day with her," I said, "while you're out at job-sites."

"You travel for work," he said.

"Not anymore. I'm done."

Lucas leaned forward on the table, reaching for my hand. I pulled it back into my lap. He said, "You wouldn't stay home when our son was alive and now you won't leave home."

The lawyer's office was dry from the forced-air heat. I took a sip from a water glass, not recalling when it had been placed in front of me. Then Lucas said something that, in the moment, I found cruel. "What are you going to do when Addie dies?"

I let all the rage rise from my belly. "At least this time I'll be prepared."

Teardrops leaked from his eyes. I knew those wide, briolette eyes so intimately, the way he focused them and pondered with them and rolled them. I'd never seen him cry before, not even at the funeral.

The lawyer was both in the room and not in the room, as if Lucas and I were floating in a bubble, and the lawyer was a silent observer. He occasionally jotted notes on his legal pad.

Inside the bubble, Lucas looked down at his hands in the way one does when he is about to confess a sin. We floated away together, backward in time.

"It's my fault," Lucas said. "It's all my fault. You kept telling me to put him down in the crib. But he was so sleepy, and he wanted Addie to curl up next to him on the bed."

"Lucas," I said. "Let's not—" I covered my heart with my hand.

I already knew everything I needed to know. Earlier in the day Lucas and Jimmy accessed the porch roof from the window in Lion's room so they could paint the trim before the weather turned. I wasn't there to help. When they finished the primer coat, they climbed back inside but left the window open, out of carelessness or laziness, perhaps because they would need to go out there again to clean up. I wasn't there to close the window. Jimmy was still at the house when Lucas's mom dropped Lion off after watching him for the morning, and she told Lucas she had just changed his diaper and he was sleepy from the car ride and ready for his midafternoon nap. Lucas carried Lionel upstairs and laid him down on the bed instead of the crib. I wasn't there to insist on the crib. Lucas and Addie stayed on the bed with Lion until they were sure he was asleep. Then Lucas joined Jimmy in the backyard for beers—I knew that too. They left the back door open so they could hear if Lion woke up and cried out, and Addie could move freely between the front of the house, where she liked to perch on the back of the chair to watch passersby, and the backyard, where she could be near them. They listened to a sports talk radio show on a small, portable speaker, just as Lucas did every day. All of this I knew; the rest I imagined.

Martin Yagla was with them too. I didn't know it that day in the lawyer's office, though. I found that out tonight.

"Addie saw him fall," Lucas said. "I know she did. She saw him from the front window."

"She's a dog, Lucas."

Lucas went on to describe the way Addie threw herself against the front door, the way she madly scraped at the wood with her claws. Her loud, sharp, persistent bark. He said, "At first I thought it was just the mailman at the door. I put my beer down and walked inside. Addie's body writhed. She thrashed against the door. I yelled for her to calm down."

His eyes remained fixed on his hands. He rubbed them together like someone applying lotion aggressively. He tugged on his wedding band.

He described Lion's little body, face up, arms outstretched, like a snow angel on our redbrick walkway. He described how he held Lion in his arms while Jimmy held Addie back with one hand and dialed 911 with the other. The doctors said Lionel's head hit first.

"Lucas, stop." I couldn't bring myself to say the thing he needed me to say: *It wasn't your fault.* Deep down I blamed him.

"Emma—"

"Do we have to do this now? In front of Doug? I'm paying him a lot of money to sit here and listen to this."

"Our lawyer's name is Doug?" Lucas looked at him, acknowledging him for the first time.

"No, Lucas, *my* lawyer's name is Doug. You don't have a lawyer."

Doug became very uncomfortable when we started talking about him. I'm sure he'd experienced worse, being a divorce attorney.

"How cliché," Lucas said. "You hired an attorney named Doug."

"What do you care what his name is?"

"It's just fucked up. Doug is the final arbiter of a great love."

"Doug isn't the arbiter of anything, Lucas." The lawyer was completely frozen. He wasn't sure whether he should agree with me or if I had insulted him.

"The point is," Lucas said, "and I don't care how much you're paying this guy, he's going to hear it—the point is that I am the one who put Lionel down on the bed. I am the one who didn't think about the window. I am the one who went out back for a beer. Addie saw everything."

"What's your point, Lucas?" My hand hit the table. I wasn't in control of it.

"You don't know what it was like," Lucas said. "*You weren't there.*"

Doug finally worked up the confidence to cut in, or maybe he just had another unhappy couple on their way in. Whatever his motivation was, he finally said, "I think I have what I need to finish up the paperwork."

"Addie saw him fall," Lucas repeated, and I knew what he did not know. It didn't matter whether Addie saw Lionel fall. It mattered that Lucas saw him fall through her eyes, and he would continue to see him fall for the rest of his life.

———————

RIGHT NOW, ADDIE IS sleeping on my bed. She has pulled back the quilt so she can curl up in my soft French linens. Lest I've led you to believe Addie is a good dog, let me clarify. Addie *wants* to be a good dog—strong is her desire to please—but she's not. She can't control her impulses, which are to eat everything and smell everything and chase everything. When I call her to come, she takes her sweet time. When I leave food on the counter, she snatches it as soon as she finds herself alone. She once slipped out the front door and forced the delivery guy into a full sprint through the yard, barking as he leapt into his truck, headfirst. Long after she could be called a puppy, she chewed through my laptop cord and my Bose headphones cord, which seemed targeted, the fact that she chose those two things, one that I use for work and the other for travel, her dual enemies, but I can't imagine she's that smart, just bored.

Every now and again, a friend will find me out with Addie and, having seen her develop over the years from a spry puppy to a languorous old girl, will say, "Have you thought about getting another dog?" No one ever completes the thought: *It might soften the blow when she dies*. People say this out of genuine concern, so I don't hold it against them, but I know another dog would not diminish my grief but add to it. Addie is the only dog I've ever had. I begged for one as a child, but my mother was such a constrained germophobe that a dog was a practical impossibility. On my own, I moved around too much, lived in rentals without yards, and was, perhaps, too capricious to slow down for the love of a creature. The fact that Lucas dropped Addie into my life was pure, dumb luck, or possibly fate, because I could not have chosen a more loyal companion from any shelter in the world. Someday I might find myself with another dog but not while Addie is still with me.

No one ever suggested we have another baby. The reason I never wished for another child is not heroic. If I had another child, I could not look at him without thinking that he didn't have Lion's bow-shaped lips, or his wide, bluish-gray eyes; that he didn't have Lion's robust, portly little body and, as a result, would never share my dad's pet name for him, *Cicciotto*, one of the few Italian musings he'd ever allowed himself, a reminder of another life and time. Every time my living child laughed, I'd miss Lion's giggle, which always came quicker and lasted longer than I expected. In our bed, I'd note his presence but regret that he didn't worm his way between us, pushing his body against Lucas's bare chest for warmth and clutching my long hair in his fingers, in exactly the way Lion once did. As horrible as this sounds, all the ways this other child was not Lion would accumulate, and the result would feel less like love and more like indifference.

———

WHEN LUCAS AND I wrapped up with Doug, divorce attorney to the stars, I had to drive back to my apartment alone. The meeting ran longer than expected, owing to Lucas's breakdown, so I was forced to endure the twenty-seven red lights that line Route 1 in traffic, not city traffic— small-town traffic, which is actually more annoying than city traffic because if you live in a city, you signed up for traffic but if you live in a small town, traffic only exists during a one-hour window when all the clock punchers drop whatever they're doing and head to the bar, or home, depending on their values.

At one of the red lights, I noticed that the pea-green Subaru Outback in front of me had a 13.1 sticker on its back hatch. I thought, *Why would anyone want to call attention to the fact that she finished half of something?* Misery emanated from me then—I can see that now—and not just misery, but failure. It was easier, or necessary, to see everything as failure—to see 13.1 miles as failure—than to face my particular failure.

My check-engine light came on, which wouldn't have fazed me— I would've just driven to the shop, which is three blocks from my apartment, next to the hardware store—but then the engine started smoking. I pulled over and found myself in the parking lot of the LongHorn Steakhouse for the second time in my life.

This time, I found the faux stone exterior distasteful—a cheap, vulgar Disneylandesque nod to the Southwest, with red neon lights lining the roof. The large, fake cattle horns above the door reminded me of the fake Texas longhorn head that hangs above the bar inside. I wanted nothing to do with any of it, but it was damn cold outside, leaving me no choice but to go in while I waited for AAA.

Later, I would pay a guy six grand to take apart my engine, clean out the sludge, and put the whole thing back together. I could have just bought a new car, but the idea of dealing with a car salesman was utterly repulsive for a number of reasons, first and foremost because the minute I walked into the dealership, the salesman would say something like, "Why don't you bring your husband in to take a look?"

In Upstate New York, AAA tow truck drivers take their sweet time, so I was forced to kill more than an hour in the LongHorn. I'd forgotten how big the place was, and it was crowded at the dinner hour. There was only one seat open at the bar next to a middle-aged man devouring an enormous Panhandle steak.

I forced a fake smile, thinking about heart disease and diabetes and the opioid epidemic, and everything that's wrong with America. Cheesy pop country, which played low in the background, numbed my brain.

If I'd come ten minutes earlier, it would have been happy hour. My twelve-dollar cocktail was a premade sugary mix with not nearly enough booze in it to accelerate time. I'd come here once before with Lucas to share time—to steal a couple of hours together—and I was here now, by myself, to kill time. Sharing time is a flash, impossible to hold on to. Killing time is slow, methodical torture. It is looking at the clock, and then looking again and again. It is waiting for something you need but you don't want.

In anticipation of the tow truck driver's arrival, I mustered my sobriety and self-restraint and told the bartender, "Thank you, the drink was just fine. I'll take the check, please." But when the check finally came, I noticed he'd fucked it up, and it wasn't fucked in my favor, so I couldn't just tip him a little extra and be done with it.

When he took back the bill, he laughed at his mistake. "*You* didn't order the T-bone, now, did you?"

I should have just paid for my neighbor's T-bone and left because the bartender took forever to bring me the correct bill, and in that time, I couldn't help but think about how much this place had changed since my last visit.

Actually, this place was exactly the same. I was different.

The first time I crossed the threshold of the LongHorn, so long ago now, Lucas called me out for being from Connecticut. I said, "Oh my God, I love you." It wasn't a serious *I love you*. It was one of those things you say when someone cracks you up. Maybe I should have said, "I love that," because it was so early in our relationship. But in a subterranean way, it was true: I loved him.

He took my hand and said, "I love you too, Emma." We didn't stop saying it until Lion died.

"WHY ARE YOU STILL here, Jimmy?" I ask.

"You're fixing me up. Then we'll both go home, and tomorrow will be another day."

"No, I mean why are you still in this town? Why don't you go back out west, practice engineering again? Lucas said you loved it."

"That was another life," he says. "My life is here now." He looks around the room, which makes me think *here* is this bar specifically.

I want to tell him that there's nothing here, that he could find the same bar in any town, but I'm afraid he'll ask me the same question: *Why do* you *stay?*

"I'm gonna open a restaurant," he says. "Not some diner making breakfast all day. A real restaurant. Tuna tartar and miso black cod and squid-ink pasta—that kind of restaurant."

The part of me that is my father's daughter wants to tell him to open his restaurant someplace else. But another part of me that is also my father's daughter wants to loan him the money to actually do this thing. Jimmy's raw, rustic cuisine would attract newcomers, young professor types, as well as tourists from Brooklyn and the Upper West Side in search of authenticity. I picture Jimmy completely in his element, swanning around long farm tables, as diners eat his food late into the night.

1AM

MARTIN YAGLA IS BACK.

Jimmy jerks away from me. We turn our ears to the stairs. The sound of chaos ricochets off the walls: shrieking, scuffling, shattering, Amelia's voice. "Get out! I'm calling the cops! You're fucking crazy!"

I look up toward the screen mounted in the corner. It's black.

The previous owner, back in the day when the bar was called Hanihand's, had installed video cameras upstairs. He did so presumably for security but most of the old regulars thought it was more of a voyeuristic thing. James Hanihand would disappear to the basement and wait for a group of college girls to wander in; then he'd do a bunch of blow and jerk off to cleavage and tight little asses. Or so goes the legend. Hanihand snorted his way into bankruptcy, before I had the pleasure to make his acquaintance.

The cameras are permanently off now because, before tonight, no one cared much about the footage—heck, we all live the footage, and when we aren't several drinks deep, it's usually mind-numbing. If the video cameras were on, I'd be tempted to keep my eyes on the screen, watch Yag implode from a safe distance, but as they are not, my impulse is to run toward the action.

Jimmy tells me to stay put. He scans the room and his eyes land on a bag of softball gear, a relic of the coed team Lucas and Jimmy organized and The Final Final sponsored. The sound of the zipper alerts me: the voices from above have gone quiet. I hear only the rhythmic thump of the jukebox. Jimmy grabs a metal bat. I scurry up the stairs after him. He's faster than me, clearing two steps at a time.

Yag walks the length of the bar, dispensing the contents of a red gas can. He looks at Jimmy, then at me, then back at Jimmy. His eyes bug out. He wasn't expecting us to come up from the basement—he thought we'd left for the night. He locks on me and mutters something under his breath.

"What do you think you're doing, Yag?" I hear the harshness in my own voice. It doesn't sound like fear; it rings of condemnation.

He says the bar is toxic. He calls it a "filthy hellhole," and I immediately think of my mother, her refusal to sit down in this place. I don't entirely disagree. Then I channel Lucas, hearing the tone his voice would take, how he would defuse the situation, and I realize: *We are in a situation.*

Cal is gone, down at the police station. So is his gun. *This is a good thing,* I think; *Summer shouldn't be here.* Maybe no one will get killed tonight. If we'd only called the police earlier, immediately, Martin might be in custody right now. But we didn't. We waited. *If only. If only.*

Death is in the air. What does that even mean? It sounds so melodramatic, like the name of a single episode of a nineties TV drama, a name that was previously unseen until Netflix invented the full-series binge, and the nature of time shifted from days and weeks and months to episodes and seasons and series. But it's so apropos. Maybe it's the way the conditioned air feels: artificially dry, ice-cold. I move away from the vent.

"Yag," I say. "Martin, come on. Martin, you're right. This place is filthy. We can clean it up. We can go down to the basement and get the bucket and the mop, and the massive container of bleach. We can take care of it."

"No, man, it's in the cracks," he says.

He empties more gas from the can onto the pool table.

The jukebox is still playing. Amelia turned the music back on when Jimmy and I were down in the basement. A newish pop song comes on, distinguishable by its chipper *beepity boppity bop, whoo-oo, whoo-oo, baby, baby*—the college girls play it over and over again. They are long gone now, and I'm sure they added the song to the queue hours ago. Aside from me, Jimmy, and Yag, there are no other patrons in the bar. Amelia huddles behind the bar on her cell phone with the police.

The late-night Chinese place next door in the adjoining building is a grease pit. If The Final Final goes up in flames, it will too—there's no way around it. We might lose the whole block.

"Emma, get out," Amelia says. She's right—there's no one blocking me. I would leave, but I'm frozen. I am both panicked and calm, or rather, the panic has tricked my mind into a state of calm. Everything happens before me in slow motion: Amelia's mouth moves; Yag waves his right hand over his head, clutching a lighter; Jimmy grips the bat and angles his body in a loaded stance, elbow up.

I AM BACK IN the Adirondacks. My hand is on my belly. I am three months pregnant with Lionel. Lucas lifts the oar. I tell him to stop. He swings at Kilo, misses.

Jimmy swings the baseball bat in Yag's direction. Jimmy's eyes are open, curious; Lucas's eyes were squinted, angry. Jimmy's jaw is slack, mouth open, poised to speak; Lucas's jaw was locked, teeth clenched, without words. Jimmy's motion is different; he's holding back, swinging to warn. Lucas was protecting his family, swinging to kill.

———————————

I WALK OVER TO the table at the front of the bar where Summer drew ponies and weed plants hours prior. I sit down slowly, as if it's a regular night, as if in a minute or two, Amelia will walk over and ask me if I want the usual. My elbows are on the table and I rest my chin on my fist.

The air-conditioning is on full blast, but Summer left the front window open. I listen to the rain, and the warm, wet air provides relief from the Freon. There isn't much of a breeze but the smell finds its way in through the window anyway. The rain has trapped all the scents of the day, a mix of grass and gravel with hints of cigarette butts and dog piss. It's not a bad smell; it smells real and familiar.

I am no longer Lucas's wife. I am not carrying his baby. There's no point in taking a swing anymore. Oar, bat, Lucas, Jimmy. Does any of it matter? Does it matter if Jimmy strikes Yag? How hard he swings? Will he give him a jolt? Knock him out? Crack his skull? Maybe he'll do none of these. He'll chicken out. And Yag's thumb will roll that metal spark wheel down to the red ignition button, and a ninety-eight-cent lighter from the corner store will be the end of us all.

There is a signed receipt and pen on the table in front of me. Amelia hasn't had a chance to pick them up. I flip over the receipt and write,

– 244 –

The filth is in the cracks ∧ *We cannot clean the cracks*

∴ *Burn the bar to the ground*

That's not a fallacy; it's just plain crazy.

The bowl of matchbooks at the center of the bar, in front of the taps, catches my eye. Fancy Pete made the bowl during his pottery phase. It's a little misshapen, glazed deep green with a drip effect. The matchbooks are branded with *THE FINAL FINAL* in Courier New, as if someone typed each one individually on an old-fashioned typewriter.

Desire strikes from deep inside: *I want the bar to burn to the ground.* For the first time in our lives, Martin Yagla and I are aligned. The Final Final has betrayed us—this old haunt, our second home. It seduced us with the illusion of family. It staved off loneliness with banter. It drowned self-blame in booze. It is, and has always been, one thing: a trap.

I want to light it up myself, and I think maybe I have it in me, maybe I could do it, except for one thing: my humanity. My mind runs through possible eventualities, however unlikely. *Amelia's lungs will fill with smoke too quickly. Jimmy will get trapped under a fallen beam trying to save Yag. A dog, left home alone upstairs, will be locked inside with no way out. A child sleeping above the Chinese place will be unable to escape the inferno.* I don't want anyone to get hurt.

Amelia motions for me to leave. The 911 operator must be telling her to clear out the bar. The phone is pressed tightly to her ear. She repeats, "Okay. I'm still here. Okay. Okay. Yes, I'm still here."

The rain stops suddenly, the way my tears always stop, which means it could always start again. The sirens are louder now. They are no longer a distant chorus. They are an urgent clamor. Everything else goes on mute. The jukebox is silent. Amelia's repetitive exchange with the 911 operator is barely audible. Yag and Jimmy appear to have reached a détente—Jimmy with raised bat and Yag with raised lighter.

Maybe we'll all walk out of here. Everyone will be alive. But Lionel will still be dead.

Then Jimmy unmutes the room with words, stupid words. "Do you hear the sirens, Yag? The police are coming. It's over. It's all over."

"Don't you see it?" Yag says. "We're all worthless! Filth. It's all over all of us." He sets the gas can down on the pool table and rubs the back of his right hand on his pants.

"What are you gonna do, Yag?" Jimmy asks. "You gonna kill us all? Light this place up and burn us alive? Come on. The police are almost here. Give me the lighter."

"You don't think I'll do it? I'm a murderer already. When we came in from the roof, Lucas fixed the screen. We headed out back, cracked our beers, and then I couldn't find my stupid, fucking phone. I left it on that damn roof. After I got it, I was trying to be quiet and forgot to put the screen back on. It's my fucking fault!" He looks across the bar at me, his eyes flickering. "Wooooooo. Splat. I knew what was going to happen and I left the screen off."

Fuck Yag, I think. Fuck him for annexing my pain, for making it about him. Fuck him for reminding everyone what I already know: I should have been there. I am responsible.

I yell, "Don't flatter yourself, Yag."

The room smells strongly of gas. Scratching his nose, Yag picks up the gas can and pours some on himself, down his shirt and jeans. He is the fuse.

"You win, Dr. Yag," Jimmy says. He extends his hands and squats down to place the bat on the floor. "You're going to let Amelia and Emma walk out of here first, okay?"

Yag shakes his head. "Why do any of you even want to live? We're already dead!"

Jimmy dips his head, like a defensive back going in for a tackle. Yag falls backward into the pool table. He pushes off and charges Jimmy, who is off balance, and manages to push him to the top of the basement stairs. Jimmy releases his arms from Yag's body and grabs the door frame with his fingertips. He holds on. Gravity carries Yag forward. The sound of his body crashing down the stairs is unbearably loud, bone on wood, again and again, picking up speed the whole way down. I'm not sure he'll survive it.

Jimmy looks at me, and it's only for a second but it's the longest second in the history of the world. He's making a decision, and even if I wanted to, I know I can't stop him. No one can. He lets go of the door frame, turns, and disappears into the basement.

Five police cars are outside now, pulled up on the curb, catawampus. The bar fills with red and blue lights.

When the officers enter, they smell gas immediately. One of them grabs me. I don't resist. My mind is slow, as if I'm in a meditative state. I can see and hear but I cannot react—I cannot speak, and I cannot move.

I hear Amelia say, "The basement. They are in the basement."

"How many are in the basement?" the cop asks.

"Two," Amelia says. "Martin and Jimmy. Martin Yagla has a lighter."

"Get them out of here now," one cop yells to the other. Amelia and I are dragged out, one on each arm. She is walking. I'm not aware of my own feet.

I smell the smoke before I see it, and I swear it smells of death, and I know what has happened: Yag lit the fuse.

Jimmy and Yag tumble out the front door. As they hit the sidewalk, Jimmy is gripping Yag, arms around his waist. They are both on fire. A firefighter, already on scene, launches on top of them with a huge fire blanket, which puts out the flames almost instantly but somehow intensifies the smell, which is smoky and acrid and fatty, flesh burning, distinctly human, not animal, and also rank with toxic chemicals.

They are alive and squirming around. Yag's body, which was covered in gas, is more damaged than Jimmy's, which, by comparison, looks normal, except he's covered in ash and he winces in pain. The gash where Yag hit him with the bottle is visible. It has opened up again. This time, he'll take the ambulance.

I think about Lucas's scenario: the house is burning down; who do you save? Jimmy had to save Yag, no matter the risk. My question—my joke—about who started the fire (*Was it your faulty electrical wiring?*) was irrelevant. Saving Lucas was the only thing I could do, the only thing I can do.

The Final Final lights up—from across the street I see the fire advance from the basement to the pool table to the bar, Yag's trail of gas. Seconds pass. I can't see anything but smoke and flames.

My hands shake. I shiver despite the hot, muggy night. Slowly my mind comes back to me. "Is this our fault?" I say aloud.

There is a female police officer by my side now. She assures me this is not my fault.

"But we could have stopped him," I say. "If we had said something different."

"My experience with cases like these," she says, "when perps are out of their minds, is that there's very little anyone can do except restrain them and wait. You look strong, but few are strong enough to hold down a grown man bent on taking everyone out with him."

The Final Final is gone. The front window is shattered and flames lick the edges of the building. An orange inferno rages inside. The sign still hangs over the door frame but it is melted out, and my mind immediately turns to word play: The Final Final *Final*; The Final Final *Finale*.

Our antique tin ceiling melts away. The wood paneling in the ladies' room feeds the fire—the heart I gouged deep: permanent, no longer. The old bar top, a steady old companion, ever faithful, is gone. The pool table's gone—no more stack of dollars on the rail, bets that will never be called. Lady Justice and her scales, the photos of the past bartenders and old regulars: all gone. About the only thing in the bar that will survive this inferno is the cheap vinyl floor, moisture resistant and impact resistant and scratch resistant—hollow to the heel, lacking in history, incapable of memory. Made to look like wood, the vinyl will outlast the real thing.

Years from now, when the regulars have moved on to other bars and other lives, the place will reopen with another name, a sports bar called SPRTS or a burger joint called BRGR, some chain that finally made it all the way upstate (an indicator to investors that it's time to sell the stock). I'll duck my head in once, just to see what became of my old haunt. The space will be gutted, entirely unrecognizable, fresh drywall painted prison gray, silver stools, laminated cocktail menus. The only remnant of what it once was will be the blasted vinyl floor, which I'll know as soon as the heel of my boot hits it. I'll turn around and walk out without ordering a single drink, and I'll remember what I know now: we are fools to believe any place worth inhabiting is permanent. To inhabit a place is to alter it in some way, to leave a mark.

The firefighters work to contain the flames. Looks like there's a good chance they will save the Chinese place and the rest of the block after all.

This never would have happened if Lucas were here. None of this would have happened. Earlier in the night, he would have put his arm around Martin, like he'd done that night at our house. He would have said something kind, something that made him feel like more than a failure, like a human being, even. He would have forgiven Yag, letting him off the hook like he let everyone off the hook, and Yag would have hated himself a little less.

As the flames turn our bar to smoke and ash, I consider why we all hang around here so much. Once upon a time, we came to The Final Final to share in Lucas's goodwill, hoping his humanistic spirit would rub off on our pessimistic souls.

TAKE AWAY THE HABITAT and . . .

The creature adapts.

Migration. Exodus. Change.

The air is wet and heavy. Sitting on the curb across the street from what's left of The Final Final, I see lights and sirens and firefighters and cops, yelling commands, hustling, doing what needs to be done, their world so far removed from my experience it might as well be playing out on a TV screen. The curb is hard under my ass. My hands are folded in front of me, covered in soot. My heartbeat is slow and steady. I recognize this calm.

"So this is the world," I say.

Like fire, grief subsumes everything. I've been so deep for so long I forgot what it's like up here. Now I can see the series of traps that caught me long before Lionel died: wealth, the big city, the small town, the Long-Horn on Route 1, the bar, the bottom of a drink, motherhood, the holdings sheet. My whole life I've been exchanging one trap for another. When Lion died, every trap collapsed into the one that came before, not unlike this bar before me, not unlike that last straw.

Every time I saw an exit, I took it: I moved upstate, I traveled for work, I abandoned my marriage. These were choices, but they weren't exits. They freed me from nothing. I believed I was autonomous. I thought movement, in and of itself, was ambitious. It was a grass-is-greener approach that worked until my son died, and then there was no more green grass, not in this world. Not anywhere.

I never wanted to take Lionel to the zoo, because every time I'd visited one as a child, I felt acutely depressed afterward. Like coming down from a hard night of drinking and cocaine, recovery took a minimum of three days. The animals were cute, but was it worth it? Maybe the animals had moments of happiness at feedings or in tender exchanges with the staff. Maybe they wanted nothing from the wild anymore. But to me, that was the problem: the wanting nothing. The dead eyes. I didn't want Lionel to see that. I wanted him to *want*.

Two years ago, my world collapsed. All trappings became one trap. I lost everything when Lionel fell off that roof. I can't explain it, but watching the bar burn to the ground feels like a commuted sentence, like the zookeeper opened the gates and said, *Best of luck to you.*

Run, I tell myself, *if your legs still work. Run.*

The pain will never go away. For the rest of my life, I will burst into tears at random times: when Addie turns left toward Catherine Street, when I catch a glimpse of Lucas and see Lionel's wide eyes and sideways smile, when I wake in a cold sweat from a dream where I am holding my baby again, naked from the bath, soft and heavy, everything I needed right there in my stupid, undeserving arms. But here on the curb, I make a decision: I will live my life to the bitter end. I want to live.

I will find Lucas and forgive him. I will tell him I'm sorry. We'll take comfort in each other, in mutual understanding, in all that we've lost. This clarity is strange and exhilarating.

I admit to myself what I've known all along. There is one place that will have me, *wretched refuse of your teeming shore.*

I can see it now. The Brooklyn town house, lamp lit. Lucas is in the backyard, throwing a Frisbee for Addie. She acts younger than she is now, bouncy and spry. He plants his feet and flicks the Frisbee sidearmed, nonchalant, at ease in his world. Through the lines on his face, I trace sadness that exists parallel to my own, side by side, separate. Lionel not being here for us to love will always be the void between us, around us. We are parents who have lost a child. We'll never be anything more, or anything less. But when I see that loss in this good man, it makes it easier to live with it in me.

In this future, Grace and I have offices in Manhattan and Boston. They look nothing like those of our competitors, not because of the architecture or interior design, but because of the people who occupy the space. Our competitive advantage is stories, after all, and we celebrate the diversity of our scars as we did at Francesca Jones's East Village restaurant.

Now that I've seen it, this life is more real to me than the one I've been living: a vision born from the ashes of The Final Final.

As soon as I allow myself to imagine it, ambition takes over. This future is the reason Grace, once head of private wealth solutions at one of the world's leading investment firms, walked away from her seven-figure compensation package to work with me. Grace exists in a state of perpetual forward motion. I imagine what it feels like to walk around in this state: alive in a world of possibility, consciously unwilling or unable to perceive a resistance level. Without awareness of a ceiling, none exists; all energy is potential. Immersion in this future feels like a drug. Without past and present, there is no pain, no struggle, only actualization and the experience of actualization—awareness of it—reality, a summit, a singularity comparable, perhaps, to Dante's divine light, everything and nothing. In the future, I see a sweep of time, a great love, a dog's companionship, *the death of my son*. All at once, I feel emptiness and terror and, though I have to fight to identify it, the possibility of joy.

AFTER HOURS

MY STUDENTS USUALLY MAKE the mistake of concluding their remarks with a financial projection or recommendation and then putting up a giant question mark on the screen in preparation for the Q&A. When they do this, I mark them down for "insufficient conclusion." Generally speaking, I find their endings too narrow, too focused on their own analysis. They don't think about the implications, what their findings really mean in the short and long term for the company, the industry, and society—and beyond society, for actual human beings. MBAs tend to forget that organizations are comprised of people, and their products and services are sold to people, and all these people live and breathe, and *to be alive is to be in pain.*

Once, I sat through a guy's entire presentation bored, but at the end he put up this giant line graph, which basically represented the apocalypse for the entire financial system. He left it up on the screen for the entire ten-minute Q&A, and by the end of it, the exponential curve of the line was burned into my memory. It was like a Bret Easton Ellis podcast: gloom to absurdity—nobody reads, film is dead, the golden age of TV is over, video games are the future of entertainment, Sony is apologizing for making light of food allergies—proof positive, civilization is doomed. That guy got an A.

The chief question of any great conclusion is, *Why does any of this matter?*

———————

ADDIE GREETS ME, TAIL wagging, at the door of my apartment.

There are more text messages on my phone from Grace and Samantha. The night at the bar felt like a supernatural intervention. I'd nearly forgotten about the ridiculous one with Elisa Monfils. I scroll through the texts with no intention of responding. From Grace, a series of stern messages about my fiduciary duty to meet with Elisa are softened by interstitial celebratory texts. The fund is performing better than expected. We're showing phenomenal numbers. Grace is raising more capital for the fund, which is exactly what my father would do (perpetual forward motion). From Samantha, the texts are more maternal, like I broke curfew, like she's just *concerned*. The most recent, from five minutes ago, reads, *I'm coming over again to check on you. I have a key.*

I grab Addie's leash from the hook by the door, and she begins to shake. She never gets walks at this time of night, after bar close. I can't tell how she senses time. She likes going to bed when it gets late. I know this because she used to follow me upstairs when Lucas was passed out on the couch, in spite of the fact that she never wanted to leave his side.

Still, the sight of the leash thrills her, even at this late hour.

The whole process of working on the hedge fund has me thinking about all these stories, the stories that make people special—Pamela's bookmaking father, my dad's Italian suit, the French mayor's death brigade—and the thing I can't come to terms with is that my story, the humanizing element, is Lionel, and Lucas, and the gravest of all loss. There's something there, though, in the telling of it, a profit of some kind that cannot be quantified.

The walk to Catherine Street takes only ten minutes—it's a small town—and it suddenly strikes me that the law of chance should have dictated more accidental encounters. Lucas must work hard to avoid me.

There are two types of people who walk: people who take pleasure in idleness, gait easy and light, and people who use the time to ruminate, gait slow and heavy. Lucas was the former; I am the latter. Addie could always sense this. When all three of us walked together in the cemetery, we let her off leash so she could roam while we strolled. She was playful with Lucas, jumping alongside him, nosing his hands, nipping his heels.

When she ran off chasing squirrels or deer, Lucas would tell me to hide, and we'd crouch down behind gravestones and laugh while she circled around, trying to get an angle on us. Her whole body bounced up and down as she cantered, and when she hit full sprint, she caught air, all fours off the ground at once. Relieved to be with us again, she'd stay close, pushing her head into Lucas's heels, watching while we read names off gravestones. Lucas liked the old-timey ones—Clementine and Eleanor. He never said it outright but I knew he hoped for a girl too. He wanted Lionel to have a sister.

I LOST A SON and then a husband. Those are the facts. If I lied about anything, I lied about Addie, about not knowing her true preferences.

Before I headed out to the bar tonight, I opened the pantry and remembered what I already knew: there was only a half cup of dog food left. I grabbed Addie's leash and we walked out the back, in the direction of the hardware store.

The store has a dog food club. Buy nine bags, get the tenth free. The clerk keeps a tally. She takes her job very seriously. The source of her authority is a maroon polyester vest with her name, Emily, pinned atop her left breast.

We lingered in the dog food aisle. I scanned the shelves while Addie sniffed around. There was a problem. The store was out of the usual. For the club, I needed to stick with the same brand—also, Addie is accustomed to this brand—and I always buy her chicken. The only other option available for a medium-size dog was lamb. So that's what I bought.

There's no legitimate reason I always chose chicken except that I myself prefer chicken to lamb. I find the flavor of lamb somewhat gamey. And I project my tastes onto her. Families like all the same things, right?

But as we walked home together, I lamented that I did not know her true preference, and then I recalled that I still had a little bit of chicken left over: a half cup. We would do a test!

I put the last of the chicken in a bowl and a half cup of lamb in an identical bowl. I placed them on the floor in front of her side by side at exactly the same time, chicken on the left, lamb on the right. Her nose dipped into the chicken bowl first. She licked up a few nuggets of food; then she turned to the lamb and devoured all of it before returning again to the chicken. Lamb won.

I made it as far as the living room, where I dropped to my knees. My upper body collapsed forward on the hardwood, the dust grainy beneath my hands and forearms. Heavy with tears, my head hit the floor, and I realized how pathetic I was, my body contorted in this yoga pose, even though I don't do yoga. *It's just dog food, you weakling*, I told myself.

Addie sat next to me on the floor, upright. Her body was still like the statue of a proud dog, a firefighting dog or a special ops K9: a hero dog. She deserved a placard: FOREVER FAITHFUL. Her brown eyes stared expectantly. Her instinct, when encountering a person at her level, knee-high or thigh-high—the height of a small child—was to play, to cuddle aggressively, to go in for the lick. She knew to suppress her nature but not what to do instead. She knew to stay close but not how close. She knew to wait but not for what. She knew but she didn't know.

I confess: I wanted her to choose chicken. I'd been buying her chicken for years, forcing her to choke it down every single day.

About a month after the divorce was final, I took Addie for a run in the cemetery and let her off leash. She lagged behind, trying to sniff as much as she could, and then sprinted to catch up, and then again, lagged and sprinted.

The cemetery has multiple entrances—we always enter through the west gate, closest to my apartment, and exit into an adjacent park, closer to Lucas's house.

Addie was chasing a squirrel when I spotted Lucas, walking toward me from the opposite direction, cutting through the cemetery on his way downtown. I slowed my pace to a walk. When he saw me, his gait changed as well. He stood up straighter and put his hands in his pockets. We had no choice but to keep walking forward toward each other.

The squirrel escaped up into a tree and Addie bounced under it for a few seconds. Then she turned her head and saw Lucas. She crouched down, pushed off the ground, and exploded toward him. She jumped up on him, putting her front paws on his jeans, then dropped to the ground again, then back up, then turned back to me, sprinted, and then back to him and back to me, until we stood facing each other, just a few feet apart. She'd been waiting for this moment.

We made small talk—I don't even remember what we said. My mind was occupied with the concern that Addie wouldn't follow me when it was time to continue on. At some point, we said goodbye. In this moment, I was aware that Addie had a choice. She could continue toward the park with me, or stick by Lucas's heels, moving in the other direction toward town. My instinct was to put her on leash, pull her away quickly. That's what I should have done. But I needed to know. I'd worked hard to prepare an argument for why she should be mine—collecting receipts and testimony—and I spent all my time with her, having given up travel. Generally speaking, unless I was at the bar or running a quick errand, I was home. On some level, I'd convinced myself that she'd grown to love me more.

I said, "Let's go, Addiecakes," and slowly walked off in the direction of the park. Lucas started walking too, in the opposite direction. Addie thought we were playing a game. She jumped up at Lucas's side, putting her mouth on his hand. He batted her back. She jumped again. "Addie, come," I said. Lucas told her to calm down. He pointed to me and told her to go. She looked confused. I kept walking. She ran over to me and nipped at my heels, a feeble attempt to herd me back to Lucas. I said, "We're going this way." I pointed to the park. She ran back to Lucas. I kept walking. At the edge of the cemetery, a dirt path led into the park. A sign read, ALL DOGS MUST BE ON LEASH. I stood there staring at it for what seemed like a long time. Behind me, I could hear Lucas telling Addie to calm down, to go, that it was time. I looked back at them and saw her sitting, looking up at him, her master. She loved us both but she loved him more. I tried hard to hold back tears but they streamed down my face. I was the chicken; Lucas was the lamb.

Lucas walked toward me. Addie followed gleefully. He didn't say anything. I bent over and clipped on the leash. Addie and I disappeared into the park.

She looked back in the direction of the cemetery, hoping, I'm sure, that we were playing a game, just like when we used to crouch down and hide behind the gravestones. She assumed we would eventually emerge, as we had always done, and we'd be together again.

———————

THE OVERCAST, MOONLESS NIGHT makes seeing the house difficult. The neighbor's front lamp is on, and looking closely, I can see the trim is half-naked, still covered only by a primer coat, just as Lucas, Jimmy, and Yag left it the day Lionel died. The paint is peeling off the siding on the front of the house. If Lucas doesn't attend to it soon, the wood will rot. The process of decay is difficult to curtail once it has begun.

Some of the neighbors have gone with fiber cement siding, which lasts longer than wood and doesn't require constant maintenance. It doesn't look as good, though. It wouldn't do justice to the stately old house, our bungalow with a weirdly tall body. Lucas would rather do nothing and watch it rot away than do something that would strip it of its character, its history: what it once was and could be again.

When I moved out, I half expected Lucas to rip out that redbrick walk. Lucas's dad replaced a portion of the brick to erase the stain of our son's blood, but I doubt Lucas was ever able to eliminate it from his mind. As I stand here now, I imagine the shape of the mark, bigger than a splotch, an ocean of blood, running off into the grass, seeping into the dirt below, still there, detectible, just not to the eye.

We put in the front walk before Lionel had even been conceived. Maybe it makes sense that the walk remains as we remain: a reminder of how we were before it happened, a reminder of it happening, and an enduring presence now that it has happened. Here lie three walkways: before, during, and after. Who would have the heart to rip out such a walkway? The walk that I envisioned, that Lucas built, that our son died on, that Grandpa Murphy partially replaced. It's a relief that the red brick remains. It means Lucas hasn't tried to forget.

My gut is twisted in knots. I think about heartbreak, how it should be either delivered or received, not both. Maybe it happens all the time, but I feel exceptional in the way I broke two hearts, mine and Lucas's, by denying myself and him the very thing we both cherished. We lost a child and then chose, freely, to lose each other.

I'd built a reputation on making other people feel worthy of change. My book sold to millions. But I never reached the people who really mattered. I see now that the only way forward, the only future that is not consumed by self-destruction, is one where I am kind to Lucas, kind to myself, and kind to the memory of our son.

There was a chalkboard by the fridge, which we'd put up for grocery lists, but we were never very good at using it. One day, I opened the fridge to grab some milk for my coffee and on the board Lucas had written a single line: *Here we find haven and haunt.* I stole it from him when I scratched it into the wall in the ladies' room at The Final Final. He wrote it before Lion was born; I plagiarized it after Lion died.

Addie and I linger. She is busy sniffing something in the grass. It's been more than a year since we moved out, but the seasons haven't washed away the scent of the place. A dog's nose is a steadfast compass, always pointing toward home.

The porch swing catches my eye, and I think about those three hand-prints on the underside: Lionel's handprint, Lucas's handprint, my hand-print, clustered together willy-nilly and sealed so they will last forever. It's not my house anymore, not my swing, but those prints belong to me, *to us*. I need to see them. Just a glimpse.

I tug Addie's leash and we turn up the walk. I lie down on the floor of the porch and scoot my body under the swing. It's too dark, so I turn on the flashlight on my cell phone. I find three prints, just where we left them.

A light comes on in the kitchen. Lucas is awake.

I pull myself up on two feet and tiptoe to the side of the picture window so I can peek in. He moves toward the pantry. He's probably just grabbing a box of cereal for a late-night snack, but I imagine him rooting around for a can of tomatoes. I think, *If he has the right ingredients, maybe he'll make pasta*. I want to try it again. I want to remember exactly what it tastes like.

Addie bounces up and down when she sees him through the glass. She pulls hard on the leash. Seconds pass, brief but expansive—enough time for my heart to make a million infinitesimal calculations.

Lucas opens the door with his arms stretched wide. We hug for a long time.

Eventually, he says, "Happy birthday," as if he'd been expecting me all along.

I don't think, *If only, if only*. My mind is quiet. My heart speaks instead: *Someday, someday*. And I say aloud, "Lord, give me forgiveness but not just yet."

ACKNOWLEDGMENTS

Ordinary Hazards was written with the support of many people and some very special institutions. To them, I owe a debt I cannot repay.

My agent, Samantha Shea, is a consummate professional and a great champion. She discovered this book, believed in it, and made it better. Others at Georges Borchardt, including Valerie Borchardt and Rachel Ludwig, helped bring it overseas.

Two weeks after the birth of my son, Lindsay Sagnette told me she wanted to buy *Ordinary Hazards* on behalf of Atria. Even sleep deprived and delirious, I knew immediately she was *The One*. Her empathy for these characters transformed this novel. Fiora Elbers-Tibbitts answered all my dumb, first-time-author questions. The rest of the team at Atria, from production and copyediting to marketing and publicity, brought this novel to the hands of readers with great care.

The Iowa Writers' Workshop provided three years to write, funded in part by the Flannery O'Connor Graduate Fellowship and a Teaching-Writing Fellowship. Sam Chang built a culture of camaraderie in place that could easily turn competitive under the stewardship of someone else. Connie, Jan, and Deb kept the place running. Deb threw the best Hawkeye tailgates. Three great writers had an enormous impact on me through their teaching: Ethan Canin, Charlie D'Ambrosio, and T. Geronimo Johnson. Brilliant, generous, and tough, all in different ways.

Roy H. Park and the Triad Foundation supported me as I pursued my first graduate degree, an MBA from Cornell University. The Park Fellowship is unique in its vision and has an enduring legacy that stretches throughout many

ACKNOWLEDGMENTS

corporations. It should surprise no one that it played a part in supporting the arts to boot. Clint Sidle gave us an education that business schools so rarely offer.

The first three readers of this book were Christine Utz, Jennifer Adrian, and Sophia Lin, women with wildly different and exceptionally beautiful souls. I cannot wait to read the books they publish. In particular, Sophia wrote a very long letter that altered the terrain of this novel in remarkable ways. Stephen Markley is the guy from workshop who I most want to grab a beer with, and Tim Taranto is a storyteller through and through. What a cohort!

Some of the banter recorded here came from the lips of good friends: Tony Pagliai, Mike and Kate Richard, Emily Salmonson and Dan Peterson, Ian and Raquel MacKay, Rachel Vanderwerff, Ryan Whiting, and Ned Carter. May we have many more long nights at the bar together.

My colleagues at the University of Iowa's Tippie College of Business, Pam Bourjaily and Mark Petterson, influenced me as a teacher and provided the sanity of a day job as I wrote these pages.

Above all, I'd like to acknowledge my family directly . . .

Lynne and Bill Bruno: This book exists because you raised a confident woman. Thank you for teaching me I have a seat at the table of my dreams. After love, you gave me a liberal arts education, from Shady Side to Stanford, where I first read Dante and Tolstoy, who endure in memory and touch these pages. Mom, you have great taste—truly finger-on-the-pulse. Thank you for always calling it how you see it.

Billy Bruno: Thank you for toughening me up as only a big brother could, lovingly. Tamara Kraljic: You read this novel early, before almost anyone, and you've supported everything I've ever done. I won't forget it.

Nancy Parker and Dwight Dobberstein: I did, in fact, hit the in-law jackpot. Thank you for all you do, especially for watching the baby while I write. Talk about a grant for the arts!

Parker: This book is dedicated to you. Without you, there would have been a book, but it wouldn't have been this book. It wouldn't have been a love story.